©2023 K. Ramsuer

To Sophie. Maybe one day we'll meet again. And to ER Lawton. Thanks for putting up with me!

CHAPTERS

❖ ❖ ❖

Chapter One: Brother
Chapter Two: Running
Chapter Three: David
Chapter Four: Unnerving
Chapter Five: Ghost
Chapter Six: Threat
Chapter Seven: Service
Chapter Eight: Ally
Chapter Nine: Captive
Chapter Ten: Missing
Chapter Eleven: Johann
Chapter Twelve: Lover Boy
Chapter Thirteen: Captive Again
Chapter Fourteen: War Party
Chapter Fifteen: Move Out
Chapter Sixteen: Wounded
Chapter Seventeen: Injuries
Chapter Eighteen: Home Bound
Chapter Nineteen: Outlaws
Chapter Twenty: Ride Away
Chapter Twenty-One: Falling
Chapter Twenty-Two: Love
Chapter Twenty-Three: Headwaters
Chapter Twenty-Four: River

Chapter Twenty-Five: Homeland
Chapter Twenty-Six: Found
Chapter Twenty-Seven: Betrayal
Chapter Twenty-Eight: Raider
Chapter Twenty-Nine: Magic
Chapter Thirty: Snake Bite
Chapter Thirty-One: Crown
Chapter Thirty-Two: Rescue Me
Chapter Thirty-Three: Shade
Chapter Thirty-Four: Warrior
Chapter Thirty-Five: Raw
Chapter Thirty-Six: Castle
Chapter Thirty-Seven: King

CHAPTER ONE: BROTHER

◆ ◆ ◆

Wilhelm Hart pulled at his fur-lined coat and tried not to think about the shrouded figure in the grave pit. A cold wind tugged at his clothing, ruffling the embroidered tunic he wore. A tall, lean wolfhound lounged beside him, panting softly as he stared at the ceremonial fire. Holly draped the shrouded figure in the pit, along with a wreath of heron feathers and wolf fangs. All were symbols of a prince, and soon they would be returned to the earth from which they came.

I miss Emil. Wilhelm wiped at his face and tried to look brave. His dog, Toman, nudged his hand as the priest droned on. He couldn't force himself to look at the grave or at the disapproving way his aunt Maria stared at the body. Wilhelm buried his hands in Toman's long, silky fur as he tried to hide the tears. Crying wouldn't bring Emil back. Nothing short of a miracle would and it was the kind the gods wouldn't perform.

Once a person died, their soul danced with the stars, it

was said, until they were reborn in the summer rains. No soul had ever come back before their time, and it was useless to even try.

The priest closed his book and released a handful of sage lily petals and holly berries. The wind caught them, billowing them out over the crowd, and Wilhelm could imagine his brother's smiling face for a few sweet seconds. He didn't know what to do without his older brother. Emil had been thirty to his twenty-three years and about to take the kingdom of Talla Gael from his parents. The bells had been cast, the white calves fattened, and all for nothing.

Maria pursed her lips as the funeral party started to break up. "I don't like the way they did things. That's not how they do it in—"

"If I cared, I would have asked you," Arlin growled. He reached up, touching the lacy crown on his head. "But I didn't and I still don't. You can be buried by your rites, but Emil will be buried by ours."

Wilhelm ducked away. He clicked his tongue, calling the brindle wolfhound to his side. Toman was a tall dog, his back coming to Wilhelm's ribs, and he trotted along at great speed. Wilhelm slipped through the tangled forest surrounding the sacred grove like he owned the place and soon came to a rush-covered bluff overlooking a river. Evergreen bushes surrounded a fallen log, along with tufts of dead sedge grass, and only the sky loomed overhead.

He wrapped his arms around Toman and cried. The dog licked his face, taking away the tears. Wilhelm clung to his dog as the river splashed over stones far below them. Emil had shown him this place. If Wilhelm looked hard enough, he could see his brother leaning on one of the standing stones playing his flute for the wild birds or naming the clouds as they rushed by. Only the wind greeted him now, and it made the rushes dance.

Toman stiffened. Wilhelm looked up. He reached for the dagger he kept on his belt now and crouched behind an ornately carved stone as the dog paced through the clearing. Toman barked sharply. He bluff-charged something, like he was trying to chase it away, but it didn't move. Wilhelm could see something large and white slide through the trees. Whatever it was moved silently, and he didn't dare speak until he saw it.

A massive white stag ambled into the clearing. Its antlers were tangled with ivy and holly, and it had eyes of pure gold. It was a massive thing, easily the size of a large pony, and its cloven hooves left no trace on the soft ground. Toman barked at it, jumping at the animal like he was going to bite it, but the stag ignored him. The beast sniffed the wind. It ambled closer to Wilhelm, and when it found him, it lowered its massive head.

Wilhelm reached out and touched a velvet-soft muzzle. "What are you doing here?"

The stag reared back. It snorted and half reared but didn't lash out with its hooves. Scars branded its pure white pelt, and something that looked like an arrow stuck out of its side. It was clearly injured, and Wilhelm wanted to help. He held up his hands so the stag knew what he was doing and walked toward it. The animal snorted. It reared its head back, sending holly berries all over the place, and took a step toward the open forest.

"Easy," Wilhelm said. "I just want to help you, honest!"

The stag eyed him. The animal lowered its head after a moment, glaring at Toman. As if on cue, the dog whined and covered his face with his paw. Wilhelm ignored him. He ran his hands along the stag's trembling flank and gently touched the inflamed and bloody spot that the arrow had left. The stag jerked back. It swung its head around like it was going to gore him, but Wilhelm grasped the arrow just in time and jerked.

Or, well, he tried to.

His fingers went right through the ghostly arrow, and he landed flat on his back in a sedge bush.

"What was that for?" Wilhelm yelped.

He wiped his hand on his pants, fully expecting to see blood, but his hands were clean. Even the holly berries the stag had scattered were gone. The stag reared as soon as he tried to approach it again and vanished into the forest. Toman jumped up from where he had been huddled and filled the air with barking. Wilhelm grabbed the dog, wrestling him away from the mist-filled forest.

"And stay gone!" he yelled. Wilhelm shook his head as he stared at the place where the stag had vanished. "Go tell your friends that I won't help them!"

Only the wind answered him. Wilhelm stared at the forest for a long time before he started heading back. Dirt and sedge marred his fine cloak, and he knew he was going to hear about it from his mother. He couldn't bring himself to care though. On a whim, Wilhelm looked at his hands. Fine white hairs softer than silk lined them like he had been petting a real stag. Wilhelm didn't quite know what to make if it.

He needed to go back to the palace. Wilhelm pulled his cloak around himself as he started to walk. A cold wind tugged at his clothing as he walked, chilling him to the bone. Toman trotted alongside him. The dog yapped playfully and snapped at the wind and falling leaves. A light mist started to fall as he approached the palace walls, and he shivered from a setting chill. Wilhelm slipped inside, unlocking a rusting iron gate as he did so, and ducked through the servant's hall before anyone could stop him.

"Wilhelm!" A young man with fire red hair came rushing down a narrow corridor. "You're in big trouble, you know! Maria has everyone going crazy! They thought you were kidnapped!"

Wilhelm stared at Henri. "Are you kidding me?"

"Do I look like I'm kidding?" Henri asked. Amusement flashed in his green eyes, and he looped his arm around Wilhelm's waist. "Because I'm not. She seriously has half the court thinking you're dead and has all her ladies doing some ridiculous prayer thing in the Great Hall!"

"I was at the cliff!" Wilhelm yelped. "Surely she knew the place!"

He darted down a narrow corridor lit by blazing rush torches and tried to imagine what he was going to say. It was just like Maria to suggest such a thing—she had thought Emil's death was a punishment for not following her god and had nearly been thrown out of court for suggesting it. Emil had died suddenly. One moment, he had been riding and playing with his friends, and the next, he had been dead in the dirt.

No one knew what had happened to him and only a few dared whisper of treason. Wilhelm was one of those few. Healthy princes didn't just collapse and die. At least, not without a little help.

He stepped inside the Great Hall, and the sudden glow stunned him. Gilt leaf covered nearly everything. Stags with roses in their horns—the Hart family crest—had been carved or painted into nearly every available surface. A tame fallow deer, wearing a collar made of golden cloth and studded with enamel roses, napped peacefully in her corner. Tapestries showing the history of Talla Gael surrounded every wall in the soaring hall, and nearly a hundred candles and rush lights filled it with a warm glow.

"Sorry to disappoint," Wilhelm said, "but I'm not dead."

His mother, Queen Iyanna, turned around. "Wilhelm! What were you doing?"

"I needed time to be alone," he said. He hugged her close and tried not to lose his composure. "I just...needed to be alone, that's all."

Arlin got up from where he had been sitting. "You can stop crying, Maria. I told you my son was fine!"

Maria raised her head, her eyes red and her kohl makeup smeared dramatically. "I told you...you play with your son's life! He might as well be dead in that cursed forest of yours!"

Wilhelm pushed away from Iyanna and pulled out his dagger. "I'm more than capable of defending myself, you know. And I had Toman with me, so it wasn't like I was all alone."

Toman took his place by Wilhelm's side and growled.

Maria flinched and drew back. She stared at the dog with distrust in her dark eyes, and she nearly tripped over her wooden carving of a dead man. Wilhelm averted his eyes. He had never liked that thing. It was made of beach wood painted white, with the torture marks covered in gold leaf. Maria and her ladies worshiped the thing, and Wilhelm wasn't surprised that it had found its way out here.

"That dog is no match for a soul protected by angels," Maria softly said. She lifted up her long skirts and lowered her head. "Come pray with me, gentle nephew. Together we can send Emil to his peace."

"Actually..." Wilhelm trailed off. He tried not to look at the other courtiers. "I just want to be alone. That's all I want."

He turned away and pressed a secret button on a carved hunting scene. Something rustled behind him. Wilhelm turned around, only to see the doe, Meera, staring at him. He held his hand so the animal could sniff it. She seemed more interested in his coat, so he tied the embroidered blue and scarlet wool around her neck, allowing her to take it off to her corner. Maria refused to look at the animal and didn't say anything when one of her ladies kicked at her.

Wilhelm grabbed Toman by the collar and pulled him up the now visible stairs before he could lunge. "It's not worth it, Toman. You'll just get us both in trouble!"

Toman growled softly. He took the steep staircase two at a time, though, and dropped down like he wanted to play. Wilhelm didn't have the heart to do that today. Instead, he walked around the dog and sat on a plush sofa in his private chambers. Toman sighed and lay down on his feet. Wilhelm kicked off his boots after a minute and patted the plush velvet so Toman would know he could take a seat.

"I miss him." Wilhelm looked over at Toman. "I don't want to be king, you know. I wanted to travel the world, see the island where my mother came from, maybe even go to one of the universities, but I can't do that anymore. I can't even marry Henri like I want to!"

It just wasn't *fair*. Wilhelm punched one of the pillows beside him and cursed when he struck golden beads instead of plush fabric. He rubbed his hand for a few seconds before getting up and walking over to a window. He leaned against the cold glass, watching as the fine mist turned to snow. Dogs barked in the distance. Toman perked his head up. For a second, he looked like he was going to add his voice to the chorus, but a sharp look from Wilhelm kept him quiet.

"They're probably chasing a rabbit or something," he finally said. "Or that stag decided to come back. I don't know. But whatever it is, Toman, it's not for us to worry about."

CHAPTER TWO: RUNNING

◆ ◆ ◆

David Troy slipped down the ravine and just managed to grab hold of a jutting root.

The rocky soil cut through his thin clothes. His boots were shredded now, and his dark hair flopped in his face. He didn't dare try to brush it back. Hounds barked and snarled somewhere behind him, reminding him that he needed to hurry. David braced himself against one of the rocks and slowly picked his way down. He grabbed at any root or strand of bracken he could find.

The harsh fibers cut into his hands. David wiped the blood off on his already work-stained shirt before jumping off his little perch and neatly landing on the rocks below. A thick mist rose around him, slicking the stones and making them shimmer in the dying light. David swore under his breath. He picked his way down the lichen-covered boulders, nearly slipping once or twice. Stagnant water pooled between the rocks. A night bird called, only adding to the noise.

"Down there!" someone yelled. Behind her, a hound bayed.

David grimaced. He pressed his body into a tangled thorn bush and tried not to cringe when the branches tore at his clothes. He dropped to his belly. David crawled through the wet, mossy mud and around the twisted roots. Yet more thorns grabbed at his hair and back. David ignored them. He crawled into the creek that splashed over the jagged stones. The current grabbed at him almost instantly, nearly jerking him into its grasp, but he fought it off and emerged on the other side.

Something moved in the tall grasses.

David froze. He reached for a large rock, fully prepared to bash whatever it was in the skull. Instead of a dog, though, or even a hunter, a white stag picked its way through the growth. Ivy tangled in its antlers like a forest hound, and its legs were scarred like the hounds had been set on it. The stag wandered over. It dropped its head down, like it wanted to inspect David, and he didn't waste any time.

David jumped up from his hiding place, used a rock as a springboard, and mounted the animal's back. He nearly slipped off the slick, white fur. The animal reared in fear. It cried out when the black hounds appeared over the edge of the cliff and turned toward the deep forest.

David held on for dear life. The animal bolted through the thick undergrowth. It jumped over ruined fences and fallen trees with dizzying speed, carrying David far away from his pursuers. The landscape seemed to blur around him like a strange oil painting. He couldn't even focus on it without his head throbbing.

He held on as long as he could. The cold wind bit at his fingers, weakening them and making them slip. David leaned on the stag's back like a burr. Its muscles flexed under his hands and threatened to make him fall. David forced his cold numbed fingers to hold on. His arms burned as the stag ran. Vines tore at his clothes, and branches snapped his face. The stag's lather soaked his arms and legs, only adding to the slickness.

The animal came skidding to a stop in a clearing surrounded by standing stones. David slipped off. He landed on the ground, hard, and crouched down. For a second, he thought the stag was going to gore him. The sunlight glittered off thick, strong antlers, and the beast was surely big enough. Golden eyes, though, shone with a strange sort of warmth as the beast's flanks heaved. David reached out his hand to touch it.

"Thanks," he whispered. "They would have killed me for sure."

The animal pressed its nose into his hand as if to say it understood before backing up. It raised its head to some unheard call and turned around. David opened his mouth to thank it again, but the stag had already vanished. He sat down on a broken stone and took stock of the situation. His clothing was ruined. The thorns had shredded the plain, well-worn material and his flesh besides.

His boots had cracked through, showing his patched and frayed socks, and nearly every inch of him was soaked with mud. David's body ached. His hands throbbed like they had been bound with rope for a few hours. David rubbed his wrists. The cuts on his head throbbed, and his back felt like it was afire. He leaned back against the cool stone, idly looking at a trail that wound its way through the dark forest.

Logically, he knew he needed to get up before the sun went down. He was likely too close to the hunters to risk building a fire, and the Tallan winter meant that death by exposure would happen faster than he cared to admit. He couldn't see any lime kilns around. David had grown up near them in his home country and knew how to sleep near one without being overcome by the fumes.

As it was, he needed to get walking.

David stood up slowly. His body protested even that little effort, though, and he found the world dancing around him. He leaned against one of the moss-covered stones for support. David relaxed against that before pushing himself off and taking a step forward. One step in front of the other. That was how he would do it. That was how he had gotten out of that hellhole and how he would find a decent place to rest.

"Let's go," he whispered. David rubbed his arms. "I have no idea where I'm going, but it's going to be a hell of a lot better than here!"

He had no idea where the trail took him. With his luck, it was going to be a ruined barn deep in the middle of the forest. David walked down the needle-thin path. The dry and dusty earth cut through the thick fern banks. Mist billowed out of little hollows and caves, further filling the air with a sick chill. A few autumn flowers bloomed in the sea of brown and dying plants. Little flashes of purple, red, and gold broke the monotony, and David could see wild grapes rotting on the vine.

Boot prints cut through part of the dust. They looked to be heeled and not good for traction instead of the sturdy, ruined boots that David wore. There were also scuff marks like someone had dragged a cloak around the path too. He could hear industry after a little bit and soon came to a rusty iron gate set in the middle of a moss-covered wall. Ancient stone gargoyles perched over the thing, leering down at him with tarnished brass eyes.

David ignored them. He tested the gate and it swung open freely, revealing a dark passage lined with furs and lit with rushlights. David paused. He almost didn't go in there, but soon he heard hounds baying and the thundering of a galloping horse. He slipped inside the tunnel quickly and locked the gate behind him. He didn't see any key, which meant that the hunters would at least be held up while he explored.

He allowed himself a small smile as he hurried down the corridor. He could hear people singing a Tallan watering song and ducked into what looked like a storeroom when someone came near. Great vats and barrels of wine lined the cool walls. Each one was marked with chalk in Tallan writing, and some of the vats were as big as the rude little room David shared with five other men.

"Henri, think you can get something for the prince? He looks a little upset."

"A little?" Someone, presumably Henri, yelped. "You don't say, Maria! His brother just died, and that witch had to make a scene about it!"

"Don't be so hard on her." Maria sighed. "She lost her husband, you know. Those Alsatian brutes murdered him!"

"It was war. People die. It was nothing personal, and besides, we invaded them!"

David agreed with Henri, but it was probably better to keep his mouth shut. He pressed his body between a great vat and a wall lined with wine bottles. For once, his simple clothing would help him blend in. This

Henri wouldn't be looking for an intruder. He would be looking for something for a spoiled prince. David could work with that. All he had to do was keep still and quiet.

A young man with fire-red hair stepped into the room. He wore a loose tunic edged in cloth of gold and his hair was pulled back from his face with an alabaster clip. His trousers were made of soft deerskin, embroidered with creeping vines and flying birds, and he wore a wolf skin cloak around his shoulders. He looked handsome enough, David supposed. If he had been a free man and not running for his life, David would have been tempted to speak with him.

"I hate Maria," Henri muttered. He took in the middle of the room, the light from his candle filling every corner of the wine cellar. "She can't let Emil rest in peace! She has to make everything about her stupid god!"

"I heard that!" Maria called.

Henri didn't answer because he was staring right at David.

David tensed. He didn't want to spring out and attack the other man, as Henri might scream. Besides, there seemed to be people nearby. Any cry would bring the entire Tallan army down on his head. The two young men stared at each other for the longest time. David fought the urge to make himself smaller and plead for mercy. He eyed the short dagger on Henri's hip. If he were faster and stronger, he might be able to reach it, but now wasn't the time to try his luck.

"What the hell?" Henri whispered.

"Don't say anything!" David hissed. He slipped out of his hiding place. "They'll kill me!"

"Who will kill you?" Henri dragged David to the far corner of the room. "You're bleeding!"

"I know," David said. "I crawled through a thorn bush and fell off a cliff!"

"I need to get a doctor." Henri touched David's forehead to inspect one of the wounds. "These have dirt all in them, and they might get infected!"

"No doctor!" David caught Henri's hand and thanked the gods that this young nobleman was as stupid as he was pretty. "What part of 'they'll kill me' means bringing an outside party in is a good idea?"

"Let go of me!" Henri twisted away and wiped his bloody hand off quickly. "Okay, fine. But if you wanna stay here, there is someone who needs to know."

"Who's that?" David slowly asked.

"Wilhelm." Henri took his cloak off and wrapped that

around David's body. "He's my friend, and he has the perfect place to hide you. No one can go in there without his permission."

"Great," David said, "lead the way."

"Come on!" Henri grabbed a bottle of wine at random and David's hand soon after. "We'll take the secret passage. I don't want anyone to see you!"

Maybe Henri was smarter than he looked. David took the wine when it looked like Henri was going to drop it and followed after him. Henri wove through the tunnels with the skill of an expert. Half of them weren't even lit at all, and the other half were covered in thick sheets of dust and grime. David covered his mouth when they went through a cobweb-draped doorway. There was a steep set of stairs waiting for him, and he didn't even know if he could make it up.

"Let me help." Henri took David's arm and slung it over his shoulder. "You look really tired."

"Thanks," David whispered. He closed his eyes as they started to climb. "You really know your way around this place."

"Yeah," Henri said. "Me and Wilhelm used to explore as kids when we could get out of lessons. I was going to marry him, you know. When he wasn't the crown prince."

"The *what*?" David asked.

What exactly was he getting into?

"The crown prince," Henri repeated. "Prince Wilhelm Kessler von Hart. You know, the royal family!"

David stared. He never kept up with the Tallan royal family—as an Alsatian, he had no interest in that—but he had never expected that he was going to meet royalty when he looked like what he was. David tried to jerk back, but Henri was stronger than he was and easily pulled him through a narrow door covered with a tapestry.

"Will!" Henri yelled. "Look what I found!"

A massive wolfhound bounded off a couch and started barking. Prince Wilhelm himself—every inch of royalty with his soft, blue eyes and golden hair—started from where he was reading a book on a window seat. David suddenly felt extremely out of place in his simple, torn, muddy, and bloody clothes. Hell, even his boots were coming apart at the seams!

"I can explain!" David yelped. At least, he hoped he could.

"I would hope so," Wilhelm softly said.

"There's no time," Henri said. He started pulling David toward what the other man hoped was a bath. "We need to get him presentable before the wannabe murderers show up!"

"The *what* does *what*?" Wilhelm asked. "Hold up. I'm missing something here."

"You and me both!" David called, just as Henri yanked him off to the other room.

CHAPTER THREE: DAVID

◆ ◆ ◆

Wilhelm rested his hand on Toman's back as he stared at the filthy man. Toman didn't growl. The wolf hound wagged his tail, even. He pulled away from Wilhelm and wandered over, nosing the man's hand. He was very thin, Wilhelm thought, and his dark blue eyes reminded one of the sky just after twilight. His dark hair was tangled and matted with dead leaves, twigs, and mud. His skin was far too pale to be healthy, and it looked like he might fall over at any minute.

"Henri," Wilhelm said, "don't pull on him! He might trip and fall!"

"Yeah," the man said. He pushed Henri's hand off his wrist and sat down on the edge of the tub. "I really don't want to crack my head in front of a prince, okay?"

"Alsatian?" Wilhelm guessed.

The man winced. "The accent, right?"

"And the way you speak." Wilhelm gracefully knelt beside the man's legs and started working off cracked and muddy work boots. He frowned. "Why is there white fur stuck to your leggings?"

"It was the weirdest thing," the man softly said. "There were hounds chasing me through a ravine, you know, and I was scared they were gonna catch me. But then this stag showed up. It let me ride it, and I wound up in a circle of standing stones on a bluff. I've…I've never seen anything like it, you know, before or since. Then I heard dogs barking and I found a trail. Henri knows the rest."

Henri shrugged. "His name is David. I like him."

"David." Wilhelm repeated the name. "It's a good name. It fits you."

"Thanks? I guess?" David squirmed and jerked back as soon as the boots were off his feet. "Look, I don't know if this is some weird Tallan thing, but I can undress myself, okay? I don't need people trying to do it for me."

Wilhelm shrugged. He wasn't in the mood for arguing. Besides, taking care of David would keep his mind off Emil. He got up, leaving David to his own devices, and found a bar of fragrant, golden soap. Bits of dried honeysuckle had been sprinkled through it, and it truly smelled amazing. Golden vanilla, the sweet nectar from the honeysuckle vine, and something earthy that came from the powdered amber that gave it its golden color perfumed the small room.

Henri pulled the curtains closed as he started to run a hot bath. David wasted no time. He stood, swaying slightly on his feet, and started stripping down. Wilhelm couldn't look away. David's lithe, bony body seemed to gleam in the warm candlelight. His moon-pale skin was scattered over with freckles and a fine layer of dusky hair. A few scars branded his back. They were thin and fading, like they had been there a long time, and Wilhelm fought the urge to kiss them.

"You must be cold," Wilhelm heard himself say. "Do you want me to show you that we Tallans aren't all bad?"

"That depends on what you wanna do," David said. He paused, like he was going to step inside the tub. "Not to be harsh, but I don't think I know you well enough to just hop into bed with you."

"David!" Wilhelm yelped. He couldn't help the flush that spread over his cheeks, and he fought to keep his eyes above David's navel. "Please...please don't insinuate those things! I–I can't do that!"

"Why?" David asked. He sunk himself into the water and sighed. "I mean, you're the prince, right? Means you're gonna be king. Then you can do whatever the hell you want."

"But I can't," Wilhelm said. He rolled up his loose sleeves and knelt on the cool tile. "Henri, the cup and soap, please."

David's eyes fluttered closed. "Fuck me. You people know how to live. First time I've been properly warm since winter hit."

"Gladly," Henri purred.

"Pardon?" Wilhelm looked at his friend. "You can't mean that!"

"And he's not offering," David said. "You two enjoying the view? Do I need to charge for this or are you gonna let me take a wash in peace?"

Wilhelm grabbed Henri's hand and dragged him out of there. He shut the door behind him before sitting on his bed. He didn't know what to say. David would need clothes, of course, and a smarter person would have been getting them. Wilhelm couldn't bring himself to get up though. Henri sat beside him. He didn't say a word; he held out his arm and let Wilhelm curl up against him.

"It's not fair," Wilhelm whispered. He screwed his eyes shut and tried to fight back the tears. "It's just not fair!"

"I know," Henri said. He rubbed Wilhelm's back and

sighed. "In a better world, Emil would be here. But he's not and you are."

"I think Maria had something to do with it." Wilhelm looked up, his mind racing. "You know they hated each other. He was going to banish her from court the second he became king, you know. And he wasn't shy about telling her."

Henri bit his bottom lip. Wilhelm searched his friend's face intently. Something bothered him, telling him that he should kiss Henri while he still had the chance. He shook his head. He didn't have the time for that sort of thing, no matter how much he might love being with Henri. Henri ran his hand through Wilhelm's soft blond hair, gently pulling at the strands and relaxing the tension that spread through him.

On an impulse, Wilhelm leaned his head back and gently kissed Henri.

Henri flushed. He smiled softly and brushed his own kiss against Wilhelm's lips. Wilhelm deepened it, fully relaxing into Henri's embrace. His traitorous mind filled itself with images of himself lying underneath Henri, allowing him to see skin that no one else had. Wilhelm pulled back after a second. He flushed, his eyes wider than they usually were, and every word died in his throat.

David pushed the bathroom door open. "Anyone got

clothes or something? I don't wanna put that filthy stuff on after I've just gotten clean."

"In–in my trunk," Wilhelm managed. "I–I think it'll fit you."

"Am I interrupting something?" David asked. He adjusted the plain white towel around his narrow hips as he walked through the room. "Because it sure as hell looks like I'm getting in the middle of your hookup."

Henri rolled over. "It's not what you think. Just…come over here. Get pants on and we'll get you warm."

"Henri!" Wilhelm hissed.

"Don't mind if I do," David said. He eyed the bed, hunger in his dark blue eyes. "That looks softer than anything else I've slept in for the past year or so."

He opened the trunk, and the towel fell off of his hips. Wilhelm swallowed. David might have been thin, but his body still rippled with lean muscle. He moved with the grace of a panther, nearly crouching down and rifling through the clothing. David dressed himself with the things he found – trousers, linen shirt, soft socks – and met Wilhelm's gaze with one that was both feral and hungry.

Wilhelm didn't know how to voice the thoughts racing

through his head. He wanted to see more of David's body, wanted to touch it, wanted to know his scent. He wanted to know what David's rough hands felt like over his own smooth, soft skin and what his kisses might taste like. Henri adjusted himself and casually covered them with a blanket. Wilhelm swallowed. He curled up close to Henri and tried to send away any traitorous thoughts.

David sauntered over to the bed and eyed them. "Wilhelm okay?"

"I'm just…I'm not used to this." Wilhelm swallowed. "The-the touching, I mean. And I find myself…I find myself very attracted to both of you, and I know I shouldn't say this because my brother died and we had to bury him today." He covered his face with his hands. "What am I saying? I shouldn't–I shouldn't be dumping this on you!"

"Hey," David said. He sat down and wrapped his arm around Wilhelm's shoulder. "It's okay, I promise."

"It's not," Wilhelm said. This time, he couldn't stop the tears that burned his eyes. "Emil's dead. I'm never going to see him again. I–I think someone killed him."

David nuzzled him and kissed the tears from his cheeks. "Do you want us to help you find them?"

"Please?" Wilhelm asked. He hiccupped and mentally

cursed himself for looking so weak. "I would be forever in your debt."

"That I would like to see," David muttered. He pressed his head against Wilhelm's and rubbed his back. "But before that, how about we try to get you calmed down. You're no good to anyone if you're upset like this."

Wilhelm nodded. He rested his hand against David's back. He could feel warm, smooth skin through the thin material, and he entertained the idea of pulling that shirt off and doing wicked things. He shook his head violently. David jerked back, something unreadable in his eyes, but Wilhelm ignored him. Wilhelm's private thoughts were his own, and he couldn't go falling in love with an Alsatian. That would throw the entire court into chaos.

"I'll get something to eat," Henri said. He sat up and eyed the door. "Might be a good idea to try and pass him off as my long-forgotten cousin or something. I have enough of them that no one's going to notice an extra one."

David took a breath. "Wait. You want me to stay here?"

"Yes," Henri said. "You're smart, I like you, and Alsatians can fight, can't they? If someone did kill Emil, what's to keep them from going after Wilhelm?"

Wilhelm froze. "You mean—"

"I mean you're getting a bodyguard," Henri said. A sly smile played at his lips. "Besides, it lets me be alone with you. Don't let Maria's priest drag you off. I swear, that man gives me the creeps. David, if he starts bothering Wilhelm, you have my permission to slap him right in the face. I don't want him anywhere near Wilhelm, understand?"

"I thought I was supposed to make that choice," Wilhelm said. "I am the prince, you know."

"I know." Henri smiled softly. "But I am going to go get you food that I know hasn't been tainted. Stay safe, you two. And leave me some of the wine, will you?"

Wilhelm watched him go. He didn't want to think that someone would try to kill him. He knew that he would have enemies—there was a list of Alsatian barons who would love nothing more than to have his head on a stick—but none of them were close enough to do him any harm. Wilhelm shivered. He curled up close to David and tried to keep himself calm. Henri was right; someone was going to try and kill him. He had to be on his guard.

David, by contrast, seemed calm and relaxed. He wormed his way under the blankets and spooned Wilhelm from behind. He rested his rough hand on Wilhelm's chest, like he was contenting himself with the strong, steady heartbeat. Wilhelm didn't move. He couldn't; the panic simply grabbed him and forced him to stay where he was. It was like a great rock sat on his chest and tried to drag him into some place where he couldn't breathe.

"Hey." David shook him. "Are you okay?"

Wilhelm shook his head. He grabbed for the man, desperate for anything that might ground him. Daggers twisted in his chest and speared his heart. He opened his mouth, tried to speak, but nothing came. All he could do was hold on as David hugged him. The man rocked him after a second, whispering words that he couldn't understand. Wilhelm took a shuddering breath. He needed Emil. Emil always knew what to say when he was scared, even if Wilhelm thought everything was lost.

"Wilhelm." David cupped his cheek with one rough hand. "Are you okay?"

"I'm scared," Wilhelm managed. "More scared than I've ever been. What if they kill me?"

"I'm not letting that happen," David promised. "You have me and Henri, okay? We're gonna protect you."

Wilhelm tried to believe that. Really, he did. But something inside—something nasty that he couldn't banish—told him that it was just pretty words and David would leave him just like Emil did. Wilhelm screwed his eyes shut as hot tears burned down his cheeks. He couldn't do this. He just couldn't. He needed to get away, and he pushed against David like a frightened deer. David caught him quickly.

He held Wilhelm close to him and sunk back down on the bed. Wilhelm couldn't stop himself from sprawling on David's chest. After a second, David patted the space beside him and made room for Toman. Wilhelm rolled over and buried his face in the dog's side. He didn't care that his shoulders were shaking or that David could hear his ugly sobs. Something twisted inside of him, something that stabbed with the pain of a thousand knives, and Wilhelm couldn't stop the ragged wail that tore itself from his throat.

"I want Emil." Wilhelm wiped his eyes off and tried not to sniffle too much.

"I know." David looked away as he stroked Wilhelm's back. "I've been there. My Emil died too."

CHAPTER FOUR: UNNERVING

◆ ◆ ◆

David didn't like thinking about Alexi. He tried to push his brother out of his mind as he curled up beside Wilhelm. The mud and mire that once covered his body had long since been washed away, and the soft clothing caressed his skin. He buried his nose in the crook of Wilhelm's neck, breathing in his scent. His eyes fluttered closed after a few minutes. He thought that he was floating on a cloud with this soft, warm bed.

Henri cleared his throat as he entered the room again. "He looks happy."

"He is," David said. He tossed his arm over Wilhelm's middle and then stared up at the redhead. "And he's very warm and doesn't want to get up unless he has to."

Henri laughed softly and sat on the bed. "Well, I do have something to eat. And I know you're both hungry. Please, eat."

Wilhelm pushed David to the side and propped a pillow them. David grabbed for the food, completely ignoring the others, and enjoying the plethora of food in front of him. Sweet rolls, thick meat stew, vegetables in broth, tea, and rice. David didn't care what it was; he was hungry and he wanted to eat. He grabbed for a china bowl and helped himself to a nice helping of stew.

"This is good." He wolfed it down and busied himself scraping the bottom of the bowl before anyone could take it away. "Really, really good."

The stew was sweet in just the right way, and the meat gave him something to sink his teeth into. David scooped himself some of the rice to sop up any of the broth that might have been left. He didn't even think that he was tasting the food; he just ate to dull the cramping in his belly. Before, he had been lucky to get a few pieces of bread and half a boiled potato, never something as thick and glorious as the stew currently burning his mouth.

"Easy." Wilhelm pushed his hand away from the bowl. "You're going to make yourself sick!"

"Do I look like I care?" David asked. His shirt slipped, revealing his bony shoulder, and he pulled at it on instinct before downing half a goblet of wine. "If I'm gonna protect you, I need some weight on me."

"But I also don't want to have anyone ask why I smell of

bile," Wilhelm said. He bit his bottom lip and turned to Henri. "I think this is enough. David needs to rest for a little bit."

"David is right here," he said. David crossed his arms and glared at the younger man. "I can hear you just fine, you know. Me being hungry doesn't mean I'm stupid!"

"He never said you were," Henri said. He took the tray, though, and gently pried the soup bowl from David's fingers. "He's not lying about you getting sick either. I don't know how we would pass it off without saying that Wilhelm was sick and bribing the doctor."

They had a point. David grumbled under his breath and snuggled back down beside Wilhelm. The wine pooled in his belly, and he slowly relaxed under the blankets. He wrapped his arm around Wilhelm once again, seeing his warmth and presence. There was something about the younger made that made his blood sing. David wanted to find out what it was and chase the sweetness he saw in Wilhelm's eyes.

Wilhelm kissed his forehead and swallowed. "I…I think I would like to get to know you better."

"Same here," David murmured. His voice was thick with want, and he traced Wilhelm's soft lips with a single finger. "What's the punishment for ravaging the crown prince?"

Wilhelm blushed. "Well, I don't think anyone has ever done it, so…"

"Perfect." David pushed himself up and cupped Wilhelm's face with both hands. "And then I shall do the honorable thing by marrying you."

He ignored Henri's pointed glare. David didn't know what his problem was, nor did he care to find out.

"David." Wilhelm pushed his hands away. "We can't."

"And why not? You want me, I want you, and it's private," David said. "Last I checked, Talla Gael didn't do arranged marriages. Sure, I might be Alsatian, but you could always spin that off as a dynastic thing or something."

"I…" Wilhelm looked away. "I couldn't do it. I'm already promised to another."

"All right," David murmured. He kissed Wilhelm's soft, fine hand and smiled. "I'm willing to wait then. It's the honorable thing to do."

Wilhelm snuggled into David's side and stared out the window. "You said you had someone you lost. Tell me about them, and I'll tell you about Emil."

David sighed and curled his fingers around Wilhelm's.

He didn't want to. It still hurt, even two years later. He didn't even know if he could find the words to talk about what happened. David shook his head, his voice dying in his throat, and couldn't meet Wilhelm's eyes. Alexi was dead. He had died as he lived, fighting the Tallans, and all the pretty words in the universe wouldn't bring him back.

"I can't," David whispered. If he listened close enough, he could hear the roaring battle and the cries of dying men. "I...I loved him, but I can't. He's dead, and I think we should let the sleeping lie."

"Then he's being reborn." Wilhelm smiled sadly. "I like to think I'll see Emil again. They choose their bodies in the great dance of souls. Some become dogs, some become horses, others men, and some want to be born as the morning rose. We live and die in our time, following the dance of the stars."

That sounded quite pretty. The Alsatians didn't believe that. They believed that one was born, lived, died, and that was it. The dead lay sleeping under the earth and would be awoken when it was their time. How or why no one knew. It was all so final, and there was no guarantee that anyone would come back. David liked the Tallan version so much better. At least that way he would get to see Alexi again.

He sighed and tried to focus on the warmth. Wilhelm's heart thudded in his chest, and he was warm, so warm. So alive and vital—a far cry from the cold, dead body that Alexi had left. David shook his head, trying to chase those feeling away from him. He needed to focus on the here and now, not the pain Alexi's death had left him with. What good would he be if he could only focus on the past? Wilhelm needed him, and this job would keep him out of a labor camp.

Someone knocked on the door. Wilhelm rolled over, covering his head with the pillow. Whoever it was knocked on the door again, this time harder, and shouted something that was muffled by the wood. David gritted his teeth. He spooned Wilhelm, protecting the younger man's body with his own. The pounding on the door increased. Wilhelm gripped the pillows with both hands and whispered something David couldn't quite catch.

"Want me to deal with it?" David asked. He kissed the back of Wilhelm's neck and decided not to wait for an answer. "I'll deal with it."

He stalked over to the door and flung it open. "What!"

A woman wearing a plain black dress stared at him. "You aren't Wilhelm."

"You're damn right!" David snapped. "Now what do you want?"

"That's no way to talk to a woman of the Sun Lord!" the woman yelped. "For your information, my name is

Maria, and I want to speak to my nephew. If you would, please leave the room so I can talk to him in private."

"About that." David fixed a sneer on his face. "Wil's my responsibility now. Henri's too. Now either you can respect this or get lost."

"Why, I never!" Maria's hand flew to her throat, and she looked like she was going to whirl away. "And where are you from, young man? I haven't heard an accent like yours."

"Wouldn't you like to know?" David asked. He blocked the door with his body and tried not to look at a man wearing a rough brown robe behind her. "Look, the prince is having a bit of a hard time right now. The death of his brother has him upset, and we would all rather if you left him alone."

"But that's what I'm here to talk about," Maria said. "Father Jakob and I wish to speak with him about the state of his immortal soul."

David gave her an unimpressed look. "He's grieving. Let him be."

Maria wasn't an impressive woman. Her plain brown hair was tied back in a severe bun at the back of her neck, and her obsidian dark eyes were lined in smeared kohl. Her skin was moon pale and lined a little, and her hands were rough and chapped. Her dress looked like it was made of poor, rough materials, and her mantle was patched and ragged. Her only jewelry was a golden sun with a ruby set in the middle. It was set on a simple leather cord and rested on a piece of worn black lace.

"But that's the best time to talk to him," Maria said. "He might be receptive to the true light. And don't worry; you could stay for the lesson too."

David took a deep breath and debated slamming the door in her face. "I'm not here for any lessons, ma'am. What I am doing is asking you not to bother Prince Wilhelm or myself. I don't know what's so hard to understand about that, but it's quite annoying and I want you *gone*."

"But you don't understand!" Maria said. "This might be his only chance! Whatever sickness that took Prince Emil might take him!"

David shut the door in her face and latched it. He figured there was another way in this room—old castles seemed to be filled with those kinds of things—and he didn't want to give this Maria any excuse to bother them. He wandered back to the bed and sat down on the edge of it. His heart fluttered in his chest. David stared at the door, trying to puzzle out why the woman unnerved him. She reminded him of every other ascetic he had ever had the displeasure of dealing with, but there was something about her that screamed of danger.

Wilhelm picked himself up and scowled. "I told her to leave me alone!"

"Who is that woman?" David asked. "And where can we get rid of her?"

"Her name's Maria and she's my aunt," he said. Wilhelm looked down and wrapped his arms around his knees. "I...she scares me too. I wish she would quit bothering me, but she doesn't take no for an answer. Father Jakob scares me too. I wish they would just leave me alone..."

"I'll make sure they will," David promised. "I don't know how I'll do it, but I promise they won't bother you again."

Wilhelm smiled. David gave him a quick kiss and tucked him back into bed. Being Wilhelm's bodyguard meant that he was going to have to get stronger. There was no use for a weak guard, especially if there were dangerous figures in the court. He stripped off his shirt and tossed it over one of the chairs before sitting down and starting a few stretches. That winded him, telling him that he wasn't ready for anything more strenuous, and he relaxed back on the thick, soft carpet.

"You know," David said, "I could get used to this."

"Thanks?" Wilhelm rolled over on his belly and blushed a little. "Where were you before?"

"That's classified." David couldn't look at him. "Let's just say that this is a damn sight better."

"All right," Wilhelm said. He tried not to smile, but that effort failed and a silly grin spread over his face. "It's better for me too. I feel safer with you here."

"That's good," David said. "Means I'm doing my job."

Even though I have no weapons, and I couldn't fight my way out of a wet paper bag.

"You said you're Alsatian?" Wilhelm asked. "Aren't we at war with you?"

"Wilhelm, if I wanted you dead, you wouldn't be here," David said in a flat tone. "I don't know what tripe they told you, but most of us are good people. We don't like our leadership any more than you do. We just don't have the means to fight. Besides that, I've been in Talla Gael for longer than I would care to admit. Folks like me ain't exactly welcomed back with open arms."

"Why ever not?" Wilhelm asked.

David looked up and prayed for strength. "Because being captured means that you're weak and less than, apparently. Don't ask me for the logic behind it; I haven't the foggiest idea, either."

"A soldier..." Wilhelm whispered. He shook his head, his eyes widening. "I've never met a soldier before. Are they all as handsome as you?"

David laughed as he got up. He sat back down on the bed again, not bothering to grab his shirt. He didn't know how to answer that question or even if he should. He caught Wilhelm's hand, covering it with a soft kiss, and offered only a roguish wink as his response. Anything to take Wilhelm's mind off of Emil's death was a good thing, he figured, and if he could come up with a few wild stories, he might just ingratiate himself further with the young prince.

"Well," David finally said, "I guess handsome depends on your taste." He dropped himself beside Wilhelm and pulled the younger man so he was splayed against his chest. "But let me tell you about that one time I stole a general's horse..."

CHAPTER FIVE: GHOST

◆ ◆ ◆

Wilhelm tried to keep his body still and his thoughts pure as he held David. The other man had all but collapsed into his arms. His cheek was pressed against Wilhelm's, and his lashes just brushed against soft skin. Wilhelm allowed himself to rest one hand on the small of David's back. Warm skin flexed under his hand as David squirmed, and it was all he could do not to rest his hand a little bit lower.

David rolled over and flopped his arm around Wilhelm's middle. "Wake me up when it's morning."

Wilhelm glanced to the window and smiled wryly when he saw the sun peaking over the horizon. "It depends on what you call morning. It's certainly starting to get light out."

"That doesn't count," David muttered. He pressed his face into Wilhelm's neck. "I meant noon or something."

"We can't stay in bed all day," Wilhelm said. He pushed at David and sat up. "I have things to do and places to be. If you want to be my bodyguard, you need to go with me."

David grumbled, but he sat up. His sleep-mussed hair stuck out every which way, and his eyes weren't all the way open yet. Wilhelm couldn't resist leaning forward and giving him a quick kiss on the nose. David reared back, almost like he was expecting to be struck, but a sheepish smile spread across his face. He blushed all the way down to his collar bone. David nuzzled Wilhelm gently, almost as if promising he'd keep them both safe. Wilhelm relaxed a little. He could get used to this, he thought.

"Do I at least get breakfast?" David asked. He slid out of bed, neatly avoiding Toman, and stretched out where the sun could catch his body. "I really could use something to eat, you know."

"In the kitchens," Wilhelm said. "And after you take a bath."

"You know, I could get used to this." David stood on a colorful rag rug and started stripping down. "A bath every day and breakfast is a hell of a lot better than what I was getting before, you know!"

Wilhelm stared. The pale morning light lit up the scars that crossed David's back. He was lean, almost too lean to be healthy, and Wilhelm could see every one of his ribs. David's scars clustered around his buttocks, and some of them dipped even lower. David turned around and smirked. Wilhelm quickly looked away. He didn't want David to get the wrong idea. After all, they were supposed to have a working relationship, and Wilhelm didn't want to get in the way of that.

"You could have changed in the bathroom," Wilhelm said. He looked down and kicked at the cold stone floor. "It wouldn't have bothered me."

"Come take a bath with me." David grinned, making Wilhelm blush. "Come on, I promise it won't be that bad. I'll wash your back; you wash mine. You do have a shower, right?"

Wilhelm nodded. He slowly took off his own clothing and carefully folded it before putting it on his nightstand. He didn't know what he wanted to do. David was clearly confident in his own body. He casually walked across the room, grabbed two towels, and waved for Wilhelm to follow. Wilhelm tried to summon all the courage he could. He was going to need it, especially when it came to showering.

He eased the door shut behind him, trying not to wince when it slammed into the frame. David ignored him. He stood in front of the glass paneled shower and adjusted the faucet until a spray of hot water pounded the tile. Wilhelm cleared his throat. He brushed his hand on David's back to let him know he was there and opened the clear door. A cloud of steam covered his body, draping him in its warm, wet embrace, and David tried to pretend that was why his body was reacting as it was.

David stepped into the shower and took Wilhelm's hand. "Why are you so shy?"

"About what?" Wilhelm swallowed and tried not to look at how the water beaded on David's lashes. "What do I have to be shy about?"

"Us." David leaned forward until his breath just brushed over Wilhelm's steam-covered cheek. "You do like me, I can tell. You don't have to restrain yourself."

Wilhelm nodded and found himself drawing closer. He rested his head on David's shoulder and let the hot spray drench their bodies. David held Wilhelm in a tight embrace, shielding him from the worst of the water, but enough slipped through to mask Wilhelm's tears. He couldn't stop himself. Emil would have wanted him to be happy, that was true, but duty required that Wilhelm marry his brother's fiancée and provide an heir.

"Hey." David kissed his cheek. "What's wrong?"

"I can't marry for love," Wilhelm whispered. "I would have to marry Katarina, and I don't want to."

"Then don't," David said. He stepped back and turned,

grabbing for a pot of sweet-smelling gel. "It's as simple as that. Marry who *you* want, not who you have to."

Wilhelm shook his head. He took the pot and scooped out a generous handful of the light blue gel. David's eyes lit up when Wilhelm motioned for him to sit down. He even ducked under the hot water first, just to make sure that his hair was nice and wet. A soft smile tugged at Wilhelm's lips as he started working the soap into silky dark brown hair. David sighed, his eyes fluttering closed, and his entire body relaxing as Wilhelm quietly worked.

On a whim, he rested his hand on David's pulse point. The other man's heart seemed to throb in his chest, and his entire body shivered. Wilhelm looked away. For a second, he thought he saw Emil staring at him. His brother looked concerned, and he opened his mouth like he was saying something. Wilhelm felt the pot slip through his hands as he stared at the cloud of mist. Distantly, he heard it shatter, but he couldn't bring himself to care.

His entire world focused on his brother. Blood seemed to stream from Emil's neck. His eyes were blank and hollow and his shirt soaked with blood. His hair was mussed and bits of leaves stuck in it. Emil gestured wildly with his hands, like he was yelling, even though the only thing Wilhelm heard was the shower. He opened his mouth, tears blinding his eyes. Wilhelm took a step forward. Pain flashed through his body, and the vision vanished when he cried out.

"Wil! Wil!" David shook him. "What's wrong? Are you hurt?"

"I saw my brother," Wilhelm whispered. He sat down the tile-covered bench, wincing as his foot started to bleed. "Emil... He was saying something, but I couldn't make it out."

David stared at him. "Are you sure?"

Wilhelm nodded. His heart wrenched all over again, and he held himself. Ugly sobs tore themselves free. All he could hear was himself crying. David hugged him and rubbed his back, but Wilhelm pushed him away. He couldn't bring himself to care. His foot bled freely, staining the water a dark crimson color, and Wilhelm just left it there. He barely even noticed when David cleaned up the mess he had made and started scrubbing his own hair.

"Maybe he was trying to tell you something," David finally said. "Like who murdered him. How did he die?"

"He was thrown from a horse." Wilhelm cleared his throat to get rid of the hoarse whisper he had now. "But the wounds he had... David, I think he was stabbed!"

"That's a start," David said. He cut the water off and helped Wilhelm up. "Now where did he die?"

"He was riding in the North Garden," Wilhelm said. "He took his favorite black stallion, and he was practicing jumping. There's a festival coming up, and it's a tradition for the crown prince to ride his horse over seven jumps. It's a recreation of the fire god's story, basically, and he was working with the horse. It threw him."

"I don't think so." David grabbed the towels and a smaller washcloth. "Hold still and let me look at that foot of yours."

Wilhelm stuck his foot out and winced when David prodded at the cut. "The North Garden is the horse garden, and the jumps aren't all that high. Maybe you're right; the way he was injured didn't look like he had been thrown. It's just...how would they get rid of the blood?"

"Like this," David said. He crouched down beside Wilhelm and started wiping up the mess on his foot. "It's not that hard to get rid of blood, especially if it's still fresh."

Wilhelm's breath caught. There was a small chapel near the garden, unused except when a couple needed privacy. Wilhelm had played in it many times as a child. The locks were old and worn, so much so that it was very simple to just pop one open whenever someone wanted inside. He pushed David away as soon as his foot was bandaged and went running for his clothes.

"We need to find that chapel," Wilhelm said. He pulled on his trousers and ran a hand through his drenched hair. "Now."

"I'm with you all the way." David grinned. He pulled on Wilhelm's clothing and Wilhelm couldn't help the swell of pride he felt when David pulled on his shirt.

Wilhelm whistled, getting Toman's attention, and the big dog went running out the bedroom and down the hall with them. Maria caught them in the hall and opened her mouth like she was going to say something. Before Wilhelm could stop and say anything, David caught him by the shoulders and all but dragged him down the hall. Henri must have seen them from the second story. He greeted them with a shout, jumped over the railing, and opened the great double doors for them.

Henri shivered as they stepped outside. "What's going on?"

"We need to find the chapel in the North Garden," David said. "Wilhelm thinks it's important."

"Oh, I know where that is!" Henri said. "I brought a Juban there last week! There are better places to be alone, you know. Like your bedroom?"

Wilhelm thought he saw a bit of jealousy in Henri's eyes, but brushed it off quickly. Henri would get over it soon enough.

"We're not doing that!" Wilhelm yelped. He flushed again and shook his head to clear his mind. "We think Emil was stabbed and the killers might have hidden there."

They ducked down a paved path and hurried between a strand of evergreen trees. Toman raced ahead of them, barking at the wind and scaring the birds. The iron-gray sky stretched heavy overhead. Wilhelm imagined it pressing down on him, smothering him, grinding him into ashes while he tried to find who killed his brother. The bands on his heart tightened again, and he forced himself to keep going.

Henri led them down a gravel trail and between intricately sculpted hedge bushes. The whales and unicorns seemed to taunt the winter sky with their green leaves, and their thorns lurked for the unwary to step on them. Wilhelm felt his foot throbbing as he wound his way through the maze. He ducked under a half-dead oak tree, before stepping into a small clearing dominated by winter dead grasses and red bud trees.

The chapel itself wasn't much. It was made of white stone blocks, and the iron door was covered in all manner of rust and filth. Bits of grasses grew between the blocks, and the steeple had long since collapsed.

The thatch roof now hosted lichens, small bushes, and dormant vines. The windows—made of costly colored glass—were streaked and spotted with grime and dirt. Wilhelm gingerly approached it, almost as if he was afraid the building would come alive.

Wilhelm gripped the lock in one shaking hand and twisted it. For a second, it didn't seem like anything was going to happen. Then Wilhelm pulled harder and the lock gave way. The door groaned when it swung open, and a rush of foul air came rolling out. Henri coughed and covered his nose. David just ignored it and stepped inside. He crouched down, just inside the place, and picked up a white silk handkerchief covered in blood.

"Found the source of the smell," David said. "There has to be a dozen of them in here!"

"Let me see!" Wilhelm pushed Henri aside and crouched beside David. He picked up one of the silk squares. "I've seen this before. Or one like it."

"That's cute," David said, "but this is better."

He picked up a slender silver dagger, the side of it inlaid with bone and mother of pearl. Dried blood covered the blade, and several bits of inlay were missing from the side. Wilhelm took it. He put it on the grass and turned it over, idly wondering why there were white hairs stuck to the hilt. He had never seen a weapon like his before—the blade was curved where Tallan blades were straight—and there were bits of orange dye clinging to the polished bone.

"So who did it?" Henri asked. He grabbed up the handkerchiefs and started putting them in his pockets. "Because I'm pretty sure that no one dragged Emil up here to save him."

"Maybe they were trying to clean up the blood," David murmured. He crouched down and traced the dried blood pooled on the swept stone floor. "If he was bleeding this bad when he was brought here, he was dead or close to it."

Wilhelm forced himself to look before he got up and backed out of the chapel. "But why would they kill him? Emil never hurt anyone!"

David looked up. "He was the crown prince, wasn't he?"

Wilhelm's hand flew to his mouth, and he leaned on Henri for support. If Emil was killed because he was the crown prince, Wilhelm knew he might be next.

CHAPTER SIX: THREAT

❖ ❖ ❖

David's chest tightened as he stared at the handkerchief. This was bad, very bad. He turned around, keen eyes searching the garden around them. Only the dancing grasses met his gaze, though, and a few birds split the air with their piercing calls. A raven soared overhead, its broad wings casting a pale shadow on the windows. David squeezed Wilhelm's hand as he stepped outside the little hut. Wilhelm, for reasons only he knew, chose to hand him the dagger in exchange for the blood-soaked square of fabric.

The knife weighed heavy in his hand. He wanted to throw it away, wanted to leave it where no one could find it. That dagger had killed Emil. There was a chance it would kill Wilhelm too. He stared at it, holding the weapon up so the weak winter light would catch it. He could smell the old blood and something made him run his fingers across the crusted patches. David had killed before. What soldier hadn't? He had just never killed in cold blood, that was all.

Something rustled in the thick bushes beside the chapel. David crept toward it. He held the dagger at the ready, fully prepared to stab whatever dared threaten him. It rustled again. He thought he caught a glimpse of white fur through that tangle of undergrowth, but he wasn't sure. Curiosity seized him and David couldn't help himself. He turned his body sideways as he squeezed between tangled branches.

The white stag turned around as soon as he stepped into an overgrown lawn. The animal's legs were covered in mud and tendrils of evergreen ivy twisted in its antlers. Its golden eyes were half closed, and it seemed to be enjoying the pool of sunlight. David froze as soon as he saw it. The animal lowered its head, as if to warn him, before half rearing. David jerked back. He held up his hand, only for the dagger to catch the light and shine right into the stag's eye.

It let out a truly pained cry and bluff charged him. David dropped the dagger as he scrambled out of the way. The animal pummeled at the thing with its sharp hooves, driving the knife into the half-frozen soil with every blow. It tossed its head in fear, eyes wide, and let out a call that could only have been impotent rage. After a minute, the stag backed off. It lowered its head, as if in apology, and snorted softly.

"What the hell?" David asked. "What was that for? We need that dagger! Someone killed Prince Emil!"

At the mention of Emil's name, the stag's ears went straight back to its skull. It snorted again and stood over the knife.

David glared. "Really?"

The stag pawed at the ground. It shook his head at him before backing off. The beast lay down in a patch of dead ornamental grasses, and David got a good look at a web of scars that covered the right side of its head. There was also a scar that went across its throat. If David had been in the forest, he would have said that this stag had been hunted and nearly taken.

Who kills a white stag, though? Aren't these kinda sacred?

"Hey." David raised his hands. "What happened?"

The stag sighed as it stretched its neck out. David crept closer to it. The beast watched him with golden eyes, and it tensed like it was going to bolt. David kept his movements slow and graceful so he wouldn't scare the beast. The stag pulled at some of the grasses listlessly, like it wasn't interested in eating. David crouched down as soon as he was beside it and carefully put his hand on the animal's shoulder.

"Thanks for saving me," he murmured. He scratched between the shoulder blades, right where a horse would like it. "I didn't get the chance to say that before."

The stag nuzzled him. There was something unreadable in its golden eyes, and it didn't seem to mind when David stroked its head. It even rested its head on his shoulders for a moment. David could hardly dare breathe as he touched it. The stag was soft, so soft. Far softer than any of the horses he had brushed. Its eyelashes just fluttered across his cheek as its lowered its head. David cupped the scarring on its face and his breath caught.

"Something hit you," he whispered. "Something tried to kill you? But what would attack a white stag?"

"What is that thing doing here!" a shrill voice yelled.

The stag bolted up as soon as Maria came storming into the garden. The stag cried out in terror and bolted through the thick tangled underbrush. David grabbed the dagger's hilt – the only thing sticking out of the grass and mud – before anyone saw. He stuck it up his sleeve, his eyes wild with terror. Maria saw that and *pounced*. She slapped him across the face, making his ears ring, and yelled something that he couldn't quite hear. When he didn't answer, she slapped him again and hauled him to his feet.

"Where is he?" she snarled. "Where's the prince?"

"In–in the chapel!" David yelled. He kicked himself for doing this and wrenched himself free. "We were just going exploring, lady! I swear it!"

Maria's eyes narrowed and madness glittered in their dark depths. "And what does a Tallan have with Alsatian scum like you?"

"He has a really good sense of character?" David suggested.

A man with long, greasy hair cleared his throat as he stepped out on to the sleeping lawn. "Let him go, Maria. If the boy wants a degenerate toy, who are we to deny him?"

"He scorns the Holy Father," Maria said. She prowled around David, and her predatory eyes raked over him. "Though why a beautiful young man would forsake his natural use is beyond me." She cocked her head like a hungry dog and then her eyes went wide. "Boy! Where did you get that knife?"

David backed up and tried to push it farther up his sleeve. "What knife? I haven't seen any knife! It must be that new silver bracelet Wil—"

The man lunged at him. He grabbed David's wrist before he could react and forced his arm up. David yelled. He tried to wrestle away, but the man was just too strong. His stench made David gag, and his greasy grip tightened as David tried to struggle. The knife came loose and clattered to the ground. Instead of letting

David go though, he forced the younger man to the ground and wrenched his arm behind his back.

"Let me go!" David yelled. He struggled as best he could, but the man was just too strong. "Unhand me right now or I swear I'll kill you!"

"Brave words for an Alsatian bed slave," the man whispered. His rough brown robe caught on David's cracked nails and greasy, stringy hair seemed to burn David's pale skin. "I thought you would enjoy this, hmm?"

"Either you let me go or I'll kill you," David hissed. He tried to calm his racing heart. "I swear it! I'll kill you!"

Maria picked up the knife and wiped it off on her simple gray gown. "You know, I was wondering where I lost this."

"Then why were you in the chapel?" David asked. "'Cause that's where we found it, and that's where Henri brings everyone he wants to fuck. Not that I blame him though. Or you. 'Cause he's just that kind of—"

The man slapped David across the mouth, stunning him. "Don't speak so poorly of your betters, Alsatian!"

David turned his head and let his eyes flutter a few times. *Okay, time for a bit of learned helplessness.* "What do you want with me?"

"The truth." Maria crouched in front of him and tipped his chin up with the dagger point. "About what you were doing there."

"But I told you!" David said. "We were just exploring." His mind raced as he tried to come up with something better. "That's all, I swear. We just wanted to explore. Henri said he knew a place that no one went. We just... we wanted to see what it was like, that was all."

He slumped against the man and tried to look like a defeated prisoner. David lowered his eyes. He bit his bottom lip and stared at the ground. He forced his fingers to relax and didn't try to scratch at the long, yellowed nails that dug into his wrist. Maria pressed the tip of the dagger in just a little deeper, like she was considering stabbing him. David prayed she didn't. For some reason, his mind sought out the white stag, and he swore he could hear the beast's haunting call.

"Let him go, Phillip," Maria finally said. She stood up and nodded. "I don't think he's any threat."

Phillip let David go, and it took all his strength to not recoil. Instead, David leaned into the man as if those rough brown robes comforted him. Phillip sneered. He kicked David in the ribs, sending the younger man sprawling, and he casually stepped over David's prone body. Phillip took his place at Maria's side before bowing his head. There was something cold in his dark eyes, something far colder than the chill wind that now filled the little garden.

David swallowed and made himself as small as he could. "Can I go now?"

"Get lost!" Maria snapped. "And don't let me catch you here again!"

"Yes, ma'am!" David only barely resisted the urge to salute her as he bolted through the tangled garden.

"David!" Wilhelm cried as soon as David found the others. "What happened? We were looking all over for you!"

"Maria." David ran to Wilhelm and threw his arms around him. "She took the knife, Wil, and nearly let her pet... I don't know what he was, and he nearly killed me! Had my arm behind my back and everything."

If only he were stronger. He cursed quietly, knowing full well that he couldn't protect Wilhelm if he was so weak. He blamed it on being sick and hungry for so long. Maybe Wil wouldn't think to ask. *And maybe pigs will fly*, he bitterly thought.

"Maria has the knife?" Henri asked. His voice jerked David from his thoughts. "David! You couldn't hide it?"

David nuzzled Wilhelm and drank in his sweet scent to calm his nerves. "Well, I tried. But they found it anyway. They were shaking me around like I was a rat and they were terriers!"

Wilhelm held him close. "We need...we need to get out of here. She has the knife now and she knows..."

David nodded grimly. He took Wilhelm's hand and guided the younger man between himself and Henri. His hand reached for a dagger that wasn't there anymore. David knew he wasn't in any shape to fight —the brawl with Phillip had proved that much. Still, though, he had to keep vigilant. He had to keep Wilhelm safe. After a few moments, he led the other two back to the castle, keeping sharp lookout for anything suspicious.

A few times, he thought he saw the glint of silver in the evergreens. Every time, he turned to look, whatever it was didn't move though, and soon he started walking again. David wanted a weapon. He needed some way to defend himself, Henri, and Wilhelm. His weakened body wasn't going to cut it. The cold started to sap what little of his strength he had left, and he found himself leaning on the others for support.

Wilhelm wrapped his arm around David. "It's just a little farther. Can you make it?"

"I'll try," David mumbled. He closed his eyes and coughed. "I don't think I can do the cold anymore…"

Henri nodded. He found another iron gate and wrenched it open. David stumbled as he walked over the threshold. Whatever strength he had slowly faded, and he could barely keep his eyes open. He clung to Wilhelm, barely even realizing it when they bundled him into the castle. Distantly, he could hear Toman barking. He hoped no one had forgotten the dog. Toman was a nice dog; he didn't deserve to be left out in the bitter chill.

"Come on, come on," Henri said. He helped David up the suddenly steep steps. "You can do this, David, I know you can!"

David nodded. He didn't want to admit it, but the fight took more out of him than he had to give. A few months of rough treatment – bad food, not enough sleep, and the biting Tallan cold – meant that he just wasn't as strong as he used to be. David didn't like his chances if he had to get in a fight for real. He didn't think he would win. David glanced toward Wilhelm, hoping that he didn't notice just how weak his bodyguard really was.

His legs shook as he walked, and he found himself leaning on Wilhelm more and more. He clung to Wilhelm with as much strength as he could muster and collapsed on the bed as soon as he was safe. Wilhelm and Henri helped him out of his boots and clothing.

He sought out Wilhelm's warmth on sheer instinct and sprawled himself on top of him.

Well, fuck. Now there's no way I can hide it! David found himself shivering as he held the younger boy close.

"Don't hate me," David whispered. "I don't feel so great."

"We can tell," Henri dryly said. "Wil, you can do better than this."

Much to David's great relief, Wilhelm seemed to ignore that remark. He petted David's hair in an effort to soothe him and chewed in his bottom lip. Did he understand just how sick and cold David really was? David liked to think he was good at hiding it, even if the evidence suggested otherwise. He wouldn't blame Wil for not wanting him if he was this sick – he'd just be an accident waiting to happen.

"He's so cold, Henri," Wilhelm said. He pulled the blankets over them and started rubbing David's back. "I don't know if he'll ever get warm!"

"Keep holding him and I'll get tea," Henri said.

"Cinnamon too." Wilhelm nuzzled David and tried to warm chilled cheeks. "I think that'll help more than anything."

The warmth slowly coiled through David's body, relieving aching muscles and easing vicious chills. David was only dimly aware of the soft skin underneath him. Instead, he just rested there, allowing the crackling fire to soothe him. He felt himself being pulled to sleep. He knew he needed to fight it, but the siren's call was just too strong. David let himself drift away, and soon, all he knew was an uneasy slumber only punctuated by another's heartbeat.

CHAPTER SEVEN: SERVICE

◆ ◆ ◆

Wilhelm held David until the other man was asleep. He clicked his tongue, getting Toman's attention, and held David's head up so the dog could take his place. David barely stirred. He curled up against the dog and drifted back to sleep. Wilhelm smiled softly. He stole a kiss, just to see what it would feel like, and forced himself to leave once it was done. They slept until dawn broke over the sky.

Wilhelm woke up first and rolled out of bed. The cold stone chilled his feet, waking him up a little, and he enjoyed the few moments of silence. Toman slept in front of the fireplace. David sighed a little in his sleep, as he always did, and gave no indication that he knew Wilhelm was up. Wilhelm watched him for a few long minutes, then he wandered over to his desk. He had work to do.

He reached into his pocket and pulled out the blood-soaked handkerchiefs. The stiff fabric clung to his hands. Wilhelm could smell the iron scent of blood, and he swore that there were strange white hairs stuck in the matrix. He lay one of them on his wooden desk and flattened it out with his hands. Some of the dried blood clung to his hands. He fought the urge to fling it away, knowing full well that this might have been used on his brother.

The handkerchiefs were very plain. They were made of white silk and embroidered with threads just a few shades darker than the material. Wilhelm held one up to the weak winter light. He could just see what he thought was an initial, though it was obscured with blood and white fur. He brushed some of it off, wondering why it now clung to his hands. Maybe there had been an injured white dog. Several of them lived around the castle, and it wasn't uncommon for one of them to be hurt.

He had just set the blood scrap of fabric back beside his companion when someone knocked on his door. Wilhelm ground his teeth. It couldn't be Henri; Henri knew he was welcome anytime and he could just come right in. On that note, he pulled on his coat and wandered over to the door. Behind him, Toman raised his head and growled. The wolfhound stared at the door with obvious malice. Wilhelm frowned.

"Toman? What's the matter?"

The dog snarled softly. He coiled his body around David and bared his teeth. Wilhelm left the dog to it. He opened the door slowly, not wanting to see who was behind it.

One of Maria's courtiers, a young man named Matthew, bowed his head. Matthew had one brown eye and one blue one and his dark hair was always neatly combed. He wore the same plain black-and-white clothing as his lady did, and his gaze was just as dour.

"Lady Maria requests you for midday chants," Matthew said. "We would like to sing a petition for your brother's soul."

Wilhelm gave him a long look. "I'm sorry, but I have other things to do right now."

"It's important!" Matthew stepped inside, neatly avoiding the door Wilhelm tried to close on his foot. "Please. If only for Maria. Why aren't you letting her mourn in the way she sees fit? Hasn't she given the kingdom her best years? She negotiated the truce with Donnhall. Doesn't that mean anything here?"

"He was my brother!" Wilhelm snapped. "Why don't you just leave me *alone!*"

Matthew gave him a pitying look and rested his hand on Wilhelm's shoulder. "And he is dancing with the angels. It's not his fault he didn't hear the Song of Truth. The Father has drawn him into—"

"Don't touch me!" Wilhelm flung Matthew's hand off of his shoulder and glared at him. "And get out."

"My lord—"

"I said *get out.*" Wilhelm's eyes narrowed, and he reached for a dagger he no longer carried. "These are my quarters!"

Matthew sighed softly and closed the gap between them. "I was told to collect you," he murmured. He gripped Wilhelm's chin with a sudden, strong grip. "I don't intend to fail this mission of mercy. Lady Maria is your aunt, and your father has not yet made you king."

"Are you threatening me?" Wilhelm asked. He took a step back, fighting the fear that built itself in his chest. "You could be arrested for this!"

"You are coming with me." Matthew wrapped his arm around Wilhelm and started dragging him out the door. "You do not have to sing, you do not have to pray. But your presence is required, my lord, and I intend to do my duty."

Wilhelm tried to fight him off. He dug his heels into the floor, but Matthew just pulled him over. Toman bounded out of bed. The dog snapped and snarled, going for Matthew, but the man took out his sword and struck Toman with the flat of it. The dog yelped. He rubbed at his nose, dark eye bewildered. David picked himself up, eyes half rimmed with sleep. When he saw what was going on, he threw himself out of bed and rushed Matthew.

"Let him go!" David almost slipped on the slick stone floor. "Let him go, you son of a bitch!"

"What?" Matthew dropped Wilhelm and held his sword at the ready. "Is that an Alsatian?"

"Yeah," David said, "it is."

Matthew stepped in front of Wilhelm and pressed the sword tip to David's naked chest. "Then what are you doing here? Were you trying to hurt my prince?"

"Um, I live here?" David said as if in a question. He backed up, eyeing Matthew. "You need to get away from *my* prince, sweetheart. Otherwise, I'm going to have to mess you up."

"You?" Matthew asked. "You don't even have trousers on!"

"That's not the problem you think it is," David hissed. He gestured to the whimpering dog and clenched his jaw. "I don't have to have pants on to kick your ass!"

Wilhelm could see how weak he was. His eyes might have blazed with white hot fire, but he clearly wasn't strong enough to win another fight.

"Stop it!" Wilhelm yelled. He held up his hands. "Matthew, we'll go. Just give David enough time to change."

"Go to what?" David asked. He scratched Toman's head. "What exactly am I being brought into?"

Matthew took a second to straighten his jacket and sheath his sword. Then, "Prayers and songs for the soul of Prince Emil. It is being hosted at the expense and insistence of Lady Maria. I do not think we've ever had an Alsatian visit, but there's a first time for everything."

Wilhelm didn't say anything. He backed away from Matthew. He didn't trust that man. He never had, not since Matthew had converted. There was something shifty about his former friend now. Wilhelm didn't like it. He buried his hand in Toman's fur and tried to calm his racing thoughts. Did Maria know? She knew they found her dagger, but that could be explained away. Perhaps one of the white carting dogs had been injured and she had tried to help it.

David grabbed his clothing. Wilhelm had draped it over the back of a chair and he hadn't expected it would be worn so soon. He hadn't even bothered to fold it. David dressed himself quickly, his movements quick and jerky. Anger twisted his beautiful face, and Wilhelm couldn't help but notice that he pocketed a small knife. If Matthew noticed, he didn't say anything. He just stared at his nails, pointedly ignoring what was going on in front of him.

David cleared his throat when he was dressed. "Right. Let's get this over with."

Wilhelm took his hand when they walked into the hall. He ran his thumb across David's hand, trying to comfort him when he felt how tense the other man was. The halls seemed to narrow in all around them. The shadows cast by the torches seemed menacing somehow, and the tapestries hung strangely still. Even the rushes on the floor were woven in bizarre, interlocking patterns. The only comforting thing was Toman as he followed them.

They crunched under his boots as Wilhelm walked, and he could only think of the snapping, popping sound that came from breaking bones. Had Emil heard that? Was that the last thing he knew? Or had he known something else—the cold terror that came from knowing you were the prey? He couldn't look at Matthew without think of his brother's last moments. He pressed close to David, trying to take comfort from the other man's presence.

A low, haunting chant filled the hall as they walked. Wilhelm couldn't understand the words, but he could feel the melody. There was something strange about it, something melancholy, and it jarred him. Wilhelm wanted to cover his ears and run away. Candles, set in brass and their own grease, replaced the flickering torches. No dogs ran through this section of hall. Every single one of the colorful frescoes had been scrubbed clean and whitewashed.

No holly decorated the exposed rafters. There were no evergreen boughs, no colorful winter wreaths. Even the tapestries were dull and sterile. They showed only pastoral scenes and sheep instead of dense forests or thrilling battles. A few pieces of crossed wood, some decorated with thorn vines, hung on the barren walls, but the halls were otherwise barren. The gray stone seemed to burn Wilhelm's eyes. He found himself hating it, and he wished he could bring a little life to these dull and broken halls.

Matthew stopped in front of a plain oak door. "Please remove your shoes. And no dog. Such things are unclean, and this is a holy place."

David gracefully knelt and unlaced his boots. "You know, your god has a lot of rules."

"Our god is the god of orders and boundaries," Matthew said. He removed his own shoes and smiled humorlessly. "There is a place for everything and a great chain of order that all have a place in."

"What's that?" David asked. He stood on the rushes in his bare feet. "And let me guess, Alsatians are at the bottom."

"David." Wilhelm nuzzled him. "Please. This is a holy place, not one to start fights."

David grumbled, but at least he kept his mouth shut. Wilhelm pulled off his boots and stashed them beside the others. He knew David should have been resting, but something told him not to send the other man away. He might not walk out if he did. Matthew opened the door silently and gestured for them to step inside. Wilhelm didn't want to, but he did anyway. Mentally, he added it to the list of things he would change as king.

The walls inside were draped with blue silk. More crosses and thorn crowns were painted on the silk, and candles were placed on every available surface. The room was filled with a soft golden glow. Maria knelt on what could only be an altar, her long brown hair unbound and all around her shoulders. She wore no gold and her plainest, most simple gray dress. There was no embroidery on it, and it fit over her body like a sack.

She rose and smiled when she saw this. "Wilhelm. And David. We met in the garden, I believe."

David tensed. "Where's Phillip?"

"Do you want to speak with him?" Maria asked. She gave them a gentle smile. "He is always available for matters of the faith."

"I don't want to speak to him unless he gets a bath," David growled. He stepped in front of Wilhelm, and his hand curled into a fist. "Unless he's going to melt, that is."

"David!" Wilhelm hissed. He nudged the man and tried not to let the embarrassment show. "Please, we're guests here. We can't make a scene."

They had to mind their manners here. He took David's hand and guided him to a row of hard, plain wooden chairs. David's nails dug into his palm. Rage shown on his face, and he looked like he was going to bolt. Matthew sat beside them and crossed his legs so they couldn't leave. Wilhelm almost asked why, but that was when a young woman dressed in white walked around, dousing the candles with a simple clay snuffer.

A man Wilhelm thought to be Phillip took the stage. "We are here to sing for the soul of a life cut short, a life lost before it could hear the truth! This soul is wandering around us even now, crying out for the righteous way and begging to not be shown eternal torment! It is our solemn, holy task to bring the Truth to every person in this kingdom! Otherwise, they shall die as Prince Emil died, lost and alone."

A small chorus of voices started to sing. The foreign words flowed from his tongue, and Wilhelm almost lost himself to their hypnotic song. Maria sang just as sweetly as any of her maidens and lifted her arms for a few moments. Wilhelm watched her with great interest. Phillip spoke in that same language, and his voice thundered through the small room. David winced. He bowed his head, covering it with his hands and whispering something in his own language.

"We need to leave," Wilhelm whispered. "David's still sick and he's overwhelmed."

Matthew gave him a nasty look. "Must you?"

"Yes. I must." Wilhelm helped a trembling David up and made sure he wasn't going to fall. "I think this is a wonderful experience, but I have to care for him. He cares for me."

Matthew scowled, but he moved back. Wilhelm didn't wait a second longer. He helped David out from that long row of chairs and guided him through the crowd. More people that ever seemed to crowd into that small, dimly lit space. They all pressed against him, seeming to suffocate him, and it was all Wilhelm could do to keep from fainting. He dragged David through it and flung the door open.

Both of them collapsed outside and pressed their overheated bodies against the stone walls as the heavy door swung shut.

David swallowed and sat up. "Let's never, *ever* do that again. Agreed?"

Wilhelm nodded. He had just opened his mouth to agree when something struck the back of his head, and all he knew was darkness.

CHAPTER EIGHT: ALLY

◆ ◆ ◆

David woke up and rubbed his head. "Ow. Whoever did that is going to get my boot up their ass!"

He turned around, fully expecting to see Wilhelm. When he didn't, his heart dropped straight to his belly. He dragged himself up, clinging to the stone wall with trembling fingers. Toman nudged his leg with his cold nose. The dog whined softly before gripping his shirt hem in his mouth. David pushed the dog away. He had to get his wits back together before they came back and tried again.

Toman barked sharply. The dog nipped his hand, making him yelp. David jerked his hand back and rubbed the aching flesh. He bent down and grabbed his boots, all the while keeping an eye on that dog. Toman paced in the halls. The dog whined and yelped. He scented the air and snarled as soon as anyone came close. David could hardly see, as someone had doused every single rushlight and candle in the hall.

"Easy!" David snapped. He reached for a sword that wasn't there and cursed when he came up empty. "I can't find him with you biting me!"

Toman barked again. The wolfhound darted forward, grabbing his sleeve and dragging him down the hall. David struggled to keep up. He could feel blood trickling down his head, and his entire skull ached. Someone had hit him. David intended to find who it was and rip them a new one. Toman let him go and the dog darted down another hall. His paws seemed to skim over the barren stone, and his baying bounced through the empty halls.

"Quiet!" David hissed. "You want them to know we're coming?!"

Toman bayed in response. The dog wagged his tail back and forth like a whip, right before he started pawing at a massive tapestry. Three entwined oaks stared back at David, and he swore he saw a white stag in the tree. He reached out to touch the animal. His fingers lingered on the yellowed white threads, and they traced over to the obsidian eyes. David shook his head. This...it couldn't be the stag in the garden!

Could it?

Toman barked again, jerking David from his thoughts. David pushed the heavy material up and slipped under it. He could just see a door, painted to look like the stone, set flush with the wall. Unlike the rest of the castle, this part wasn't plastered. No white chips clung to the uneven stones like this had once been plastered, nor could David smell any lime. Toman whined. The dog scratched at the door and tried to push, but his efforts were to no avail.

"Let me try," David whispered. He found the place where a keyhole should have been and he pressed. "This is one of those things I need to do."

Something clicked and the door swung open. David could just see a dim golden light at the end of the hall and wilted rushes covered the floor. He held it open for Toman, allowing the dog inside, and stepped over the threshold. The door slowly closed behind them and cut the pair off from the outside world. The air reeked of mildew and rot. Every single rush smeared into the stones underfoot. Some of them popped, and David gagged on the stench.

"You know, back in Alsace, this sort of thing wouldn't be allowed," David said. He petted Toman's back, trying to calm himself. "We would get someone with a broom up in here before the door shut again!"

"But this isn't Alsace," a soft voice said. Phillip stepped out from behind a rotting curtain. "This is Talla Gael."

"Yeah, I know." David eyed the man, shivering when he saw the bloody lines that crossed moon pale skin. "You okay, Phillip? Do I need to get a doctor or something? Because it looks like you got hurt real bad and—"

As much as he disliked the man – and hardly knew him – David didn't want to leave him to die.

"No!" Phillip held up his hands and the soft candlelight glittered off his broken fingernails. "These are holy wounds, wounds that I took for the soul of this nation. Treating them would be spitting in the face of the living god!"

"My gods believe that hurt people should get healing," David said. He held up his hands, noting the fear in the man's eyes. "And that people should get a bath. I don't know if you noticed this, but you stink."

Phillip bristled. David figured he didn't like being told he stunk, but David had never been in the habit of mincing words, and he wasn't going to start now. He just plastered a smile on his face and grabbed the man by the shoulders. The fierce man seemed to melt under his touch, and David could feel the bones under his skin. That skin seemed to be pale and clammy, like he was sick, and the back of his neck felt feverish.

"You're sick," he softly said. David shook his head and tried to get Phillip to sit. "You needed a doctor *yesterday*. I would know that you're sick, cause I'm kinda sick, too."

"I'm fine!" Phillip snapped. He staggered on his feet, and

fresh blood bubbled up under his nails. "I don't–I don't need a doctor."

"You're sick!" David said. He grabbed Phillip by the shoulders and shook the man, trying to rouse the man's fighting spirit. "And being in this rot-infested dump isn't helping!"

"Rot-infested dump?" Phillip didn't try to keep the scorn from his voice.

David rolled his eyes. "And, speaking of, you know anything about Wilhelm? Someone whacked us both on the head, and now he's gone. The dog brought me here."

Phillip looked at him like he had just suggested murder. "You think I would do anything to hurt the prince? Are you mad!"

"I mean, you terrorized me in the garden," David said. "So yeah, I think you would."

Toman growled softly and nipped his hand. David jerked away. He didn't know what had gotten into that dog. Before he could say anything, though, Toman reared up on his hind legs and started covering Phillip's face in licks. The man yelled and pushed at him, but the dog pushed him toward the wall and kept licking him. David grabbed the dog's collar. Toman was almost as tall as he was and twice as strong—all Toman did was lock his legs and refuse to move.

"Get him off!" Phillip yelled. "Get him off me!"

"Toman!" David tried to drag the dog back. "Stop it!"

The dog whipped around. He dropped to the ground, his hackle fur up. David quickly held up his hands. The dog didn't growl, but David swore he had eyes like molten gold in those few moments. Phillip groaned softly. He staggered against the wall, and his eyes fluttered closed. David stepped around the dog. He grabbed Phillip and threw his arm over his shoulder just like Phillip was a wounded soldier.

"We are getting you out of here, like it or not," David said. "I might not like you, but I know when a man's hurt. And you're hurt."

Phillip said something like he was going to protest. He tried to draw away and dig his legs into the filthy stone floor, but David just started dragging him along. He wasn't going to take no for an answer. He had seen enough death in his time, and he knew that being in this fetid trap was doing nothing good for Phillip's health. Every single one of the man's candles were drowning in their own grease, and all of his possessions were covered in a thin layer of grime.

Something moved behind them.

David dropped Phillip to the floor, pushing the man aside. He stood in front of the man. There had to be a weapon somewhere around here. He grabbed a rusting candelabra from where it had been left on a rotting ledge. Toman growled softly. He stood in front of David, his ears pinned to his skull. The massive wolfhound snapped at the air. David waited. Whoever it was would get bored soon enough.

"You can come out now!" David called. "I know you're here, whoever you are!"

Something moved in the corner of his eye. David turned around, just as a staff came toward his head. He dodged as best he could, slipping in the rotting reeds. Toman leapt at the figure, and his jaws sunk into the soft gray material. The figure wore a robe in that soft, silky material, and it clung to their body. The staff was made of strange dark, oiled wood, and it was set with ribbons of polished iron.

"Leave us alone!" David yelled. He swung the candelabra around like a wild man. "He's hurt! You'll kill him!"

"That's the idea!" a female voice hissed. She lunged again and swung the staff. "I have orders to get him out of the way!"

"For what?" David snapped. He grunted when the staff caught him in the ribs and he went down. *Hard*. "If there's anyone here who should kill him, it would be me!

He roughed me up the other day and really pissed me off!"

"I have my orders," the woman said. She drew back and ice-blue eyes glittered behind her veil. "And you would do well to get out of my way."

"How about no?" David gave her a cocky smile and tried to ignore the hammering in his own chest. "See, I've seen enough death in my time. I don't want to let this one die too!"

"Do that and you'll never see your prince again," the woman said. She had to be smiling behind her veil, and she lashed out with the staff, driving David to his knees. "Phillip isn't the only one with secrets in this castle!"

Toman snarled. The dog bit her in the wrist. He snarled, trying to drag her over, and jerked her around like she was a rabbit. She struck the dog again and again with her staff. Toman whined through his clenched jaws. The world swam in front of David's eyes, and he could hardly stay upright. Dizziness sunk its fangs into his mind. He heard himself crying out, and he leaned on the filth-blackened walls.

The woman threw Toman into the wall. The dog cried out when his body collided with the wall, and he didn't move for the longest time. She lunged toward David and struck his body with the butt of her staff. David tried to catch the second blow, but the wood caught his hand

and he dropped his weapon. He forced himself to stand. Anything to keep her away from Phillip.

The next blow sent him sprawling right through a wall of cobwebs.

"Would it kill you to clean in here!" David screamed. "I've been in rat holes cleaner than this!"

"This is a place to sleep and pray," Phillip slurred. "Nothing more, nothing less."

"He is right," the woman said. She dropped her staff and allowed David to struggle to his feet. "You could have given this place a decent scrubbing. You live in a castle, man!"

"You know, I don't like agreeing with people who tried to kill me and my dog," David said, "but she's right. This place could use a good scrubbing. And new rushes. These are rotting! No wonder you're sick!"

"He's sick?" the woman asked. "Why didn't he tell me? The sickness could take care of him!"

David lunged. He covered the ground faster than he thought he could and tackled her to the ground. The woman yelled. She struggled, punching him in the stomach and making him gag, and nearly threw him off more than once. David pinned her to the ground. He didn't weigh enough to keep her down for too long, but he could make her struggle some. He settled himself on her chest and held out his hand.

"Stick, please," David said. Phillip struggled up and handed it to David. David pressed it over her throat and cocked his head like a hungry dog. "Now, we're going to start this easy like. Where's Wilhelm? And who are you?"

"Go to hell!" the woman spat. "Hurt me and you'll never see your prince again!"

"You've already said that." David sighed. He pressed the staff down so it started cutting into her air. "And sweetheart, I survived being an outlaw. Hell ain't got nothing on that, so don't threaten me with a good time."

"I'll never tell you anything!" the woman yelled. "I'll die first!"

"Toman," David softly said. The dog picked himself up from where he lay and whined pitifully. "Take Phillip to the castle doctor. There has to be one. Phillip, tell the person in charge that the prince is missing."

"You'll never find him," the woman snarled. She struggled against the staff and raked her nails down his wrist. "You'll never find him alive! We made sure of that!"

"Yeah," David said, "I'll bet you did."

He settled back, like he was going to let her up, when her body seized and a strange sound came from her throat. David yelled. He ripped the scarf from her face, trying to see if there was a way he could help, but she was dead before the gray silk even hit the floor. David didn't wait to see if anyone else would show up. He dropped the body and bolted for the door.

CHAPTER NINE: CAPTIVE

❖ ❖ ❖

Wilhelm awoke in little pieces.

The first thing he knew was that he was lying on the ground, his cheek pressed into a bundle of half-rotted reeds. The next was that he was lying in the dark. The air smelled heavy and musty, like stagnant water was pooling in some distant place. Wilhelm kept his eyes closed. He could hear the distant murmur of some conversation and soft footfalls. There was someone here, he knew it, and he didn't want them to know he was awake.

Someone crouched beside him and ruffled his hair. "Do you think we killed him?"

"Nope," the other said. It was a soft voice, female, and the accent was strange. "His chest is still moving. He just got a nice hit on the head; he'll sleep for a good long time. When he does wake, he'll have a headache too."

Wilhelm tried to keep as still as possible. The man turned him over. Wilhelm forced himself to stay limp. He could hardly keep his eyes closed. He wanted to spring up, wanted to demand to know where he was, but he forced himself to stay still. The woman placed a cool hand on his forehead. She whispered something that he couldn't understand, and her words sounded like they came from a distant desert place.

"What does the lady want?" the man asked. "Naomi, we just can't leave him here. He is the crown prince, you know."

"I know," Naomi said. She slapped Wilhelm roughly. "Get up! Now!"

Wilhelm grabbed her wrist. He didn't know how he found the strength, but he sprang to his feet and tried to yank her over. Blue eyes widened in shock. Naomi yelled something. She reached for a curved dagger, and seconds later she tried to thrust it at him. Wilhelm dropped her wrist. He stepped back, his eyes wide. He could hardly see in the darkened chamber. Shadows pooled in every single crevice, and rats crawled in the little spaces.

The man held up his hands. Like Naomi, his hair was the color of spun gold. They both wore loose fitting gray tunics that hung off their bodies. Their skin was moon pale, far paler than Wilhelm was, and they were lithe where David was broad. Wilhelm swore under his breath. *David.* He was nowhere to be found, and Wilhelm couldn't help but fear the worst. *If they killed him...*

"Let me go and I swear nothing will harm you," Wilhelm said. He bristled and looked around for a weapon.

His heart hammered in his chest. He could hardly hear for the roar of blood in his ears, and he wanted to vomit from the terror of it. These people were going to kill him. He was going to die, just like Emil died. Only there would be no body this time. Wilhelm thought he saw something out of the corner of his eye. He swore he saw a white stag—a hart, just like his family name—and he almost tripped over something.

He picked it up on instinct. The shed antler fit perfectly in his hand, the bone smooth and worn, and the points made for a perfect weapon. On instinct, he lunged. The man yelled when the antler collided with his arm. Each one of the points ripped through his sleeve and skin. Wilhelm jerked it back. He eyed Naomi and that dagger. She moved like a wild cat, her steps sure and true, and she came at him like a wild thing.

Wilhelm ducked. He could feel the wind from the dagger, and the steel nicked his ear. He cried out from the pain of it. Blood—hot and wet—dripped down his neck. He tried to ignore the wound. He had to; there were people who wanted to kill him, and his only weapon was a piece of bone. Naomi snarled a curse.

She lunged at him again and barked an order in her language. Wilhelm slipped on a patch of rotten reeds and went down *hard*.

"Get him, Klaus!" Naomi yelled.

Klaus neatly avoided the swinging antler and kicked it out of Wilhelm's hand. Wilhelm just lay there. He looked up, silently waiting for the end. These people were going to kill him. Klaus put his bare foot on Wilhelm's chest. Wilhelm tried not to stare at him too much. He wanted them to just get it over with. This waiting was going to be the death of him, if not the dagger in Naomi's hand.

"Just kill me!" he spat. "Just get it over with!"

"You're more valuable alive," Naomi drawled. She stepped toward Klaus and nodded sharply. "Lucky for you, I might add. Get him up and in a cell. We can't risk him getting loose."

Klaus grabbed him up roughly, nearly sending him sprawling over again, and gripped his hands behind his back. The gesture wrenched his arms back. Klaus didn't seem to care about the pain, nor did he care that his breath reeked of dead things. Wilhelm tried not to gag. He also tried to lock his legs, but Klaus was stronger than him and simply frog marched him down a narrow, dark corridor.

Every part of this place (*Is it a castle?* Wilhelm didn't know) was cloaked in darkness. Cobwebs wrapped around every surface. The stones were covered in windswept leaves and pools of stagnant water. Light poured through broken windowpanes, and the glass glittered like jewels among the leaves. Wilhelm caught glimpses of dead limbs and trees covered in curled ferns. There weren't any standing stones near the castle, at least not any that he could see.

"Where are we?" Wilhelm asked. He paused in front of a rotting tapestry. "I've never seen this place before."

"And for good reason," Klaus growled. He kicked Wilhelm's right leg, making him stumble, and forced him to start walking again. "Winterhelm hasn't been used in nearly a hundred years!"

"Winterhelm," Wilhelm whispered. He stared at a crumbling fresco and shook his head. "I've never heard of it. I think it would be beautiful though."

Klaus grimaced. He didn't say anything; he just forced Wilhelm to keep walking along. Their footsteps stirred up clouds of dust and filth. Wilhelm coughed as they walked. He wanted nothing more than to get out of here, but that was just going to have to wait. He needed to figure out where he was for one and see if he could get a horse. Wilhelm didn't like wandering around without a map, but it was probably better than whatever they had planned for him.

He waited until they were on a flight of steep, algae-covered stairs before he dropped his weight. Klaus yelled. The sudden shift made him slip, and he fell against the stones with a terrific *crack*. Blood splattered the walls, the stairs, and Wilhelm. Wilhelm stared. The back half of Klaus's skull had caved in, and his eyes were wide and empty. Wilhelm forced himself to back off. He didn't want to look at that dead man.

The fact he had died without a single cry made Wilhelm shudder. Had Emil died like that? When he fell off his horse, had he hit his head and known nothing else? Wilhelm shuddered more and felt the bile rise in his throat. He couldn't stop now; Naomi was probably coming. He forced himself to step over the body. Great holes poked through the tower walls, and several stone steps were missing all together.

Wind tugged at his clothing as he walked. Wilhelm swore he could hear the whispers of the damned as he walked. Evergreen trees poked through the foundations when he was down to the base of it. The dying sunlight filtered through and pooled on the floor. White quartz —hundreds of thousands of polished pebbles set into the clay—reflected the light back with a kaleidoscopic brilliance.

Wilhelm didn't say anything. He pressed his body against the ragged stone wall and waited. He could see a bay roan horse tethered to a large tree in the clearing near the castle. It was a sturdy thing with thick, feathered legs and a bobbed tail, and it seemed to be calm enough. A tan dog with a curled tail sniffed around the edges of the forest clearing. It seemed to be decently tame—Wilhelm doubted it would bite him if he tried to dash out past it.

He could hear someone coming. Wilhelm slipped through a gaping hole and tried not to curse when he had to climb over a black thorn tree. The thorns ripped at his clothes and skin. It was all he could do not to curse, and he found himself stumbling across the hard ground as soon as he was through. He wiped the blood off on his pants. Wilhelm ran through the clearing as fast as he could and grabbed the horse by the halter.

The animal reared its head back and snorted in alarm. Wilhelm ignored it. He jerked the tether until it came free and cut the rope with a sharp piece of broken glass. He nearly sliced his hand to the bone in the process. He tied the tether to the other side of the halter, making a crude bridle, and mounted the horse's back. It was clearly a draft horse. It felt like he was straddling a barrel, and he winced every time it moved. He didn't have time to complain. He spurred the horse into a trot and hung on for dear life.

"After him! He killed Klaus!"

"Come on!" Wilhelm lashed the horse in the side with the rope. "Let's go!"

The animal half reared before it set into a heavy gallop. Wilhelm knew the horse couldn't run fast for very long, and its hoofbeats shook the earth around it. Still, he clung on for dear life. The horse dashed blindly through the thick forest. Heavy creeper vines covered in furry roots clung to twisted oak trees. Mist rose from the marshy ground as they ran, and the fetid water soaked Wilhelm's ruined trousers.

A wolf howled in the distance and was answered by its mate. Wilhelm pulled the horse to a stop. It shifted around nervously, ears pinned to its skull. The moon rose high and bright in this new little clearing. Dead sage grass crowded the place, and rune-covered stones poked through the tangle of brush and bracken. Something rustled behind them. The horse tossed its head again and backed up.

"Easy," Wilhelm whispered. He petted its neck as he looked around. "Is anyone there?"

"Now what's a pretty young boy doing in a place like this?" An older man, half his face covered in scars, picked his way out of the mist and held an old lantern high. "And how the hell did you get my horse?"

"I didn't steal it from you, if that's what you're asking," Wilhelm lied. "I was kidnapped and held at Winterhelm."

"Winterhelm," the stranger repeated. His eyes were the

color of new ice, and his orange-red hair was slicked back and braided with gold. "Now that's a name no one has used in, oh, about a century?"

"Well, I was there!" Wilhelm said. "And I'm not a boy! I'm a man!"

"Apologies, apologies," the man said. He held up his free hand and caught the horse by the bridle. "And I'm not doubting your story. This isn't the first time someone was held at that cursed place. But to find my horse there—my horse that was stolen from my corral—well, you have to wonder things."

"Wonder what?" Wilhelm bristled. "And who are you?"

"Johann." Johann gave him a sardonic smile. "I was a traveler here, much like you, though I was banished instead of kidnapped. I started a war that I couldn't win."

"My father always told me not to do that," Wilhelm said. He slid off the horse and winced when his legs touched the ground. "Do you always ride cart horses?"

"If I must. Now come on, night is falling and these woods are full of monsters." Johann took the horse and started down a winding, needle-thin trail. "What's your name, by the way? It seems fair; you know mine, so I should know yours."

"Are you Faerie?" Wilhelm asked. "I charge you by the sun, moon, and stars to answer that truthfully!"

Johann rolled his eyes. "I'm very human, thank you very much."

"Wilhelm." Wilhelm stuck beside the man and tried not to cringe when the wolves howled again. "Why do you live here? It seems so dangerous."

"Like I said, I started a fight." Johann ducked under a low hanging branch. "A fight that I had no chance of winning, but I was too arrogant to see it. Hubris, my people call it. That's my fatal flaw. I hide here so that no one can find me."

"Why don't you come back with me?" Wilhelm suggested. "I'm sure that Talla Gael could protect you."

"That's very kind, but you would not be able to." Johann sighed.

"Well, I would like to get back in one piece," Wilhelm said. "I need someone to go with me. I'm...not that good at fighting, and you look like you are. And then you'll have the gratitude of the entire kingdom."

"Pray tell, why?"

"Because I'm the crown prince," Wilhelm replied. He

smiled softly. "And my only brother is dead, killed by the same person I think took me."

Johann pinched the bridge of his nose and thought for a minute before saying, "Fine. I'll take you back. But don't expect me to fight any dragons for you, okay? I've had enough of heroics; my style is cut and run!"

Wilhelm just smiled. "We'll leave in the morning then?"

"I'm going to regret this," Johann sighed, "but fine. We'll leave at first light tomorrow morning."

CHAPTER TEN: MISSING

◆ ◆ ◆

Soldiers swarmed the castle, but there was no sign of Wilhelm. Even Toman couldn't find a trail. It wasn't for lack of trying either. David tried to stay at the back of the pack. He was Alsatian. They were going to suspect that he had something to do with it. David shivered and wrapped his coat around himself. If they thought he had done this—and there was every chance they might—being sent back to that camp was the least of his worries.

"What happened?" Henri came up behind him and pulled David into his arms.

"We got hit on the head," David said. "When I woke up, he was gone."

"There's a horse missing from the stables!" One of the servants, an older man with gray-streaked black hair, came running into the Great Hall. "One of Lady Maria's!"

Henri turned to look at David. "Are you thinking what I'm thinking?"

"Where's Phillip?" David whistled, getting Toman's attention. "I think he knows more than what he's telling. We have to find him!"

David dodged two soldiers and nearly ran into a third. No one paid him any attention. Another led in a pack of snarling, barking dogs. The animals growled at Toman. They were sleek bloodhounds, tricolored, and they had cropped ears that stood straight up. Toman was tall and shaggy, a true wolfhound, and it was clear that they didn't like each other. David didn't wait for the dog fight. He grabbed Toman's collar and dragged the dog after him.

Henri neatly wove his way through the crowds of people. It seemed that everyone in the castle and the surrounding village came out to find the prince. The woods would be crawling with soldiers, possibly some from the work camp. David pulled his hood over his head and tried to blend in. Some of them had that same gray-brown mud on their boots, and another looked like he was wearing the uniform.

"He's just around here," Henri said. Henri ducked into a side corridor and took David's hand. "It's not far now."

"Good," David said. "Because there are people back there I don't want to get a good look at me."

"Why?" Henri asked. He knocked on a plain wooden door and waited. "They're not going to hurt you, are they?"

"Has it escaped your notice that I'm Alsatian?" David asked. He crouched beside the door and tried the handle. "It's locked. Is this usually locked?"

"No, and I don't know why it would be."

David cursed. He tried it again, just to make sure, and went through his pockets once he knew the door was locked. Toman whined. The dog pawed at the door. He barked sharply and reared up before raking his claws all down the front of it. David didn't bother trying to figure out what he was doing. Instead, he grabbed a piece of wire from his pocket, straightened it out, and inserted the sturdiest end in the lock.

"What are you doing?" Henri asked.

"Get me one of the torches, will you? I need light for this." David bit his bottom lip as he worked. "Thanks, Henri. You're a doll."

He felt around for the mechanism and adjusted Henri's arm with his other hand. He could just barely smell blood. His belly rolled when he thought about it. If Phillip was dead... He didn't want to think about it.

David forced his hands to steady as he worked on the lock. After a few agonizing seconds, the door swung open. He straightened up. Henri put the torch back on the wall and drew his dagger before stepping inside.

The place didn't look like much. The walls were whitewashed, and the floor was made of neatly swept clay. A fireplace sat at the far end of the room, blazing merrily. The high, vaulted ceiling was free from dust and cobwebs. Even the windows that lined the far wall were clean and allowed a large amount of sunlight to filter through. The air smelled of herbs and something sweet, along with an iron undertone that unnerved David.

Toman darted into the room. He headed toward one of the cubicles at the back and started barking sharply. David followed him. He reached for a weapon that wasn't there, and his heart raced in his chest. The scent of blood became stronger as he walked closer. If he listened closely enough, he swore he could hear something dripping. Chills raced down his spine. A growing dread gripped him, and somehow he knew Phillip was dead.

Henri knelt beside a sheet-covered lump on the floor. "Uh, David?"

"What is it?" David stayed back.

"He's dead." Henri drew back, his face as white as the

linens and his hands covered in drying blood. "Someone stabbed him."

"I knew it!" David snarled. "Whoever took Wilhelm must have killed him! We need to see if there's a trail in the forest. Come on; let's get horses from the stables."

"Are you crazy?" Henri asked. "Someone cut his throat!"

"Yeah and they might do it to Wilhelm," David said. "I owe him my life, okay? I'm not about to leave him to his fate. Now are you with me or not?"

"Okay," Henri said. "Fine. We go to the stable and look around the forest. It shouldn't be that hard, you know."

"Good. Let's go." David whistled to get Toman's attention and started running.

His heart raced in his chest. Phillip was dead. That man had known something about Wilhelm, David knew, and someone killed him to cover it up. Maybe he even knew something about Emil. David's mind went wild as he ran. His heart pounded in his chest, and he could feel a stitch in his side, but he still kept on. A few of the ladies yelled at him as he hurried past them. He didn't care though. He had to find Wilhelm, and he needed a horse.

"You!" Maria grabbed him by the collar as he ran. "What did you do to him!"

"Nothing!" David yelled. He struggled to get away from her and gagged when she twisted his collar. "I swear it, lady! I didn't do anything to him!"

"Let him go!" Henri yelled. He grabbed Maria's arm and tried to drag her back. "He had nothing to do with this!"

"Let go of me!" Maria slapped Henri across the face with her free hand and dropped David in the process.

David picked himself up quickly. He rubbed his throat for a minute and then took off running. Henri followed him. One of the soldiers yelled, like he was going to try and stop them. Toman bit the man's hand right before he went running after them. David burst into the stable first. One of the stablehands yelled, and the horse he was holding reared. The animal was mostly white with a few black spots, and it was fully saddled up.

David grabbed the reins and mounted the horse as soon as it came down. The horse snorted. It tossed its head and tried to pull away from him, but David didn't give it the chance. He kneed the horse in the side. The animal surged under him and galloped out into the courtyard. Henri followed him on a blue roan. That stallion reared as soon as it exited the stable. One of the soldiers tried to grab David's horse and force the animal to follow him.

David kicked the man in the head. He dropped to the ground. David kicked the horse again, and it galloped toward the gate. People screamed and scattered in front of them. Toman only added to the chaos by barking as he ran. The horses' hooves clattered over the flagstones as they galloped. Someone slipped and fell, right in front of the horses, and both animals smoothly jumped over her.

They burst out of the castle gates and galloped through the village. Chickens shrieked and scattered in front of them. Ragged-looking dogs kept on chains snarled as they raced past. Ponies half reared and backed up. They nearly upset their carts, and people yelled and shook their fists. The crowd parted in front of them. It closed seconds later, just as the other soldiers started coming after them.

David guided the horse into the thick forest and pulled it off the path as soon as he could. Branches and vines tore at his breaches. Thick branches slapped his face. He crouched down against the horse's back to shield his face and let the animal have its head. The horse splashed through a deep stream. Icy water soaked David's legs, making him yell, and the horse scrambled up a bracken-covered bank.

"I think we lost them!" Henri called. He slowed down his panting, snorting horse and turned the animal around. "And we got lost ourselves."

David slowed down his own horse. "Well, at least we aren't being chased anymore."

Toman's ears pricked up and he growled. The dog raised his hackles. He stared at a gap in the underbrush, and a low growl rumbled through the air. David's horse shifted nervously. The animal pawed at the ground and tossed its head. David petted its neck. The animal ignored him and stared at that same spot. The shadows seemed to wreath something large. It moved toward them, and David heard Henri gasp.

A white stag—the same stag he had seen in the garden—stepped out into the little clearing. The animal's eyes seemed to glow gold in the half light, and hyacinth blossoms were tangled in its ivory antlers. Henri stared at it with wide eyes. Golden streaks now covered the scars that ran through the stag's coat. It turned around and started walking away before turning back to look at them.

"I think it wants us to follow," David said. He nudged the horse. "Are these things normal?"

"I've never seen a white stag before," Henri whispered. "Just in pictures. But never one in real life."

David nodded. He patted the horse's shoulder again. He thought he was going to call this one Snowflake—it had a white base with a few darker spots scattered around. The horse's pattern reminded him of that for some reason, and he decided to go with it. The stag snorted, jerking him from his thoughts. After a few seconds, the animal started picking its way through the forest.

David nudged Snowflake again, and the horse started to follow.

Darkness started to fall as they walked. Only birdsong filled the air now. David couldn't hear any sounds from the castle. The forest seemed to swallow them up even as it drew them in deeper. The stag found an old road, one filled with holes and missing stones, and started walking down it. Tree branches arched over it and twined together, forming a dense, dark canopy. Those thick and twisting branches were covered in coiled ferns and half-melted snow.

No one spoke for the longest time. David shivered and pulled his coat tighter around himself. The cold settled into his legs, especially where he had gotten wet. Snowflake turned around to look at him. The horse nickered softly, as if to comfort him, and soon went back to walking. A ruined village started cropping up all around them. Dark stone walls loomed in the air like broken, jagged teeth, and thick, furry creeper vines were hard at work pulling many of them down.

"We need to stop for the night," David said. He tried to hold the stag's golden gaze. "The horses are tired and so are we. Please, we can find you in the morning."

The stag lowered its head like it understood and vanished into the underbrush. David slipped off Snowflake. He led the sweating mare into a ruined stable and found a decent-looking corral. There was a pile of hay under a shed, meaning that the horse would be able to eat something, and the water pump still worked. David took her tack off and draped it over the fence before he started on the water.

"What is this place?" Henri asked. He paused, his eyes wide with fear.

David shrugged. "Some kind of city, I guess. I'm not from Talla Gael, so don't ask me."

Henri grinned softly. "Yeah, I get it. I've just... It's so near the castle. At least, I think it is. And I had no idea it was here."

David nodded. He helped with Henri's horse and locked the gate behind him. Both horses started on the hay. There was only a little bit of fighting over it, nothing to be worried about, and David left them to it. Instead, he found a cottage that was mostly standing and eased the rotting wooden door open. Cobwebs hung in sheets from the ceiling. Foul black rushes covered the floor. David grabbed a splintery twig broom and started sweeping the cottage out before they could sleep.

Henri winced when he found the bed. "This doesn't look like it's been used in a hundred years!"

"At least it's not covered in mud," David said. He straightened up and wiped the sweat off. "I've seen worse, you know."

"I know." Henri stood in front of him and nuzzled David. "Trust me, I know."

David couldn't help it. He cupped Henri's chin with one shaking hand and gave him a soft, gentle kiss that had the potential to turn into more.

CHAPTER ELEVEN: JOHANN

❖ ❖ ❖

Johann took Wilhelm through the dark forest. Only the tepid lantern light lit the way. Massive tangles of thorns clawed at them from the trail. Neither one of them rode the horse. It was already tired, and lather clung to its sides. To ride it like that would have been a great cruelty. Wilhelm wanted Johann to like him, so he forced his tired legs to walk and slogged his way through the rancid, freezing mud.

Owls called and pierced the night air. Thick clouds covered the moon and plunged the swamp into intense darkness. Wilhelm could hardly see the vines before they tripped him. The stones also made him stumble, and the trail was as thin and winding as a piece of sewing thread. Johann picked his way through the swamp with the ease of someone who knew his way. Wilhelm wasn't so lucky and found himself nearly falling on his face more than once.

Johann caught him after the last one. "Easy there. You're

going to break your neck if you keep doing that."

"Not my fault I can't see," Wilhelm grumbled. He rubbed the mud from his face and sat down right in the middle of it. "It's so dark here and there are vines and I just can't!"

"I know," Johann said. He sighed and offered Wilhelm his hand. "Come on, it's not far now. Then you can get clean and rest a little."

Wilhelm almost said something about patronizing him, but he managed to keep his mouth shut. He took Johann's hand and slowly stood. The mud clung to his body. He shivered as he started following the man once again. More wolves started howling somewhere in this dark mire and owls answered them. A cold chill settled over his shoulders. Wilhelm reached for a cloak that wasn't there and cursed softly.

"Are you all right?" Johann asked. He helped Wilhelm through a particularly dense patch of sedge and allowed the horse to graze for a second.

"I'm tired, cold, dirty, and hungry," Wilhelm said. "I want to go home. I have an appointment with my bodyguard and a massage and I am overdue by several hours."

Johann laughed softly. The ground started drying out under them, and the trail started widening. Soon, they were walking over what had to be an old road, one that hadn't been maintained for years. There were deep pits dug all through the center of it, like someone had been digging through the stones for the clay beneath, and they shone in what little moonlight there was. Johann avoided all of them, and soon they came to a hovel in the middle of a ring of standing stones.

"This is where I live," Johann said. He led the horse through a few more of the stones and turned it loose in a ragged corral. "I know it's not a palace, but it's better than nothing."

It was also better than Winterhelm, that was for sure. The hovel was made of local stones, piled on top of each other and plastered with mud. The roof was thatched and a piece of embroidered cloth served as the door. Johann ducked inside and gestured for Wilhelm to follow him. Inside, there was just one room and the floor was covered in woven rushes. The walls had been plastered with pale clay, and a circle of stones protected a dead fire.

A large white dog raised its head as he walked in. Wilhelm held out his hand, letting the dog sniff it. The big white dog lowered her head and went back to sleep after a second. She was so different from Toman. Her fur was slick instead of coarse, her legs weren't feathered, and her tail arched at the end. Her head was wedged shaped like the herding dogs in the village, and she had a wide, broad chest like she was made for running.

"Her name is Myla," Johann said. He took out a small box from a hiding spot and opened it, revealing flint and tinder. "Here, get me some of the hay sticks. We need to get a fire started."

Wilhelm searched around and came up with a pile of slender, braided straw sticks. Those he handed over and watched as the older man struck the stones together. A few sparks landed on the hay, and soon there was a fire in the little hearth. Johann fed the little fire with some of the larger sticks until it was larger and filled the hovel with warmth. Then he stood, searched around, and came up with a small package wrapped in hide.

"I'll get some water. You cut the carrots and the potatoes," Johann said.

Wilhelm started. "I don't know how to do that. Could you?"

"Son, I don't have the time," Johann said. He sighed and rubbed his face. "But of course you wouldn't know how to do that. You're royalty."

Wilhelm shrugged. "I've never had to do it before."

"I'll show you after I get the water," he said. Something passed over Johann's face as he stood. "It's not that hard. I had to learn the hard way too."

"Were you a prince?" Wilhelm asked.

Johann shook his head as he turned for the door. "No," he finally said, "I wasn't. But I was someone famous. I couldn't be who I wanted, and I think I resented that. So I took it out on others. But here, the only one here who could hate me is Myla. I'm pretty sure my own dog would never do that!"

Wilhelm nodded. He didn't know what to say to that. He could see a small bag of red potatoes hung on the wall, along with another bag of carrots. Wilhelm's breath caught as he slowly thought things through. Those potatoes and carrots might be the only food this man had. It wasn't like he could just go to the market either. Johann might not have had the coin needed for such a trip.

If Johann truly was an exile, there was a chance that going to town could put him in danger. It could even get him killed.

Johann came back with the water. "The big pot, please. And the juniper berries and some of the rosemary. Maybe salt too. I almost killed myself out here because I didn't have enough salt."

"Will you have enough food?" Wilhelm asked. "Later, I mean. After I'm gone."

"I'll be fine," Johann stiffly said. "Now get what I asked

for."

Wilhelm knew a closed subject when he heard one, so he backed off. He wasn't quite sure what some of the herbs were, but he found what he thought they were and handed it over. Johann snatched it. His lips were pressed in a thin line, and his eyes were narrowed. Wilhelm didn't know what was wrong. He wanted to ask, but part of him feared the answer. What if he had said something? If he pushed too far, Johann wouldn't take him back.

"Skin the carrots with the boot knife," Johann said. He showed Wilhelm what to do. "I'll deal with the rest of it."

Wilhelm nodded. He did his best to copy Johann's motions and not waste too much. It was far harder than it looked, and the knife slipped more than once. Johann steadied his hand after a moment.

"Easy," the older man whispered. "Let the knife guide you. Don't try to force it."

"That's easy for you to say," Wilhelm grumbled. "You know what you're doing and I don't!"

"That's why you're learning," Johann replied. He smiled crookedly and sat beside him on the straw. "You'll get it soon, I promise."

Wilhelm didn't believe him but nodded anyway. After he was done with that, he added it to the pot of simmering water. Soon, a warm fragrance filled the hovel. Wilhelm found his belly rumbling, and he couldn't look at Johann. He didn't want to take from this man. Johann had very little, and here he was, offering his food to a stranger. Wilhelm wasn't even sure if they were in Talla Gael right now.

"I wonder if they're trying to find me," Wilhelm said. He looked up and tried to meet Johann's gaze. "Maybe they sent out search parties, I don't know. But I know my parents have to be frantic."

"You said Talla Gael, didn't you?" Johann asked. "We're only a few miles outside the border, you know."

Wilhelm frowned. "But what day is it? How did we get so far?"

"The river." Johann stoked the fire and stared at it for a few long minutes. "At least, that was what I would do. I would let the river carry me as far as I could and then go over land. Probably with a fast horse."

Wilhelm shook his head. "But the time it took to get me out of the castle and down the river. Surely it couldn't be that long!"

They sat in silence for a long time, perhaps an hour or so. Wilhelm watched the flames as he sat there. He tried to wrap his mind around everything that happened – being kidnapped, dragged into the wilds, and trying to find his way home. Johann must have noticed how unnerved he was, because the older man cleared his throat and kept glancing his way.

"There are secret passages, right?" Johann asked. He got two small bowls and started ladling out the stew. "If it's anything like the castle I grew up in, that thing is riddled with side chambers and tunnels that don't show up on the plans. It's not hard to think of them getting you in a side chamber and taking you out during the chaos."

"Someone must have seen," Wilhelm said. "They must have!"

"I hate to say it, but they're probably dead." Johann handed out the stew and tucked into his own bowl. "Go on and eat. You'll need this later."

Wilhelm picked at it. Despite the salt, juniper, and rosemary, the stew was bland. He couldn't even tell what kind of dried meat he was eating. It was still tough and stringy even after being boiled in the water. At least the carrots were nice. The potatoes still had the skin on them and Wilhelm forced himself to eat it all. It wouldn't do to turn down this generous gift, especially when this was all Johann had.

Myla pricked her ears. The white dog wandered to the

front of the hovel and poked her head out into the courtyard. She growled softly. Her hackles went up as the fabric pooled on top of her. Johann swore softly. He grabbed a sword Wilhelm only just noticed in the rushes and went to see what was going on. Wilhelm followed him. He heard a man yell and a blond man wearing armor burst into the hovel like he owned the place.

"You!" the man snarled. He drew a sword and struck Johann with the flat of it. "So this is where you've been hiding!"

"Leave him alone!" Wilhelm yelled. He jumped up like he could defend them both. "He's not hurting anyone!"

Something dark flashed in the blond's eyes. Johann picked himself up. His cheek bled a little, and he gripped his fists like he was trying not to punch this man in the face. Myla barked sharply. The dog lowered her head like she was going to lunge. The blond struck her, making the dog yelp, and grabbed Johann by the collar. Johann glared at him. Hate smoldered in his blue eyes as Johann finally freed himself from the knight's grasp.

"I have no quarrel with you," Johann growled. "Leave this to your master and me."

"My master's battles are mine," the man said. He gripped Johann's arm hard enough to make the man groan. "By right, I could kill you right now. What were you doing with that boy?"

"We were eating!" Wilhelm yelped. "I was taken from my people, and he was going to take me home tomorrow! He knows the way!"

"Do you know who this man is?" the knight asked.

"His name is Johann, he's an exile, and he's my friend." Wilhelm set his jaw and glared. "We don't have a fight with you!"

"That's for Lord Antonio to decide," the knight said. He sneered and kicked Johann, making the man stumble and groan. "You may call me Sir Steven if you like. And I'll call this one what he is—a traitor!"

Johann picked himself up and brushed the straw from his tunic. "You'll call me by name or you won't call me at all."

Wilhelm had enough of this. He glanced into the courtyard, and his heart froze when he saw five knights. All of them had strong, fast horses under them. One of them even took Johann's horse from the corral and laughed as it tried to spook. Another dismounted and came to his master. He carried a length of strong chain and proceeded to roughly manacle Johann. That knight wrenched his arms to tightly behind his back that Johann cried out.

"Take the boy," Steven ordered. "I'll take the traitor."

"Let me go!" Wilhelm struggled as he was grabbed again. "Let me go! I am Prince Wilhelm of Talla Gael, and I order you to let us go!"

The knight laughed coldly. "Oh yeah? And I'm King Antonio. We'll deal with you later, little boy!"

Wilhelm bristled, but a sharp look from Johann made him quiet down. He didn't like this one bit. Some dark part of him wondered if this had all been set up. And if it was, just who was behind it?

CHAPTER TWELVE: LOVER BOY

◆ ◆ ◆

David sat beside Henri on a pile of dusty straw. He tried not to look at the holes in the roof too much—they reminded him of that hellhole he had escaped from. Starlight shown through the gaps in the thatch and pooled on the filthy floor. There was what looked like a broken cook pot in one corner, along with a ring of stones in the center. Filthy leather pillows were stacked beside the far wall. They were leaned against a cracked and damaged cedar chest.

Henri sprawled against him. "Look at the stars, David. I've never seen so many of them before."

"You should see where I come from," David said. He brushed a kiss against Henri's cheek and held his hands. "There are thousands of them, far more than this, and they paint the sky silver with their light."

"That sounds beautiful." Henri snuggled closer to him and let a smile cross his fine, pretty face. "Show me some day?"

"If the war ever stops." David tried not to let his pain color the words.

"I wonder what happened to all these people," Henri murmured. "Look at this place. It wasn't abandoned that long ago, you know. The roof is still decent. A thatch man with a few hours could fix it, you could get new rushes, and people could live here. I wonder what happened to them."

"Maybe they moved," David said. "The river might have rerouted, a well might have dried up, hell, maybe they got bored of the place."

Something, though, didn't feel quite right. Shadows danced on the wall, and it was all he could do to not watch them too much. A question lingered on the tip of David's tongue: Why had the stag brought them here? There had to be a reason for it. David just didn't know what, and he had no way of finding out. Something rustled outside of the little house. David reached for a sword that wasn't there, cursing himself for being unarmed, as he got up.

Yet instead of a monster, a white dog streaked with mud stumbled inside. Toman got up quickly. The wolfhound snarled, his ears pinned to his skull, as he stalked toward the other dog. The white dog snapped at him. She looked like some type of herding dog, and her beautiful coat was marred with blood, mud, and all kinds of filth. Her belly was covered in stinking stagnant water like she had been running through a swamp, and she flopped down on one of the pillows like she owned the place.

Maybe she does. Maybe this is a shepherd's hut that we've intruded on.

"Easy, Toman," David said. He got up and caught the big wolfhound by the collar. "I don't think she means any harm."

Toman barked sharply. He strained against the collar, and he was almost strong enough to yank David off his feet. David forced the big dog back. Toman's paws rent up great strips of rotting rushes, revealing the stained clay beneath, and his baying filled the air. The white dog just ignored him. She rested her head on her paws and stared at the firepit. Henri scrambled up. He grabbed Toman and, together with David, dragged the nervous wolfhound outside.

"She's not a Faerie, that's for sure," Henri said. He crouched beside the dog and scratched her large, bat-shaped ears. "I would feel better if you started a fire though. Everything I've heard says that Fae don't like those."

David had his own ideas about Fae, but he kept his mouth shut. Instead, he dug around by the circle hearth and came up with a small case made of cracked and worn hide. He bit his bottom lip as he flipped it open. Inside, he found a small, rusting piece of steel and a piece of colorfully banded flint, along with a handful of tinder. David took a few pieces of the shredded cedar bark and some dry rushes before he crouched over them and started striking.

"Henri, can you go see if there's any wood in that shed?" David asked.

Henri nodded. He got up quickly, his expression nervous, and he didn't make a sound as he slipped out into the night. A wolf howled in the distance. It was answered by some strange night bird, and the song chilled David to the bone. His hands shook as he started to work. The tinder caught after the second shower of sparks, and soon a thin tendril of smoke crawled through the air. After a few minutes of careful blowing, it caught and thin orange flames crept through it.

"Here." Henri handed him a small bundle of sticks. "There's more, but I wanted to get this dealt with before we did anything else. The wood's dry too."

"Good." David tried not to look at Henri too much. Then, "Do you think he's dead?"

"Gods above, I hope not," Henri said. He shuddered as he sat down. "Now that would inflame the war. Maybe even take it to a new level. If someone did that…"

"Henri, if Wilhelm were to die, who would be the next ruler?" David asked. He dropped a few of the smaller sticks into the fire.

Henri shrugged. "I think Lady Maria."

David gave Henri a long look. "Lady Maria? The same person who owned that dagger? And the same person who had Phillip as her priest?"

"Are you suggesting..." Henri trailed off. "No! I don't think her religion lets you murder people! Even if they don't believe the same things you do!"

"It hasn't stopped them before," David said. When he saw Henri's look, he continued. "Back in Alsace, we had a group of people who came preaching the same things as Maria does. Only they used it to try and take power. I don't know the details because I wasn't born yet, but they spoke of the same things and even sang the same songs."

"I don't think she could do that," Henri said. He ran a hand through his red hair. "Look, I know she can be a bit much, but I don't think she's capable of murder."

David nodded. He built up the fire a little more and curled into Henri's side. He was a little taller than Wilhelm, a bit more broad in the shoulders, but it felt nice to hold someone and know that he was cared for. He slipped a hand under the man's shirt and enjoyed his lithe, lean body. He couldn't help but press a kiss over Henri's pulse point. He groaned softly, angling his head so David could have better access.

"Damn," Henri whispered, "you are needy."

"It's been a long time," David admitted. He stripped off his shirt and let the firelight dance over exposed skin. "I've...I've needed someone. And no one was there for me."

That wasn't the half of it, but Henri didn't need to know that. The man caught his hand, pressing it close to his own chest. The warm firelight reflected in Henri's eyes. His expression was something unreadable, not that David cared too much, and he soon found himself straddling Henri's chest. Henri pulled him down, running a hand over his back and cupping David's ass. He could feel the heat of Henri's fingers through the material, and he couldn't help but push back against it.

Henri kissed him fierce and hard. David deepened the kiss as best he could. He clutched the other man close to him. Henri broke off the kiss, his eyes dark with desire. He stripped off his own shirt and tossed it away from them. David didn't know where it landed, nor did he care. All he knew was that his body ached for something he hadn't had in a long time. His cock throbbed where it was trapped inside his trousers.

David undid the laces with one trembling hand. Then, on a whim, he did the same for Henri. Both of them clung to each other, and soft sounds spilled out when David wrapped both of their cocks with his fist. His own dripped with arousal, and his legs shook when he started to stroke. Henri's eyes fluttered closed. He let loose a quiet groan and bared his neck like he was surrendering himself.

David didn't waste any time. He leaned over and grazed that soft skin with his teeth. He sucked a mark as he stroked their cocks. Henri's soft panting was music to his ears. Henri gripped him, his nails scratching down sweaty skin, and he said something in a breathy whine. David didn't understand him. He didn't care to. He lost himself in the slowly building pleasure and tried to imagine what it would be like to slowly sink down on Henri's shapely cock.

It was slender, just like the rest of him, and throbbed with arousal. David didn't waste time admiring it. He groaned softly, holding Henri close to him, and started to tense up. He could feel it coming, building at the base of his spine, and it was all he could do to let out a small warning. He jerked as he came, his body arching in pleasure, and he could hear in some distant way his own voice calling out Henri's name.

He slumped over Henri, his heart racing. The other man squirmed under him. He opened his mouth like he was saying something, not that David was paying attention, and grunted something when he came. David threw a lazy arm around him. He didn't want to move. He buried his nose into the crook of the other man's neck and breathed in his sweet scent. Warmth from the fire washed over him, slowly lulling him to sleep.

For the longest time, all he could hear was the crackling fire and Henri's soft breathing. He tried to imagine that Wilhelm was here too. If he listened closely enough, he could hear Wilhelm's own breathing and feel him curling up between them. David tried to tell himself that he deserved this, that there was no use punishing himself for something he couldn't prevent. After all, he wasn't strong enough for a pitched battle.

Not yet, anyway.

Dawn slowly crept over the horizon. Both men lay curled into each other's arms, their clothes still scattered across the floor of the little hut. The fire had long since died down into ashes. Only a few strands of smoke coiled into the air now. Outside, frost had fallen and the world sparkled like it was covered in thousands of diamonds. Sunlight pooled through the tangled canopy of branches. It pooled on the frosty ground and in between the gaps in the roof.

David woke up first and nudged Henri. "Wake up, sleepy head."

"Lemme alone." Henri rolled over and reached for a

blanket that wasn't there. "Quit hogging the blankets too."

David laughed softly. "Henri."

"What?" Henri rolled over, his hair mussed and his eyes half open.

"We aren't in the castle anymore." David laughed. He smiled softly and shook his head. "Come on, we need to see if we can find that stag."

Henri looked down and frowned at the mess on his belly. "First, we need to get clean."

"Do you see a bathhouse?" David asked. He gestured to the rotting house around them. "Because I don't see one anywhere near here. There is a well, though. Toss me one of the rags."

Henri gave him a long look, but complied. The rag itself was old and moth eaten. It had probably been there for ages. David stepped outside into the cold air and cursed as it burned his exposed skin. He didn't know what he had been expecting though. It was winter and there was frost on the ground. He found the well and pulled up a bucket of water before wetting the rag. David yelled when it touched his soft skin. He forced himself to clean off with it and rinsed it out before taking it back to Henri.

Henri crouched beside the now steady fire and took the rag. "Thanks."

"No problem," David replied. He sat beside the other man and waited. "So. Do you think we'll find the stag again?"

As if in response, the white dog slipped back inside. Toman followed her. His legs were scratched like he had been in a fight and one of his ears was bloody. The white dog looked perfectly fine. She sniffed around the rushes and started digging. Soon, her claws hit on something metal. David jumped up. He raced to the dog's side and helped her unearth a copper box. The sides were covered in elaborate scrollwork, and the burnished metal gleamed in the bright morning light. He grabbed his shirt and coat while he was thinking about it, slipping them both on.

David tried the top. "Well, it's locked."

"Here." Henri handed him a smooth stone. "Break the lock with this. A few blows to the center of the top should do it."

David nodded. He couldn't see a lock on the box, but that didn't mean there wasn't one there. He struck the box hard several times, wincing when he saw dents spread across the surface. Then something clicked. The lid sprang open, revealing a few scrolls set against the sides and nothing else. David took one just to see what it was and set the rest of them down. He ran his finger across the picture at the top of it.

A white stag reared, framed by standing stones and a copse of fir trees.

"What the hell?" he whispered. He rolled the scroll back up and stuck it back in his coat. "Henri, are you ready to go?"

Henri nodded as he stood. "As I'll ever be."

David nodded as he stepped outside. Unease settled over his shoulders, and for the life of him, he couldn't figure out why.

CHAPTER THIRTEEN: CAPTIVE AGAIN

◆ ◆ ◆

Steven tied the rope around Wilhelm's wrists tightly enough to hurt. He did the same to Johann's manacles and kicked the man so hard that he stumbled. Wilhelm tried to break free to comfort the man, but one of the other knights struck him. The blow sent him sprawling, and Wilhelm struck the ground, hard. He couldn't stop the cry that spilled from his lips. Johann yelled something, but Steven slapped him across the face and drew a dagger.

"Either you calm down or I'll stick this between your ribs!" Steven snarled.

"Sir!" One of the knights pulled down their visor, revealing a woman with closely cropped red hair. "The dog just went running off into the night. Should I catch it?"

"Leave the dog alone," Steven ordered. He gestured to Johann and Wilhelm. "We have what we want. Let's get moving before anyone else shows up."

Another knight, this one wearing leather armor, grabbed Wilhelm by the collar. "Let's go, pretty boy."

"My name is Wilhelm!" Wilhelm snarled. He struggled as much as he could, but the man was just too strong. "Let me go!"

"Sorry," he said, "but orders are orders. Taliya, make sure they can't come back to this dump!"

"Right, sir!" The woman saluted and grabbed a small leather pouch from her saddle bags. "Sir Steven, are you ready?"

Steven paused from forcing Johann on his horse. "Go ahead and burn it. I don't care either way."

Wilhelm shivered. He allowed the other knight to drag him on his own horse. This one was a bay charger, its shoulders broad and strong, and it stood patiently until the knight mounted it. Wilhelm tried to hold himself steady. He didn't want to curl up against this man. His cheek ached from where it had been struck. He wanted nothing more than to fling himself off the back of this horse and go running for the hills, but his hands were tied and he knew he wouldn't get far.

Taliya knelt beside the thatch and pulled out two familiar looking rocks. She struck them a few times, producing a shower of sparks, and the dry thatch caught. Seconds later, flames raced across the roof. The entire structure seemed wreathed in flames only a little after that. The bright orange glow filled the night with its light, and a perverse warmth washed through the little clearing.

Wilhelm turned his head in shame. Had he led these men here? Was it his fault that Johann had been captured and his home burned? He looked at the assembled knights again, noting their travel worn faces and how weary their horses looked. Dried mud clung to saddles, skin, and fur. Wilhelm wanted to feel sorry for them, but he couldn't stir the emotion. Once that might have made him feel sad or even scared him, but now he didn't even care.

"Flint!" Steven snapped.

Flint, the man guarding Wilhelm, jerked his head up. "Yes, sir?"

"You take point," Steve said. He gestured to the others. "Move out! We have a long way to go!"

Johann gritted his teeth and cocked his head to the right when Wilhelm looked at him. Wilhelm frowned. He knew the man was trying to tell him something, but he couldn't quite figure out what it was. His wrists twitched as he thought. Wilhelm was just about to open his mouth to ask Flint where they were going when a massive white stag charged out of the forest. The horse he was on reared, sending him sprawling to the ground.

"What the hell?" Flint wrestled with his horse. "Steven! Do something!"

The stag charged him. The animal caught the horse by the chest with its antlers. It drove the points into the stallion's body and tossed the screaming horse into the ground. Flint jumped free. He grabbed his sword and yelled, brandishing at the animal. The stag ripped his head free with a sickening sound of tearing flesh. It stamped the ground before rearing. Flint-sharp hooves lashed out, nearly catching the cowering knight.

Wilhelm didn't wait any longer. He jerked his hands, cursing when the rope cut into them, and smashed the ties into Flint's spare sword. The metal might have cut his wrists, but he didn't care. He grabbed the sword and lunged, stabbing Flint in the neck. Someone yelled. Seconds later, Johann twisted around. That man bashed his wrists into Steven's head. He fell out of the saddle, just as Johann dismounted the horse.

Wilhelm cut the ropes with the weapon he still held. They had already cut into Johann's wrist, making his skin slick with blood, and the man was grim-faced from pain. Wilhelm bashed the manacles with his dagger. Seconds later, they came undone. Johann grabbed the sword from Wilhelm's hands and lunged. He traded blows with Taliya, driving the woman back and toward the stag.

The stag caught another knight. It drove those sharp, bloody antlers through the man's padded armor and lifted him from the saddle. The man screamed and lashed out, trying to get free, and the stag tossed him into the ground. Wilhelm grabbed the man's panicking horse. Johann's horse had already galloped into the chaos, leaving them far behind. Wilhelm mounted the white stallion midstride and turned it around.

"Johann!" he screamed. "To me!"

Johann paused. The other knight lunged, scoring him across the cheek. Wilhelm kicked the stallion in the side. The animal charged right at the two men. It nearly ran over the other knight. Johann grabbed the saddle with his free hand and dropped the sword. Seconds later, he was in the saddle, one arm wrapped around Wilhelm's middle. Wilhelm spurred the horse in the side and sent it galloping down the trail.

"After them!" Steven screamed. "Bring me that boy!"

"What the hell was that for?" Johann snapped.

Wilhelm lashed the horse in the side. Only moonlight lit the way now. The horse just barely stayed on the trail as they ran. Narrow, tangled vines yanked at their clothes. Blackened branches slapped at their face. Mud splattered them as they ran. The wind seemed to tug at his clothes, threatening to yank him off, and Wilhelm could hardly find the words for what he had done.

The trail led them to clearing filled with moonlight. Grasses stained silver waved in the wind, and barren trees reached up to the sky. The horse stumbled to a stop. Its sides heaved as it tried to catch its breath. White lather caked its sides, and it seemed to shake as it stood. Wilhelm dismounted it as quickly as he could. Johann followed him. The man whispered something to the horse as he pulled the tack off.

The horse looked at him with tired amber eyes as it swayed. Wilhelm watched it closely. He didn't know what to say. The horse was clearly hurt. It stumbled as it took another few steps until it fell to its knees and lay down. Johann crouched beside it. He caught the animal's big head in his arms and petted its nose. Wilhelm sat beside him. Some strange part of his mind said that the horse was dying and that it was his duty to watch.

"You did well," Johann whispered. He petted the horse's muzzle as it struggled for breath. "Brave war horse. May your soul run forever free."

Wilhelm looked away. "I didn't mean to kill it."

"He ran for days before this," Johann said. He held the

horse until its sides stopped heaving. "It's not your fault."

"Who's Steven?" Wilhelm asked. He stood up and helped Johann do the same.

"He was a friend." Johann looked away, and it was a long time before he spoke again. "He made his choices and I made mine. We both have to live with it."

Wilhelm nodded. He didn't know what else to say. He just took the older man's hand and squeezed it. A house stood in the middle of the clearing. It was little more than a few walls and a rotting thatch roof, but it would do. Wilhelm wandered toward it. A cool wind drifted through the clearing. It made the grasses dance like the sea as he walked. He wanted to ask more about these men, but something told him it wasn't the right time.

Johann sat down as soon as they were inside the house. "How did you get all the way out here?"

"Someone kidnapped me," Wilhelm said. "That same person killed my brother, and now she's trying to kill me."

"She?" Johann gave him a long look. "My agreement was getting you to your kingdom, not getting involved in a domestic quarrel."

"I know." Wilhelm didn't look up as he squatted on the dirty floor. "As soon as we get back, I'll pay you."

Johann nodded as he pursed his lips. "Thanks. Might need a place to stay, too, until all this blows over."

"I can do that," Wilhelm said. "The court is big enough for a guest."

Johann looked away. Something distant and sad crossed over his expressive features. He pulled his cloak around his body as he sat. It draped over his body like it was made from the finest silk. A thousand questions danced on the tip of Wilhelm's tongue. He wanted to ask who this man was or where he came from. How had he gotten to this place and why had Steven even bothered to track him down? Wasn't exile enough?

"We'll need horses," Johann said after a long silence. "That one's dead, and only the gods know where mine is. Steven will track us as soon as it gets light."

Wilhelm glanced at the older man and chewed his bottom lip. "Can I ask you something?"

"Go ahead," Johann said. He scanned the marshland, like he was looking for something only he could think of.

"Steven hates you and you hate him," Wilhelm said. "Why didn't you kill him? I didn't kill him because I'm a bit of a coward, but you're different. Well, I like to think so."

Johann took a breath. An eternity seemed to pass before he spoke.

"I'm tired of killing," he finally said. "I'd like for you to stay that little bit of a coward, too. Once you start killing..." He trailed off and shrugged. "Anyways, I have no idea where the hell I am and if I'm pissing someone off right now."

"I thought you knew the swamp," Wilhelm slowly said. "Why don't we live here for a time?"

Johann made a face. "Because I made a pact with a tribe of kelpies. I stay off their turf, and they stay off mine. We don't like each other very much, and most of the swamp belongs to them. Not that I blame them for being wary—people used to hunt them back in the day."

"Surely they might make an exception," Wilhelm said. "After all, you're being hunted yourself!"

"If you can get Iron Heart to see my way, I'll kiss you," Johann dryly said. "And don't go looking for Xe either. Xe doesn't like being bothered, especially by humans."

"So how do we find kelpies and ask?" Wilhelm asked. "Someone has to go looking for them!"

Johann laughed softly. "Oh, don't worry. Iron Heart already knows. I'm actually pretty sure I'm trespassing right now, so expect a visit soon enough."

Wilhelm nodded. He pressed into the wall and stared at the empty door frame. He didn't like the way this place looked now. He could almost imagine a kelpie bursting through the door and killing them all. Would this Iron Heart do that? Wilhelm knew next to nothing about the swamps and less about kelpies. He had never even seen a kelpie before, much less even talked to one. He was just about to ask what this Iron Heart looked like when a dark figure stalked into the room.

"What are you doing here?" the thing demanded. It had eyes like glowing red coals and had hooves instead of feet. "I thought I told you to stay away!"

"Hello, Iron Heart." Johann stood up slowly and crossed his arms. "A thousand pardons for trespassing, but we seem to have been burned out."

"That's no excuse," Iron Heart hissed. Xe lashed a long, snake-like tail and prowled around the room. "I told you to stay away on pain of death, and this is how you repay me? By marching into my sacred lands and leaving a dead animal in the clearing?"

"Easy." Johann raised his hands. "Sorry about the horse, by the way, but a band of knights is here, and they're looking for us. They'll take shots at your people too."

Iron Heart snorted and lashed Xir's tail. "As if."

"I know they will," Johann said. "Their leader is Lord Steven of Robardhall. I know him very well. He's like a mastiff; once he gets his jaws locked in on something, he never lets go."

"And what of it?" Xe asked. "If this Lord Steven comes here, we'll go deeper into the swamps. You know they can't follow us in there!"

"Not this one," Johann said. "We need a horse to get out of here in a timely manner, by the way. Steven and his men are closing in."

"Hi." Wilhelm waved shyly and tried not to stare at Iron Heart. "Are you really a kelpie?"

Iron Heart looked like a mix of horse and human. Xe had skin covered in fur the color of a dark emerald and long, tapered ears that flicked at every sound. Xir's legs had hooves instead of feet and hands that tapered into wicked sharp claws. A mane and tail made of darker fur was draped over Xir's shoulders and tied into an elaborate braid. Xe wore no clothing, and the edges of Xir's form seemed to grow fuzzy and indistinct the longer Xe stood in one place.

"I would like to think so," Iron Heart snapped. "Now. What was it about you getting out of here?"

"We need a horse," Johann said. "Two of them would be better though."

"Granted." Iron Heart gave them a long look. "It will be given to you in the morning, and you will leave not long after."

Johann nodded. "I understand. Thank you for giving this to us."

Iron Heart scowled as Xe turned to leave. Wilhelm hugged himself and prayed to anything that might hear that no one would find them until they had those horses and they could flee.

CHAPTER FOURTEEN: WAR PARTY

◆ ◆ ◆

David looked around for the stag as Henri caught the horses. The white dog raced into a copse of trees and started frantically barking at something only she could see. David ignored her. On a whim, he reached down to the discarded box and picked up the other scrolls. He unrolled another out of curiosity. He couldn't read the writing, but it looked important, so he tucked all of those in his coat along with the first one.

Henri walked back with the horses. "Let's see if we can find that damn deer."

David stroked Snowflake's side before he mounted. The horse snorted as she shifted, her ears pinned to her skull. David patted her neck. He had just opened his mouth to call for Toman when the big wolfhound came bursting out of the brush. His fur was matted to his sides, and he was covered in mud and all sorts of debris.

Toman barked sharply. He shook himself out, ignoring the white dog as she came trotting back, and took his place by David's side.

David gestured to the strange dog. "We should find out who owns her. Maybe they know where Wilhelm is."

"I don't see a collar." Henri dropped the roan's reins on the ground and wandered over. "She's some kind of shepherd, though. Must be herders near here."

"Great," David said. He clicked his tongue, getting the dog's attention, and gestured to her. "Take us home, sweetheart. We're lost."

The dog gave him a long look. Then she sat down, nibbled on her paw, and scratched behind her ears. David winced. Toman gave a short, almost huffy bark. He lunged forward, like he was going to nip her. The white dog snarled. She jerked her head up, her ears pinned to her skull. Her amber eyes seemed to rake over the wolfhound, and her hackles went straight up. David swore under his breath.

"Henri..." he softly said. "Get back."

He didn't dare look and see if the other man had obeyed him. He focused on the dogs and hoped there wasn't going to be a fight. The white dog snapped at the air. She stalked forward, the tip of her tail shaking just a little, and snapped at the air again. Toman stood his ground.

The wolfhound was easily twice as tall as she, but he was leaner and made for running. The white dog had the type of scars that only came from fighting streaked across her face and muzzle.

Something crashed in the forest behind them. Snowflake reared, forcing David to grab her reins. Behind them, the roan took off. David didn't pause to see what it was. He spurred his mare in the side and took off after the fleeing stallion. The roan seemed to gallop into the heart of the woods. He took off down a tiny, narrow trail that wound through walls of bracken. Snowflake snorted as she ran, and her hooves pounded that dry and dusty ground.

The roan reared when its half of its reins caught in a bush. The horse screamed, pawing at the air. It tossed its head wildly and thrashed, but the branches held firm. The horse reared so hard that it went over backward. One of the leather straps wrapped around the horse's leg. It started kicking, tangling it even more. David jerked Snowflake to a stop and jumped off the horse. He caught the roan's head, covering the animal's eyes with his hands, and waited for the terrified animal to stop jerking.

"Easy," he whispered. "Easy. It's going to be okay. I'll get you out of this."

Snowflake snorted and butted his shoulder with her head. David ignored her. The roan shook. It let out a terrified, half-silent whinny and kicked its back legs.

David moved his hands, watching the horse intently. Slowly, he stood up from his crouch and unwrapped the leather strap from where it was tangled. He moved out of the way, allowing the roan stallion to scramble to its feet and shake off as much of the dust as it could.

"And this," David said, "is why I hate split reins."

He grabbed the other end of the rein and jerked it free from the thorn bush. The roan followed him easily enough, swishing its tail back and forth. Snowflake raised her head from where she had been grazing. The spotted mare's ears swiveled as she looked for a sound only she could hear. David swore under his breath. He grabbed her reins, too, just in case she decided to bolt, and tied the roan to his saddle.

"Not you too," he groaned. David touched the mare's shoulder and quickly mounted her again. "I've had enough heart attacks for one day, okay? Let's go find Henri before he thinks we up and left him."

Snowflake snorted. She pawed at the ground and half reared when a bloodied golden horse wandered into the clearing. The animal had no rider. Its saddle hung off of its body and something with horns had gouged it in the side. Great smears of blood dirtied its sandy gold coat, and its wide eyes were wild with pain and fear. Snowflake snorted again. She jerked her head back, ears against her skull, and lunged like she was going to nip the wounded animal.

"Hey!" David yelped. He tugged his reins, trying to draw her back. "Easy! Let it alone!"

"Halt!"

Three men came stumbling out of the forest. Every single one of them was armed, and it looked like they had been through a battle. David's heart froze in his chest. He rose his hands slowly as he debated his options. He had no idea who these people were. For all he knew, Maria had sent them and they were going to kill him. Snowflake must have picked up on his unease, because the mare whinnied and started pawing up the ground even more.

The leader, a man with cropped golden hair and a bloodied face, grabbed Snowflake's bridle and jerked her head. "I am Lord Steven, and we are chasing a pair of dangerous criminals."

"Um, I'm David and I'm chasing my boyfriend's horse?" David said. He gestured to the roan. "Because someone kidnapped my other boyfriend, and we're trying to find him."

Someone also tried to kill me, but that might be a bit too much information for right now.

Steven narrowed bright blue eyes. "Was he a young

man? With eyes as blue as mine and hair the color of spun gold? If he was, we had him with a common criminal."

David's heart dropped. "What–what did he say his name was?"

Please don't let it be Wilhelm, all you little gods out there...

"Wilhelm." Steven's face twisted like he had bitten into rotten meat as he said that word. He let Snowflake's bridle go and took a step backward. "Apologies for startling you like this, but that criminal—a man named Johann—took your...*friend* with him last night. We lost their trail during the night."

David swore under his breath. "Look, if you need the help, Henri and I would be more than willing to go with you."

"We need it," another man said. This one had a thin, pinched face, and his shifty eyes roamed around the tangled forest. "If you know him, you could talk some sense into him. Johann has him under some kind of spell; he seems to think that wretch is helping him! Instead, Johann's probably going to feed him to the kelpies!"

David had no idea what a kelpie was, but it sounded dreadful. He watched as the last knight—a shorter man wearing rusted, tarnished armor—vanished back into the dense underbrush. He came back with two horses. One was a chestnut and white pinto, while the other was a deep bay. These two hadn't been wounded, meaning that whatever little scuffle they had been involved with must have been recent.

The golden horse limped after the others. David winced when he saw the rat-faced knight mount it, but it wasn't his place to scold someone. He needed to keep his mouth shut—his Alsatian accent could very well get him killed. Steven grabbed the bay. The horse shifted nervously as the man mounted it. Steven slapped it across the head and yanked the horse's mouth back when it tried to jerk away from him.

"Let's get going," David softly said. He clicked his tongue and urged Snowflake down the trail. "Henri has to be looking for me."

He had a bad feeling about this, but he forced himself to ignore it. Sure, Steven was a hard man, but most knights were. They had to be—their lives were ones of fighting and killing. Anything soft and kind in them was probably destroyed quickly. David tried to hold on to that thought as he rode. The golden horse jerked its head when its knight struck it in the side. The roan horse jerked its head back at the sound, so David grabbed its reins.

"Hey, now," he whispered. "It's okay."

"Why're you babying that stupid animal?" the rat-faced knight asked. "It's just a horse!"

"Because that's what I do," David slowly said. "My name's David, by the way. Who are you?"

"Joshua." Joshua gave him a long look before he gestured to the man in the fouled armor. "And my brother here is Thomas."

"Pleased to meet you," David lied. "Are you Tallan?"

"Nope," Steven said. He turned around and gave his men a long, hard look. "And we don't want to bother these good people with our problems, do we? The sooner we find Johann and go home, the better it will be for all of us."

David gave the man a long look, but he kept riding. He didn't think he could send these people away, for one, and he didn't want to give the impression that he was unfriendly. The ride back to their camp seemed far longer than the mad dash it had taken to get here. Soon, though, David heard Toman's barking. The brindle wolfhound came running through the brush and started barking like mad as soon as David came into view.

Henri followed after him and stumbled over a thorn vine as he did so. "David! There you are! What took you so long?"

"Ran into these people," David said. He gestured to the knights. "The leader is Steven, the one with the cleaner armor is Joshua, and his brother is Thomas." He tossed Henri the roan's reins and waited for the other man to mount up. "Come on, they're trying to track down the bastard who kidnapped Wil."

Henri gave him a strange look, then nodded. "Right. We need to come on, then."

David nodded and gestured to Steven. "Well, sir, show us the way."

"I was hoping you would have a way to track them," Steven slowly said. He eyed the white dog as she came running and touched his sword like he was going to draw it. "Our tracker was killed during a scuffle with the criminal and your prince."

"Criminal!" Henri yelped. He bolted upright in the saddle and his eyes went wide. "Why, he's going to kill Wil!"

"He hasn't yet," David cautioned. He winced and hoped he could keep a lid on these people. "Apparently, his name is Johann, and he's good at fighting. He must have managed to escape earlier."

Personally, David hoped he found this Johann. He would

have Henri take Wil somewhere else though. He had an idea about how he was going to wrench answers from an unwilling mouth. David patted Snowflake's shoulder as they walked. The forest seemed to loom around them in some kind of dark, impenetrable tangle. The daylight could hardly reach the densely covered forest floor. Even now, the shadows were pooled in every available place.

Steven clicked his tongue and took the lead of their little patrol. David let him. He didn't know what was going on here, and unease settled over him as the ground became more and more marshy. Soon, the horses were splashing through a dark marsh. Birds fluttered through the air. Their cries rang out in the still, dense air. Snowflake jerked her head some and started staring at a patch of densely tangled vines.

Something was watching them. Its gaze—whatever it was—seemed to carve a hole straight into his back.

CHAPTER FIFTEEN: MOVE OUT

◆ ◆ ◆

Wilhelm nudged Johann as soon as dawn broke over the horizon. "Come on, we need to go. I don't think Iron Heart wants us to overstay our welcome."

Johann cracked open one blue eye. "Do you mind? I'm trying to sleep here."

The older man had sprawled out over the wet clay floor like he was used to it. Maybe he was. Now that dawn crept into the little hovel, Wilhelm could get a good look at it. It was nothing more than four crumbling stone walls, laced with vines, and a bare clay floor that had seen better days. There weren't even rush mats to sleep on. Mud clung to Johann's clothing now, and his hair had been tangled into knots.

Johann slowly stood up. The man brushed a little of the muddy mess from his trousers and ambled over toward the window. The window was little more than a hole in the wall now. Wilhelm could see shards of broken glass, meaning that there had once been glass here, but now it was little more than a gaping wound in the building's side. Golden light combed through the long grasses.

It reflected off the new dew, and the long, thin reeds danced in the wind. Birds started to sing somewhere in the distance. Wilhelm could hear the trickling water and something that sounded like hoofbeats. His breath caught. He pressed beside Johann as he watched a kelpie emerge from the dark forest. He couldn't see much of the creature, as they stayed as close to the dense plant cover as they could, but soon two dun horses came trotting out from a hidden forest trail.

They were short things, about the size of a large pony near the castle, and they picked their feet up high. One of them had a white face and blond hairs sprinkled about in its fuzzy, black mane. The other was a darker color, almost chestnut, and its mane was a darker shade of brown. Both horses wore saddles and bridles, though both were far different from anything Wilhelm had ever seen before.

The bridles were little more than leather straps braided with copper thread, and the saddles little more than hide stretched over wood. Both horses moved through the fading mist like some kind of ethereal creatures. Their hooves—tiny and narrow—hardly made a sound as they walked toward the little hovel. Both animals had the smallest, foxiest ears that Wilhelm had ever seen, set as they were in thick wreaths of dun fur.

Wilhelm slipped out of the hovel and caught one of the bridles. Wise, golden eyes stared into blue. The horse —a mare, now that Wilhelm was looking at her better —lowered her head and nuzzled his hands. Wilhelm smiled softly. The saddle both horses had didn't have any stirrups, but that was no matter. Wilhelm was just about to mount the chestnut mare when Johann cleared his throat.

He caught the dun horse—this one a gelding—and examined the saddle. "We probably can't use the saddles."

"Why not?" Wilhelm asked. They looked perfectly fine to him.

"Because these are made for kelpies," Johann sighed. He looked over the saddles and undid the leather girth strap. "And if you sit on it, you'll get splinters in your ass. Ask me how I know."

Wilhelm had an idea. He held the reins for Johann as the man mounted his horse. Johann did the same for him. The mare started some. She jerked her head up, her ears pinned to her heavy skull, but soon she settled down and ambled after Johann. The forest seemed to watch them as they started down a narrow trail. Tree branches twined together above them, and dense strands of bracken blanketed both sides of the trail.

Johann seemed to know where he was going. He clucked

his tongue, getting the gelding's attention. The horse perked his head up and fell into a heavy trot. The mare followed him quickly enough. Her narrow hooves avoided the deep rents in the muddy trail. Roots broke the packed clay surface every few feet, and there were holes like someone had been digging clay. A cold chill settled into the air even though the sun hung high in the sky.

Neither man spoke. Wilhelm watched the land around them and did his best not to pull on the mare's mouth too much. He thought he saw narrow, faint trails that peeled into the underbrush. Someone had carved strange symbols into large, twisted trees or tied beaded ribbons in the branches. Those branches danced in the light breeze. Wilhelm thought he saw shards of pottery in strange clearings, along with little cairns made from bleached and carved bone.

Time seemed to slow in the swamp. Brackish water stretched as far as the eye could see and glittered like polished obsidian. Dry sedge bushes and sage grass poked out of the pools of water. Privet hedges filled with fragrant flowers clung to the dry spots. Soon, the trail they were on became an ancient road. The edges were filled with ragged black rocks, and the center was nothing more than crushed gray stone.

Something rustled behind them. Wilhelm froze. He jerked the reins back unconsciously, and the mare reared. She reared again when Toman came running out of the underbrush. The dog's fur was matted with burs and mud. He didn't seem to care, though, and he jumped up on the mare's back. The mare bucked. She lowered her head and almost went all the way over. Wilhelm yelled. He gripped her neck and barrel as best he could as the mare plunged up and down.

"Wilhelm!" David came charging out of the forest riding a mud-splattered spotted horse. "Wilhelm!"

"David!" Wilhelm kneed the mare in the side to urge her toward his lover. "Did she take you too?"

David froze. He must have seen Johann, because his eyes went very wide and he reached for a weapon that wasn't there. Johann cursed. The man wheeled his horse around, like he was going to flee into the forest, only for Steven and his men to come galloping from the forest. Wilhelm didn't pause to see what would happen. He spurred the mare in the side and followed Johann back down the old road.

Some dim part of his mind realized that Steven had fresh horses. The dog, Myla, barked as she ran up to them. She tried to catch her master, but Johann paid her no mind. That man charged his horse straight through a thorn bush. The animal screamed as the brambles raked through its hide, but no one paid it any mind. Wilhelm guided his mare around the strand of bushes, only for her to suddenly leap over a fallen tree.

For a second, it seemed like he was flying. Wilhelm

seemed to hang in the air for the longest time. Then he lost his grip on the mare's back and went tumbling into the ground. His shoulder collided with a piece of carved stone. Agony lanced through his body. Dimly, he heard himself screaming, and he clutched at the throbbing, pulsating wound. The mare snorted. She tossed her head and reared as he reached for her, but calmed as soon as he reached his feet.

Just as he was about to mount her, a hand grabbed his wounded shoulder and *squeezed*.

Bits of broken, shattered bone seemed to grind together. Wilhelm made a wounded animal cry as he fell to his knees. Steven straddled his body and pulled out a long, wicked looking broadsword. He put the edge of it under Wilhelm's chin, forcing him to tilt it up. Wilhelm's heart froze. He could hardly think for the pain, and the only sounds he could make were broken, pitiful whimpers.

"Johann!" Steven screamed.

"Let him go!" Johann slowly his horse and turned the nervous, snorting animal around. "Just let him go, Steven!"

"Never!" Spit sprayed from Steven's mouth and landed on Wilhelm's collar. "Either you submit yourselves to us like these Tallan boys or I'll kill him!"

One of the other knights dismounted his horse and

walked over. "Why don't we just kill them now, sir? It's not like we're going to need spare princes after Talla Gael is ours."

"What?" Wilhelm whispered. Surely he hadn't heard what he thought he heard...

The knight gave a sick, twisted smile. "Didn't you hear? Your kingdom is being given over to ours as we speak."

"That's not true!" Wilhelm tried to struggle free, but Steven's grip just tightened. "That's not true! Who would do this?"

"Take a guess." Steven nodded, and David was dragged him his horse, followed by Henri. "Your kingdom is a rich jewel, you know, and they've been having such bad luck with princes. It seems that the Alsatian boy decided he was going to kill both of you in a fit of rage, and a common criminal helped him."

David bristled as he knelt on the ground. "You won't get away with this, and neither will she!"

She? What does he mean by that? Wilhelm couldn't keep the wild thoughts out of his mind as his heart raced a thousand miles a second.

"My dear," Steven laughed, "I already have. And there is no "she" to speak of."

His voice echoed like it was coming from a deep well. The world seemed to swim around Wilhelm. Faint numbness pulled at his veins, drawing him into something he could hardly fight off. Wilhelm struggled. Really, he did, but the strain was just too much and his body collapsed to the ground. He heard sharp hooves pounding on the ground. The stag exploded out of the brush and charged right at Steven.

The knight snarled. He swung his sword wildly and buried the weapon to the hilt. The deer jerked back. Scarlet blood covered snow-white fur now, but the stag didn't even flinch. He reared up on his hind legs. Wilhelm heard pounding hooves. He looked up, just in time to see Johann charge his horse right at him. Johann grabbed his arm. He yanked Wilhelm up with one fluid motion and seemed to throw him against the back of the horse.

Wilhelm clung on with all his might. His shoulder screamed as he moved it. His fingers were swollen now, and he could hardly move them, but still he clung. Toman, David, Myla, and Henri raced behind him. Their horses covered the ground far quicker than Johann's did, and soon they were almost free from the swamp. Henri had Wilhelm's horse galloping behind them. The mare half reared more than once, but no one paid her any mind.

Johann pulled his horse to a stop on the outskirts of a village. "We need to get back to your people."

Wilhelm sighed softly as he slipped off the back of the horse. The pain swelled around him in some kind of perverted dance. It felt like red hot pokers were jammed into his shoulder. The bones grated as he tried to move them, bringing only more pain. He heard himself whimpering, and he clung to the first thing that tried to hold him. David stroked his back, whispering something that Wilhelm couldn't understand.

"It hurts…" Wilhelm whimpered. He wiped off his tears and snot with one muddy hand. "I wanna go home."

Toman licked his face. Wilhelm hiccuped. He didn't know that he had been crying before and now he couldn't seem to stop. He hung his head in shame. These people had come after him when common sense said they should have stayed away. He was just going to get them killed, he feared. Wilhelm hung his head in shame. He hardly had the strength to get off the ground now, even if he wanted to, and he just lay there.

"He can't go on like this." David must have been looking at Johann. "We have to find help."

"One problem with that," Johann said. "I'm a wanted man."

"So?" Henri snapped. He dismounted and pulled Wilhelm into his arms. "He's hurt! We need to get him to a doctor!"

"We have no idea where we are!" Johann snarled. "I lost my compass. Without it, we might as well be in Cascadia. They want to kill me too."

"Damn." David laughed. "You sure know how to pick fights, don't you?"

"Oh, shut up," Wilhelm grumbled. He staggered to his feet and leaned on David for support. "I don't think I can ride though. I can't move my fingers."

"We're finding a doctor." David gave Johann a long look and a pregnant silence followed. "Either you come with us or you don't."

Johann paused. For a second, it looked like he was going to ride into the mist. Not that Wilhelm blamed him. Myla even perked her ears like she was going to follow her master. The gelding stood at the ready. He even pawed at the ground, like he wanted nothing more than to gallop into the sunset. Johann petted the horse's thick neck for a few seconds before he slowly dismounted.

"Get him walking," the older man gruffly said. "We need to be ready to bolt. Just in case."

CHAPTER SIXTEEN: WOUNDED

◆ ◆ ◆

There was one problem with Johann's order: Wil wasn't going to be walking anytime soon.

David swore under his breath. He caught the strange-looking dun mare again and cursed again when he saw she didn't have a saddle. Wilhelm wobbled dangerously on his feet. His face turned pale and wan, and his shoulder had swollen. His fingers on that side quickly curled. David had no idea what was going on there, but that was a serious injury. He grabbed Snowflake from where she was grazing and led the spotted mare over.

"See if you can ride her," he softly said.

Wilhelm shook his head. "I can't," he whispered. "I don't think I could even get on a horse right now."

"Well, you don't have a choice," David said. He grabbed Wilhelm by the shirt and started lifting him up. "See if you can get your foot in the stirrup."

Wilhelm struggled. He whined softly, clearly trying to bite back the pain, and fumbled around until he managed it. David adjusted his foot so he was at least sitting correctly and did the same for the other side. His bad arm hung uselessly at his side. He panted now, his soft hair plastered with sweat. David swore under his breath. He grabbed the dun mare by her reins and mounted her quickly with the aid of an old fence.

"Let's get going," he said. He nudged the mare down the old forest road. "There has to be a village around here somewhere. Henri, make sure he doesn't fall off his horse. I'll scout ahead."

David kicked the mare in the side before the others could protest. She had a heavy gait, much unlike the high-stepping, smooth Snowflake, and she wasn't nearly as fast. Her mane was stiffer, too, and it was frosted on the outside. David noticed that her bridle had no bit, meaning he had no real way of controlling her if she decided to bolt. *Where on this green earth did they find this horse? She looks like something out of a storybook!*

The mare stopped short, jolting David from his thoughts. She pulled at the reins some, like she wanted to run, even as David held her back. The forest stood silent around them. David couldn't hear anything out of the ordinary, nor could he see it, but unease washed over his body anyway. He nudged the mare forward. She obeyed, but pawed at the ground before she did. David patted her shoulder.

"Easy," he whispered. "Easy."

The mare snorted. Her ears pricked forward, and she stared at a spot in the brush. The walls of bracken, vines, and sedge moved ever so slightly as they looked at it. The mare backed up. Her ears went back against her skull and she whinnied. David petted her again. He tried to ignore the fear building in his body. Some primitive instinct told him to bolt, but he forced himself to ignore it.

A long, lithe cat slipped out of the brush. It was easily the size of a small pony, and ghost spots decorated its tawny hide. It had the barest hint of a mane around its broad, flat head. Its long, sharp-looking fangs seemed to glitter in the soft, almost diffused light. The mare backed up. She snorted in fear now and pawed at the ground. The cat stared at them. It turned like it was going to slink into the brush on the other side of the road before it whipped back around and ran at them.

The mare bolted. She galloped headlong down the forest road, her hooves barely touching the ground. David hung on for dear life. Branches and thorns grabbed at his clothes and whipped across his skin. The cat snarled behind them. It chased them all down the road, its golden eyes wild. David had enough of the horse running, so he grabbed the reins and jerked her around. The mare almost fell over as she turned, her hooves churning up the clay and gravel.

She reared up as the cat came near. Toman bolted out of the underbrush. The dog snapped and snarled, fastening his jaws around the cat's front paws. The white dog followed him. She bit the cat twice around its neck, her long fangs leaving a trail of blood in their wake. The cat screamed. It tossed its head and thrashed around. Toman sunk his fangs in tighter. The two dogs worked as a team, biting it and driving the screaming, thrashing cat back.

Toman screamed when the cat slashed him across the shoulder. David urged the mare forward. The mare reared again, and her sharp hooves slashed the cat across the face. The white dog lunged again. Her fangs ripped into the cat's side. The animal whipped around. It slapped the dog upside the head and shredded her ear. The white dog yelped. She shook her head wildly, blood going all over the place.

The mare kicked the cat in the side. The animal groaned. It seemed to collapse under the mare's sharp hooves, and David forced the horse to go right over it. The cat jerked as the hooves struck it. As soon as both the horse and dogs backed off, the cat picked itself up and dragged itself toward the underbrush. David let it go. The mare trembled under him. Blood splattered her front and she favored her left foreleg, but otherwise, she seemed to be fine.

Toman and the white dog weren't so lucky.

Both animals limped. Toman's shoulder was flayed open to the bone, and the white dog was missing half of her right ear. Blood matted both dogs' fur. Still, though, they growled when David urged the mare toward them. David let them be. He nudged the shivering mare into a trot and yelled when he came to the first hut in the forest. It was nothing more than four wattle and daub walls covered in thatch, but it was a sign of civilization.

A woman wearing a loose blue tunic started when he jumped the mare over her woven willow fence. A long-haired dog lounged at her feet. The dog climbed to its paws quickly and barked as soon as he came too close for comfort. There was another dog behind her—this one short haired, black and tan, with a stub tail and pricked ears—and it fixed the mare with a cold, sharp gaze.

"We need a doctor." David tried to keep the nervous mare under control. "One of my friends is badly hurt and we need help. And my dogs got hurt."

"A doctor?" the woman asked. "What do you want that for?"

"Because he's hurt," David repeated. "He got thrown from his horse and broke something in a funny way. My dogs tangled with some kind of cat and now they're hurt too. We need to get them help. *Now.*"

The woman made a face and petted the long-haired dog. "If you must... Go down this road, hang a right by the mill pond, and keep going until you hit it. It isn't that far."

"Great." David started backing the mare out of the woman's yard. "I'm going to gallop right back to the others and get them to that doctor."

He didn't give her time to argue. The prick-eared dog snapped at him as the horse cleared the fence. The mare kicked the dog in the skull, making the animal scream and collapse in a heap. David didn't bother trying to circle around. He raced the dun mare back to the others. She slung up gravel with every step, and her body stretched out low to the ground. Her ears pricked as she ran. She all but jumped over the dogs when she passed them again.

They both followed. The white dog barked all the way and howled when they came back to the others. Wilhelm sagged against Snowflake. He was bleeding now, and his eyes fluttered closed. Someone had tied him to the saddle so he wouldn't fall. Snowflake started when David drew near her. He ignored the big mare and pulled the snorting, sweating animal to a stop. Wil's mare danced under him, her hooves pawing at the ground.

"I found a doctor," David said. "Also, we need to be careful. I fought with some kind of wild cat."

Blood colored the lather on the mare's chest. Her wounds had already clotted, as had the dogs'. David didn't waste time. He dismounted the dun mare, handed the reins to Henri, and grabbed Snowflake's bridle. The mare jerked her head back. She pinned her ears to her skull, snorting and pawing at the ground. David ignored that. He swung up behind the saddle and kicked her in the side.

Snowflake all but exploded under him. She galloped down the trail, racing toward the tree line. David jerked her away just in time. She jumped over the dead cat as soon as they came upon it and did the same when they came to a creek that crossed the road. The mare snorted as she ran. Her hooves seemed to pound the earth. David found the millpond. He pulled the mare into a hard right and jumped her over another retaining wall.

Through it all, Wilhelm didn't make a sound.

David cursed. He spurred the mare on faster and jerked her around a man with a donkey cart. The donkey half reared. It cried out in fear and jerked the cart backward. David ignored them. He urged the mare on faster. Snowflake snorted as she ran. She had the bit in her teeth and she didn't intend to let go. David didn't intend to take it back anytime soon. The horse seemed to pant under him.

Her sides were soaked with lather now and her gait not as high, but still she ran.

"Hey!" David yelled. He saw a sign with the word *Doktor* written on it and took his horse right into that man's yard. "I have a wounded man! I need help!"

An older man wearing thin glasses stepped out on the long, thin porch. "What?"

"He fell off his horse and hurt his shoulder." David jerked Snowflake to a stop and cut the cord on Wil's wrist. "It's bad, real bad, Doc. He needs help."

Snowflake shivered. She lowered her head down and seemed to shudder as David tried to get her to walk. David's heart ached when he saw her. He hadn't meant to run her out like this, but he had little choice. Wilhelm collapsed to the ground as soon as David stopped supporting him. The doctor ran out and grabbed him. Seconds later, he picked up the younger man and started carrying him toward the house.

David took Snowflake's saddle off. He let that fall to the ground and started walking her. There was a pond in the front yard, so he let her drink for a few seconds before walking her again. Steam seemed to rise from her body. She clearly wanted to rest, but David feared that he wouldn't get her up again if she went down.

"I'm sorry," David whispered. He petted Snowflake's side as he let her drink again. "I'm so, so sorry."

After a few minutes, she seemed to recover. She didn't shake like she was, and her ears were pricked forward now. She wasn't blowing like she had been, so she had to be getting better. David let her graze after a few minutes. He was finger-combing the knots in her mane when the others showed up.

"What the hell!" Henri yelled. "Was the devil chasing you?"

"Might as well have been!" David yelled. "Wil needed help. I did what I had to do. I would have done it for any of you."

Henri shook his head as he dismounted the roan. "That's nice, but you shouldn't have run the horses out like that. What if they got hurt?"

"They didn't." David hoped, at least. He climbed over the fence and took the dun mare's reins. "This guy seems pretty nice, so I think he'll take care of the dogs too. Get Toman and the other one."

"Her name is Myla." Johann dismounted from his dun gelding and picked up Myla. "You know, you could have just opened the gate. You probably don't need to teach that horse how to jump over fences. That's a bell that can't be unrung."

David shrugged. "I had to do what I had to do. Get Toman over here, so we can get him inside too. I don't want to get Wil's dog killed, all right? Henri, you need to take care of the horses. See if there's a stable around back or something like that."

Then he clicked his tongue and signaled to Toman. He had to get in there with the dogs and Wil. Just to make sure everything would be okay.

CHAPTER SEVENTEEN: INJURIES

◆ ◆ ◆

Wilhelm woke up in little bits and pieces. Someone had draped a thick blanket over him, along with propping a pillow under his head. His shoulder had been bound with a sort of stiff bandage. It itched and he wanted nothing more than to just rip it off. He picked himself up slowly, wincing as the world swam around him. He was in some small room tucked away in the back of an old house.

The walls were painted a rich blue color with golden trim. There was a fire blazing in the reddish stone hearth, and the creaking wooden floor was covered in a large, ornate rug patterned with trailing vines. There were two large bay windows, both of them with a small sitting area, and the heavy golden curtains were drawn. Toman rested on the rug beside the fire. Someone had brushed the big dog and even cleaned his collar.

"Toman?" Wilhelm coughed and rubbed his throat. "Toman!"

The dog jerked his head up. Toman wandered over, his tail wagging slowly. Wilhelm winced as he pushed himself up. The bones in his shoulder grated together as he did so, and it was all he could do to keep from crying out. Toman whined. He scrambled into bed beside Wilhelm and rested his head in the young man's lap. Wilhelm scratched his ears with his good hand as he looked around.

He had no idea where he was or how he got there. The last thing he remembered was passing out and collapsing against David. After that...*nothing*. He tried to swing his legs over the side of the bed, only to be struck by a dizzying wave. He doubled over, holding himself. Wilhelm waited until the tide passed and buried his hand in the thick, colorful crazy quilt. Bile rose in his throat when he tried to stand again.

Silence draped over the little room. An almost irrational fear wrapped around him, the terror that the others were dead and he was all that was left. Wilhelm almost called out for David. The house groaned as it settled around them. Wilhelm clung to Toman. The big dog rested his head on Wilhelm's lap and whined softly. The door eased open. Wilhelm jerked his head up, his heart in his throat.

If that was Steven, then there was no way he would

get out of this. He couldn't run. He couldn't fight. If that man was there, waiting just outside the door, then Wilhelm was going to get it. His belly cramped. He grabbed the dog and prayed that no one would come. And, if they did come, his death would be swift and merciful. Perhaps the others were already dead and Steven was just saving him for last.

David eased the door open and sat beside him. "Are you feeling any better?"

"You're...you're not dead?" Wilhelm stared at him and could hardly believe his eyes. "But I–I thought—"

"I think you would hear if we had a fight," David laughed. "Besides, Johann probably kicks ass."

Wilhelm curled up in his arms when David sat down on the bed. He rested his head on the other man's shoulder as his heart started to slow. David squeezed his good hand. Both of them curled up on the bed together, and David shielded Wilhelm's body with his own. It felt... natural. And good in a way that Wilhelm couldn't describe. He tucked his head under the other man's chin and sighed as the tension left his body.

"Steven kicked Johann's ass," Wilhelm murmured. "So I don't think he's going to be able to keep us safe."

"What about Henri?" David patted the space behind him, and Toman draped his body over both men.

"Henri?" Wilhelm laughed. "Are you mad? I don't think he knows how to swing a sword. I was surprised he came out to find me too."

David took a breath. "Speaking of, I think Maria killed Emil."

"I think it was Steven," Wilhelm said. He shook his head at David's disapproving expression. "When I was... before you rescued me a second time, Steven told me the kingdom was already being given over, that there was nothing I could do. And then he said that Talla Gael was...was having a bad run with princes and—"

Horror blossomed across his face as he looked at David. How would Steven have known that Emil was dead if he didn't have help? The palace was usually closed to outsiders. It wasn't like someone could just wander in. Well, unless their name was David. Wilhelm gave David a long look as the thoughts started racing through his head. How exactly *had* David gotten into the castle? He had never thought to ask before, but now...

"David?" Wilhelm asked.

"Hmm?" David paused from nuzzling Wilhelm's neck. "What is it?"

"How did you get in the castle?"

"Didn't Henri tell you?" David asked. "He found me in the cellar."

"Well, I know that part." Wilhelm pushed David away and propped himself up on his good arm. "But how did you get in the cellar on the first place? You didn't hide in a wagon, did you?"

"No, I..." David trailed off and cursed under his breath. "Oh, stars above..."

"What?" Wilhelm asked. He needed to know.

"There was a gate in the curtain wall," David softly said. His eyes filled with horror. "A gate that was unlocked. The stag—the same white stag that saved us before—let me ride it and carried me to safety. I was being chased by dogs, you know, and I thought they were going to kill me. I pulled on the gate and it *opened*."

"A gate?" Wilhelm shook his head. "I know my castle inside and out. There are only supposed to be two gates, both of them guarded."

"Well, this one wasn't." David sat up and cursed again. "It really wasn't. It takes you right up to the wine cellar, and there's enough brush around the entrance that you could get an army through there if you tried."

"You wouldn't need an army," Wilhelm said. He sat up quickly and swung his legs over the side of the bed. "You would just need a few. There aren't many guards in the palace proper."

"We need to get back." David helped Wilhelm up and gave him a quick peck on the cheek. "Wil, I love you, but we can't wait here for you to get better. Think you can ride?"

"I can ride." Wilhelm wobbled some as he stood. "I'll need help with my boots though. I think I hit my head."

David grunted. He grabbed Wilhelm's boots and helped him sit on the bed. Wilhelm hated this, hated having his boots put on him like he was a child, but he feared he would pass out if he tried it himself. David laced his boots quickly enough and helped him to his feet. Toman ran around the room. The dog barked his head off and scratched at the door. Myla barked on the other side, probably answering him.

David opened the door and helped Wilhelm through it. "We need to move out!"

"What about my fee?" The doctor stood up and gave David a long look. "I didn't patch your friend up for free."

In response, Johann drew a dagger from someplace in his coat. He grabbed the man and pulled him close, the wicked sharp blade at the older man's neck. The action pinned the older man's arms to his side, and the dagger at his throat completed the deal. Johann pressed the knife in just deep enough to draw a tiny amount of blood. No one said anything. Wilhelm's breath caught. Henri looked like he was going to faint.

"Your fee," Johann growled, "is going to be keeping your life."

"Johann—"

"Shut up." Johann didn't bother looking at Wilhelm. "Last thing I want is for my friend to bite it or lose his kingdom because you want a few gold coins."

"I—" The doctor looked like he was going to soil his trousers. "You can't do this to me!"

"I just did," Johann snarled. He threw the man to the ground and wiped the dagger off his own trousers. "And we're going to get our horses and head out. Bill the Tallan treasury. I'm sure that you'll get a pretty penny, you greedy rat!"

Wilhelm tried not to look at the doctor. He didn't know what to say after that. They did need to hurry, but that didn't mean Johann had to be cruel. Wilhelm searched Johann's face as they walked to the stables. The world swam around him after a few steps. He groaned and sagged against David's side. David propped him up. He helped Wilhelm on his mare before he grabbed his own horse.

"Hold on, darling," David said. He blew a kiss to Wilhelm and smiled sadly. "We'll get you home, I promise."

Wilhelm nodded. He clung to the saddle horn and didn't say anything when David tied the dun mare to his saddle. He wanted to know what the spotted horse was called and tell David that his horse was beautiful, but he didn't have the strength. He slumped forward, bracing himself against the mare's neck. Her stiff mane irritated his face. He forced himself to ignore it and sunk his hands into her stiff hair to steady himself.

"Let's go!" Johann snapped. He smacked his gelding on the rump. "No idea what's going on, but you two seem to be worried, so let's get going."

"We think we know why Steven went after us," David said. He nudged his spotted mare and pulled the dun mare after him. "Someone's promised his kingdom to Steven. To get it, though, he has to kill us."

"Because you don't need the old prince," Johann said. He shook his head as he urged the horse faster. "Let's get moving! Steven's an asshole and he's gonna run your people into the ground!"

Wilhelm groaned. He watched as the dogs raced beside

them. Toman and Myla snapped and bowed at each other as they ran. Joy seemed to flow off of every bit of their bodies. The dogs raced under the horses, making his mare half rear. She tossed her head sharply. The leather holding her to the saddle groaned, and a thin part of it looked like it was going to snap. Wilhelm had just opened his mouth to warn David when the mare jerked her head again.

The leather snapped. The mare reared for real this time, the leather wrapping around her legs, and Wilhelm clung to her mane. His fingers slipped as she pawed at the air. She tossed her head like a wild thing and bolted toward the forest. Toman snapped. He barked as he ran after her. David cried out, too, and spurred his spotted horse into a full gallop. The dun mare whinnied. She crashed right into a thorn bush and bucked Wilhelm off.

He landed on his bad shoulder.

The world seemed to collapse in on him. The trees moved overhead of their own accord, and the shadows danced across his skin. Pain seemed distant to him now, and he tasted blood. He could hear the others as they chased after his mare. The dogs filled the air with their cries. They seemed like wild things to him, something that he could never understand. Something rustled behind him. Wilhelm started, almost expecting to be attacked.

The stag slipped out of the forest and hung its scarred head down.

Wilhelm lifted his hand to touch its face. "Emil?"

His voice was nothing more than a whisper. Something familiar lingered in its golden eyes. It nuzzled his hand before lowering its head and resting the tines of its antlers on his mangled shoulder. Wilhelm's breath caught. His eyes met the stag's, and its hot breath warmed his hand. Some strange feeling wrapped around his shoulder. Fire seemed to bubble up inside of him. It spread from his ruined shoulder to his hand, and he swore that he saw bits of flames dancing at the ends of his fingers.

"Thank you," he whispered. He lowered his hand and watched as the stag took a step back. "You saved my life, you know."

He slowly picked himself up. The stag watched him with sad golden eyes and allowed him to stroke its face. He wanted nothing more than to hug it, but something told him to give the beast its space. If this was Emil —and stranger things had happened in Tallan myth— he still couldn't pressure it too much. The stag nuzzled him. Something passed between them, something no one could truly describe, but the feeling of *Emil* draped over both of them.

"Wilhelm!" David yelled. The man's voice shattered the silence and made the stag bolt back. "Will! Are you okay?"

"It's okay," Wilhelm said. "You can go."

"Wilhelm!" David charged both horses into the clearing, startling the stag and making it vanish into the forest. "What the— Are you all right?"

"The stag healed me." That was all Wilhelm could say. He caught his mare's reins and mounted her. "Now we need to go save my kingdom."

CHAPTER EIGHTEEN: HOME BOUND

◆ ◆ ◆

The stag...healed Wil? Had David heard that right? He pulled Snowflake to a stop. The mare danced under him, swishing her tail back and forth. Her head jerked back, and her ears pricked forward. She could clearly see something in the dense underbrush that he couldn't and it scared her. David patted her neck. Snowflake ignored him. The mare snorted a warning. Whatever it was, it ignored her and slipped back into the brush.

David turned his head and glanced at Wilhelm. "Did you hit your head? How could a stag heal you? It's an *animal*, Wil."

Wilhelm shook his head as he turned his horse toward the road. "I don't know how, but it did. Maybe it's one of the old gods."

"Old gods?" David asked.

"We have stories about them," Wilhelm explained. He clicked his tongue and urged his mare back to the others. "They were from the time before all of this. Talla Gael wasn't even a country yet, but there were gods. There was Donnhall, a force of great evil. He wanted to steal, kill, and destroy. Bernice was his opposite in every way. She was the light to his darkness, the warmth to his cold, everything like that. Finally, there was Josef. True neutral—able to go whatever way he needed to in order to accomplish his goals."

"That sounds fun," David said. He pulled Snowflake to a stop and looked around. "Do you see anything?"

He didn't care much about the old Tallan gods. They were nothing but stories to him—stories from a savage time that was best forgotten. Snowflake pricked her ears. The big mare snorted, her nostrils trembling. Then three horses slipped through the dense forest. They were the color of a snow-heavy sky, and their long, stiff manes were jet black. The stallion—an ancient beast with scars crossing his hide—paused and tossed his head in warning.

"Uh oh." David backed Snowflake up. "Wil, I think we have a problem."

Wild horses were the last thing he wanted to deal with right now. Snowflake shivered. The mare pawed at the ground and snorted. The stallion took a step back. The wild ones were only a little taller than a pony, and they had hair that was matted and clotted with dirt. The two mares vanished into the forest on the other side of the road, right before the stallion charged. The animal pinned his ears to his skull and lunged.

Snowflake reared. The mare lashed out with her front hooves, catching the stallion in the jaw. The dun mare bolted. She galloped off down the forest trail, and Wilhelm held on for dear life. David kicked Snowflake. She took off too. The stallion chased after them. The much smaller horse nipped at Snowflake as she ran. The mare bucked, nearly throwing David. David clung to the saddle as best he could and gave up all hope of guiding his horse.

Myla came crashing down the trail. The white dog sunk her jaws into the horse's nose. The stallion jerked its head back. It threw her to the other side of the trail and charged like it was going to trample her. Toman came out of nowhere and bit the horse in the flank. The animal screamed. It suddenly bucked up like it was going to go backward. Toman dropped back. Myla picked herself up slowly, her legs shaking.

"Leave them alone!" David yelled. He grabbed the reins and wheeled Snowflake around. "Just leave them alone!"

The stallion bared its teeth. Its ears were pinned to its skull, and it pawed at the ground. Snowflake trembled. The mare bared her own teeth and pulled at the reins. David petted her gently. He didn't know what he needed to do. If he turned the horse around, they were going to get chased. He couldn't leave Myla to be killed either. The white dog leaned on Toman as she limped back behind Snowflake.

The two horses stared at each other for the longest time. Time itself seemed to stretch into infinity. David swore he could feel himself growing older as he waited. Then, as if by magic, the stallion backed up and vanished into the dense forest. Snowflake dropped her head. She sighed, her flanks suddenly trembling. David petted her again. Her rump bled where the stallion had bit her. His teeth seemed to be just as sharp as any arrow, and they would leave the same kind of scar.

"Let's go find the others." David turned her around and walked her back down the trail. "Toman! Myla! Let's go!"

The dogs walked beside him. Myla favored her right foreleg, but she looked otherwise fine. Her scratches from the cat were well on the way to healing, as were the ones on Toman. David knew he should have felt fine. Unease, though, settled across his body. He sat upright in the saddle, trying to understand what the threat was. The forest seemed to close in all around him, and frightening shadows danced across the trees.

Snowflake chewed on the bit. She snorted as they walked and pawed at the ground. Small blue lights suddenly popped into existence on the edges of the trail. They cast an eerie, sickly light across the entire forest. David swore that they moved of their own accord. They were small things, about the size of a cider apple, and rays of light surrounded them in a miniature corona. David forced himself not to look at them. They seemed...entrancing, somehow. Like they wanted his complete attention.

"Wil?" he called. "Wilhelm!"

Only silence answered him. David shook his head. A strange sort of calm wrapped around him. Something pulled him toward the lights. He could just dimly hear the others—almost like they were underwater—but the hypnotic dance on the trail seemed to pull him in. Snowflake snorted in fear. The mare half reared, her hooves striking the dry ground more than once. David could just hear the dogs barking. It sounded close, yet, oddly enough, he couldn't see them.

"What the hell?" he whispered. He urged the mare forward. "Snowflake!"

The mare refused to move. She ignored his urging and even when he swatted her flank. He could just see something edged in gold behind one of the trees. It was a beautiful thing, he thought, something dipped in gold leaf and swirled through with silver. The figure had alabaster white skin and eyes that looked like chunks of polished obsidian. Its lips were as red as blood, and its teeth—sharp and white—were long, thin, and hollow looking.

"Who are you?" David whispered. "No, *what* are you?"

The thing had orange gold hair that was plastered against its forehead, and it seemed to hover over the ground. David stared at it. Something pulled at him, trying to draw him closer to the being. Its hair fanned out in a fiery corona. Its lips—blood-red things like a gash across its lips—moved, but no sound came out of them. Snowflake reared. The mare cried out in fear and lashed out at the thing.

It hissed and drew back. That alone drew David from his stupor. He kicked Snowflake in the side. She bolted and raced down the trail. Branches that looked like claws seemed to close in all around them. One of them lashed out at him, drawing blood on his cheek. David heard himself yelling in pain. He jerked his head away and watched as blood splattered Snowflake's neck. The mare reared as a root seemed to claw its way out of the packed clay.

It lashed out at Snowflake, raking its way across her chest. The mare lashed out with her hooves. She dodged the clawing root and galloped her way down the trail. Tendrils of light started piercing through the malaise. David could hear the others yelling. They sounded closer now, like they weren't coming from the bottom of a well. He could hear the dogs barking, and it seemed like they were coming closer to him.

The orbs hissed. It sounded like jets of escaping gas, and they clustered around him now. David batted them away. He could hear the thing behind him. It babbled a song made of nonsense and dragged itself across the rent-up ground. Snowflake's flanks were covered in bloody sweat. The horse jumped over a rocking outcropping and exploded on to the road. The dogs jerked back. They barked and snarled at something only they could see and raced toward that cursed forest trail.

David slid off of Snowflake and knelt on the ground. He glanced back to the forest, his eyes wide and terrified. He didn't know if that thing was going to come out after him. And the orbs...those things were something he would rather not see again. He rested against Snowflake's legs. The mare shifted backward. She swished her tail and held her head high. David gripped her leg. He didn't know if he had the words for what happened.

"David!" Johann dismounted and helped him up. "What the hell?"

"There was a thing back there," he whispered. "I think it tried to kill me."

"Yes, these aren't the gentle woods of Talla Gael," Johann said. He shook his head and held David close. "There are things here, you know. We're close to the WildWood."

"The WildWood?" Wilhelm asked. He slid off his own horse and frowned. "I didn't know we were so close!"

David didn't know what they were talking about, nor

did he care. He curled into Johann's arms and choked back a broken sob. He didn't care that he was showing emotion that would have him ridiculed by Alsace. Johann petted his hair and let David curl into his side. David sunk against the ground. He shuddered as he thought of those long, thin fangs sinking into his flesh. Whatever it was, he feared that it wanted to eat him. He looked around, half expecting to see Henri, and mentally cursed when he didn't.

Wilhelm took his hand. "We're going to get home soon, I promise."

"You're probably going to need an army." Johann gave Wilhelm a long look. "If they've taken your palace, you're probably not going to get it back without a war."

"But I don't know how to lead an army!" Wilhelm yelped. "I wasn't supposed to be the crown prince! That was my brother!"

David gave him a long look as he stood up. "You're going to have to learn, then. And stop the damn war with Alsace."

"War with Alsace?" Johann asked. "Damn, I've been out of the loop for a long time. Last I heard, Talla Gael was turning inward. Things have changed."

David nodded weakly. "We need to hurry, then. I'll be fine. I just need a moment. That was...I don't know what it was, but I just need a moment."

Wilhelm pulled him into his arms. David almost collapsed into him. Henri held him from behind and stroked his hair. David couldn't stop the shaking. If he let his mind wander, he swore he could feel the things' claws digging into him. It had wanted to kill him. It probably wanted to eat him or do something horrible to his protesting body. Now that he was safe... Well, he didn't know what to think.

Snowflake butted his shoulder with her head. David petted her nose. She had saved him, even if she probably didn't know it. Her own scratches had already started to heal. There would be some interesting scars on her, but David couldn't bring himself to care. He just melted into Wilhelm's embrace and let the tears finally flow. To his credit, Wilhelm didn't say anything. He just held David close and rubbed his back.

"We need to get moving," Johann said. He stood and looked around the little road. "If there's a nasty thing in those woods, we don't need to hang around. It might get brave."

"Brave?" Henri's voice quavered as he came out of the forest. "Why would it get brave?"

"Because David here pissed something off," Johann grimly said. He caught his gelding's reins and mounted the horse. "Move out!"

David's hands shook as he stood. He could still feel that thing bearing down on him. Snowflake must have sensed his nerves, and she moved around. David petted her side to calm them both down. Then he mounted the mare and urged her down the road. He couldn't keep from looking over his shoulder as he rode. The dogs ran at the side of the road, seemingly as carefree as they always were, but even that didn't calm his nerves.

That thing was out there. And it was probably still looking for him. David couldn't shake his growing unease, no matter how much he tried. Something told him to keep an eye on Henri. There was something that unnerved him about that man and he couldn't quite put his finger on it.

CHAPTER NINETEEN: OUTLAWS

◆ ◆ ◆

Wilhelm clung to his dun mare and tried to calm his racing heart. These weren't the friendly trees of Talla Gael. Seeing the stag didn't mean that he was safe here. Wilhelm scanned the tangled trees for any sign of a threat as he rode. Dark shadows, their ends shaped like claws, hung over the forest path. David rode beside Wilhelm and jumped at every single sound that echoed through the underbrush.

David couldn't stop the fear that shone in his dark blue eyes. Wilhelm wanted to comfort him, but he didn't know how. He turned around in the saddle, glancing back to Henri. The man's blue roan stallion seemed to tremble under him. Henri pulled on the reins, likely trying to calm his mount, but the horse ignored him. Wilhelm hoped it was the dogs that had the horse unnerved. If this forest had another one of its nasty surprises waiting...

Something snapped behind them. The dun mare started, snapping her head up. Her ears swiveled around as she tried to locate the sound. The dogs paused. Myla darted to the left side of the road, her body low to the ground. Her hackles came up, and she pinned her ears to her head. Toman followed her. The big wolfhound growled softly as he paced. Johann slid off his horse.

"I've got a bad feeling about this," Johann said. He grabbed his sword and motioned to the others. "Get ready for anything."

Wilhelm agreed. He held his nervous mare steady and looked around. A forest of dark green stretched around him. Shadows pooled under fern covered boughs and thickets of sedge hemmed in the road. There were craggy rocks on the other side—perfect for a horse to catch its foot—that effectively forced them to stay on the road. The dun mare shifted nervously under him. She chewed on her bit and pawed at the dusty clay ground.

"Easy," Wilhelm whispered. He patted the horse's side and watched nervously. "It's going to be all right."

Toman started barking. The big dog paced back and forth, his tail wagging. Myla followed him. The white shepherd pressed her body to the ground as she did so and suddenly darted into a thicket. Seconds later, two men darted out. Their swords glittered in the light, and one of them struck Toman with the flat of his blade. Toman yelped. Myla darted from her spot behind the horses and fastened her jaws around the other's hand.

Johann swung his sword. He started forcing the other one back to the forest with swift, deadly blows. The mare danced under Wilhelm and bolted when a lean dog darted at her. The dog leapt up, like it was going to bite him, and the mare galloped toward the forest. She reared when a vine wrapped around her legs. The dog jumped at him again, its fangs barred. Wilhelm couldn't see the others. All he could do was cling to his horse and pray.

The mare ripped herself free. The thorns raked across her legs, drawing blood and splattering it all over the ground. Wilhelm lashed her with the reins. The mare galloped through the forest with a pack of dogs at her heels. They were lean things, rangy animals with black masks and too-long legs, and they snarled as they ran. Wilhelm could hardly breathe for the fear of it. He clung to the mare's thick mane as she ran.

A rider on a fuzzy white pony galloped up behind him. Wilhelm couldn't see who it was, but he knew they were trouble. The pony snorted as it ran. It pressed its body low to the ground and seemed to float over the ground. Wilhelm kicked the mare in the side. She snorted in fear, her nostrils quivering, and reared when she came to a wall of hedge. The other rider grabbed the reins before Wilhelm could wheel her away.

A dog fastened its jaws around his arm and dragged him off the saddle. Wilhelm landed *hard*. He lay there, his eyes wild. His chest heaved as he tried to gulp in air. Two more dogs surrounded him. Their ears were pinned to their skulls, and they growled softly. The mare shifted. She tossed her head, her eyes wild, and she stamped at the ground. The other rider dismounted, dropping the pony's reins to the ground, and grabbed the mare by the ear.

The rider's hood fell, revealing a long braid of blonde hair. Her eyes were a startling blue color, and her ears were long and pointed. The woman—girl, really, she couldn't have been older than Wilhelm—had well-worn dark leather trousers and a loose gray silk shirt. Her cloak was lined with wolf fur and made of a strange type of oilcloth that shifted in the half light. Wilhelm swallowed. He tried not to stare, as that was rude, but his eyes were still drawn to her.

"You have one sword among you," the woman said. "It's like you were asking to be robbed."

"We don't have any money," Wilhelm whispered. "I swear it!"

The woman snorted as she led the dun mare toward her own mount. "Oh, I'm well aware of that. The horses you ride? We would have eaten them. And your dogs are stupid, slow things."

Wilhelm bristled. "Hey, watch it! Those are my dogs you're insulting!"

"Do I look like I care?" the woman asked. She had a strange, lilting accent that the gave Wilhelm chills. "Your horses are useless, your weapons aren't much better, and you didn't even give us a good chase."

Wilhelm slowly picked himself up, eyeing the brown and brindle dogs. "I'm called Wilhelm," he slowly said, "what about you?"

"Holly." She didn't even bother looking at him. "Let's go meet the others. Hounds!"

The dogs perked up. They wagged their tails like a hunting dog did before it lunged. One of them—a massive black-and-tan beast—nipped at him like it was some kind of herding dog. Wilhelm couldn't help but walk along. He didn't like this Holly very much, and she probably returned the favor. One of the dogs nipped at him. Wilhelm just barely resisted the urge to slap the dog. There was a good chance the dog would rip out his throat if he tried.

Holly moved through the forest like she was born in her. Her boots were soft and without hard soles; they didn't make a sound on the forest trail. Even the white pony didn't make a sound. The pony wasn't very big—it was less than half the size of a Tallan horse—and it had a round, fat belly. Its fur was covered in mud and leaves, and its stiff, upright mane was all tangled and matted. Wilhelm's fingers ached for a curry comb.

Two more elves—each of them wearing the same type of loose, soft clothing that Holly wore—emerged from the forest. They were hard-bitten creatures, the male covered with scars and the female with one white eye, and they were just as armed as Steven's knights. They came to the road soon enough, and Wilhelm stopped when he saw Johann sitting on the ground. Someone had tied his hands behind his back.

His right eye was swollen shut. His sword had been tossed away. Henri was also tied to his horse, as was David. Both men were bleeding from gashes and cuts. Poor Toman and even Myla had been tied snout to feet and draped over one of the fuzzy, small ponies. Wilhelm counted six elves and nearly twenty dogs. His heart sank when he realized how thin and scarred they all were. He needed to say something, anything, to try and help.

"What happened to you?" he softly asked.

Holly whipped around. "Why do you care?"

"Because you're hurt," Wilhelm said. "You're outlaws, aren't you?"

"Why do you care?" one of the male elves asked. He was lithe, his face almost gaunt, and his amber eyes were wary. "You're *human*."

He spat the word *human* like it was some kind of vile curse. Wilhelm winced.

"I'm not like that," Wilhelm said. "My kingdom was taken by a band of renegade knights. I would like to get it back. I...I don't have any money, but we do have the forest lands near the coast."

Something caught his eyes. There was a flash of white in the deep forest, and Wilhelm swore he saw the stag. He wanted to run over and grab it, to ask it if it was his brother, but he held himself back. He couldn't draw attention to the stag. If it was his brother, he didn't want to risk the stag's life. Could you kill a spirit? Wilhelm didn't know if you could, and he didn't want to find out the hard way.

"Forest lands," the man said. "Yeah, right."

"He's telling the truth," David said. He shifted in his saddle and grimaced. "Think you can let us go? We're not going to hurt you, I swear."

"They're telling the truth, Bracken," Holly softly said. She nodded to the dogs, and they backed off. "We might as well take what little forest they give us. It's better than living as outlaws."

Bracken snorted as he started untying the others. "You might say that, but I don't trust them."

That was fine; Wilhelm didn't trust them either. He helped Henri up and nuzzled the redhead's cheek. He couldn't dare to do much more. David slid off of his spotted mare and rubbed his wrists. His sharp, dark blue eyes surveyed the little group. He snapped his fingers as soon as the dogs were released. Toman and Myla trotted to his side. Both dogs almost looked like they were about to go feral, and they snarled at the elven dogs.

"Easy," David whispered. He petted Toman's head and held his mare's reins. "Look, let's get moving. We need to get back to Talla Gael—"

"Talla Gael?" Holly yelped. "That's a hundred miles away!"

"That's where we're from," Wilhelm said. He mounted his dun mare again and tried to calm his racing heart. "We need to hurry; there's no telling what's going on right now."

He blinked back tears as he spurred his mare into a gallop. He didn't want to think of Steven right not or how thirsty that man's sword was for blood. The wind lashed in his face as he rode. Wilhelm could hear the mare snorting as she ran. Her hooves pounded the muddy road, slinging up filth that had to be covering the others. Wilhelm didn't care. He let the wind whip his face and pretended that was why tears streamed down his face.

A painful cry tore itself from his throat. He lashed the mare's side again to spur her even faster. He had to get home. He couldn't explain it, but he had to get home. Iron bands wrapped around his heart as he rode, and bile seemed to crawl up his throat. *Dead.* They would have to be dead. If Steven came to the castle... Steven's sword was sharp and his mind sharper. The mare suddenly stopped short, nearly throwing him.

"Go!" Wilhelm screamed. "Go, you stupid horse!"

The mare jerked her head back. She pawed at the ground and swished her tail. Wilhelm couldn't help the sound he made. He just wanted that stupid mare to *gallop*, dammit! His kingdom—his *family*—lay at the end of this road. He looked around, trying to figure out why the mare had stopped. Her sides were covered in lather, and her ears were pinned to her skull. Her legs seemed to tremble, and her nostrils trembled as she snorted.

Wilhelm twisted around. He couldn't see the others. He would give them a chance to catch up and rest his horse while he was at it. Wilhelm dismounted and walked the mare toward a stream that trickled beside the road. The water splashed over brightly colored rocks. Willow boughs—winter dead now—dipped into the water. A few dormant rushes clung to both sides of the bank, and water dripped from a large boulder a few centimeters from the stream.

Silence draped around them. It settled across Wilhelm's shoulders like a leaden blanket and seemed to choke him. Not even the bird calls shattered the air in this part of the road. The mare nibbled at some of the reeds, completely ignoring the water. Wilhelm petted her side in apology. He shouldn't have yelled at her, nor should he have lashed her like that. Hopefully she would forgive him.

He could hear the others. Wilhelm dried his eyes and braced his shoulders. Maybe, if the gods were truly with him, no one would mention his emotional outburst.

In the distance, he thought he saw the stag. That alone gave him a little hope.

CHAPTER TWENTY: RIDE AWAY

◆ ◆ ◆

David grimaced when Wilhelm galloped away. "You think he's okay?"

"He's in a snit," Henri lightly said. "He gets like that. It's been a hard few days for him. Emil's death didn't help anything either. Give him time; he'll get over it."

David gave Henri a long look. "You know, if Steven's going after his kingdom…"

He didn't want to say the words. In Alsace, if you said words like that, you had a decent chance of making them come true. David shook his head. He spurred Snowflake into a trot and followed the tracks Wil's mare had left. He pursed his lips as he rode. Snowflake seemed to pick up on his unease. She snorted, tossing her head, and tried to pull the reins from his hands. David pulled back just enough to remind her who was in charge.

Unease prickled across him as Henri rode away. David turned around, keen eyes scanning the forest. He couldn't see the elves, the dogs, or the others. Just a quiet, dark forest that stretched around them into infinity. Ideally, this wouldn't have unnerved him. Much of Alsace was covered in forest, with Wattling Street running through the heart of it, and the villages were little more than islands of clear space in a sea of green.

This, though, didn't feel like home.

A cool wind filtered through the trees, heavy with the promise of rain. Branches creaked and groaned as they swayed and the dead, dry leaves rustled on sleeping branches. Ivy and lichens clung to the rocks on the sides of the road. Tree roots broke through the packed clay surface and potholes were cut into the middle of the road. A dog barked in the distance, followed by its mate, but no other sounds broke the heavy silence. Johann was a few feet away, his gaze distant. He seemed lost in thought to the point that David didn't want to bother him.

"David!" Henri came trotting up on his roan horse. "Just leave him alone! He'll get over it, I swear."

"You sure about that?" David asked. He tried to force away the unease, only to have it grow. "He seemed pretty upset to me. I think we should go and see if he's all right."

Henri snorted. "Look. David. I get that they might do things differently in Alsace, but he's got to learn to be a man."

David gritted his teeth. He wasn't going to answer that one. He spurred Snowflake in the side and galloped the horse over the next ridge. As much as he liked Henri— the man had saved his life, so David owed him one— he had to admit that it was off-putting to hear him talk about Wil like that. There was a very good chance that the unthinkable had already happened. Steven might have been an idiot, but he was good with a sword.

The Tallan nobility, much like the Alsatian kind, didn't seem like they were that good in a fight.

He slowed Snowflake as the mare picked her way down the hill. Her ears pricked forward as soon as she was on level ground and she whinnied. Another mare—this one with a deeper, almost throatier voice—answered. David hoped it was Wilhelm. He petted Snowflake's neck to calm her and slid off her back. Wil couldn't have gone too far. Sure, he had been galloping, but that mare of his was too stocky to run forever.

"Wil?" he called. "Wil!"

Something rustled behind them.

Snowflake jumped. The mare half reared and pawed at the air as she cried out. David caught her bridle. He tried to listen, but all he could hear was the wind and creaking trees. Something inside of him screamed *danger*. He could hear the leaves rustling and the bracken swaying, but nothing that sounded like a human or an elf. His heart leapt to his throat. He backed up, ready to get back on Snowflake, when something flew through the air beside him.

Snowflake reared. She cried out and tossed her head, ripping the bridle from David's hands. The mare bolted, running toward the forest, but she caught her foot in one of the rocks. David ran toward her. An eerie silence stretched over the road. He could hear his heart beating, the trees moving, and the wind. Snowflake whinnied again. She popped her head up, trying to jerk her foot free from the craggy rocks.

"Easy, girl," David whispered. He grabbed her reins again and started digging at the close compacted soil with his free hand. "Easy, I've got you."

The dogs barked in the distance. Something came up behind them, almost silently. Snowflake didn't try to bolt, telling David that it was likely a friend rather than foe. He tensed inexplicably. Something screamed at him to turn around. He was just about to do so when something struck him upside the head and he found himself collapsing to the ground. For the longest time, he felt nothing.

A strange sort of cold settled over his body. He could feel the wind as it drifted across over sensitive skin, but nothing else. Blood tricked from a gash at the back of his head. It flowed in a warm rivulet that would have annoyed him before. Now, though, he couldn't bring himself to care. He just lay there, his body unfeeling, as Snowflake grazed a few feet away from him. He felt like he lay in the bottom of a deep well instead of the grassy margins of a road; every sound seemed to echo around him in an inexplicable way.

"David!" Someone shook his shoulder, urgency in their voice. "David! Wake up!"

"What the hell, man!"

"One of you people did this! I knew we couldn't trust you!"

"These are all that's left of my people, asshole! If we wanted to kill you, we would have done it before!"

"You tried to kill him!"

"Bullshit! We were here with you all the time!"

"Yeah? Well, I don't trust a fucking *elf*!"

"Everyone, shut *up*!"

That last one made David open his eyes. He groaned softly. His head throbbed like it had been used to play a drummer's song. His body ached and mud clung to his already filthy clothes. He picked himself up slowly, leaning into the hands that helped him. A large, wolfhound came into view, and before David could stop him, the dog covered his face in licks. David shook his head. He nearly opened his mouth to protest, only to think the better of it at the last second.

"Easy, Toman." Johann crouched beside him and pulled at David's right eyelid. "Well, that's one hell of a concussion. Whoever hit him was trying to kill."

Henri ground his teeth as he took Snowflake's reins. "Where's the prince?"

"The prince wants some privacy," Johann said. His voice was tight and hard. "I suggest that you leave him be."

"How would you know that?" Henri sneered.

"Because I lost my kingdom too." Johann sighed. He looked away. "I know what Wilhelm is going through. It would be better to let him come back when he's willing instead of chase him down like he's a rabbit."

David leaned his head on Johann's shoulder and swallowed. "Think we can stop for the night? Please?"

"If he has a concussion, we do need to stop," Holly said. "As much as I hate to admit it, he's got a nasty head injury. That can kill him if we're not careful. I'll get tents up."

"Thank you," Johann said. He petted David's hair, careful to avoid the bloody spot. "Henri, take Bracken and see if you can find Wilhelm. If he doesn't want to come with you, at least make sure that he knows we're going to be staying here for the night."

"Right." Bracken urged his horse toward the bath. "Toman! Let's go!"

The big wolfhound barked and trotted off after the elf. Henri followed slowly. For some reason, Toman wouldn't get near the man, nor would any of the other dogs. Even Snowflake pinned her ears to her skull and ignored him. David couldn't bring himself to care. His head still hurt something awful, and it was all he could do to lie in Johann's arms. He could see why Wilhelm liked the man—Johann was strong and his touch brought nothing but pleasure.

"Who do you think hit him?" Another elf, this one male with long, braided red hair, crouched beside them. "You don't have anything to steal and your horses are...not good."

"Ruari, if I knew, I would have killed them myself," Johann growled. "But since I don't...I wouldn't put it past Steven."

"He a prick?"

"Yup." Johann grinned crookedly. "I heard your people are good at fighting. Is that true?"

"Not for a head-on assault, no," Ruari said. "But getting in and taking out the enemies? We can do that. Besides, it'll be nice to have a place to call home again. I'm tired of living rough."

"Indeed." Johann helped David stand, careful to support the younger man's weight, and started walking him toward a plain gray tent beside the road. "Easy now. Watch your head. You already have one goose egg. No need to make it two!"

David nodded weakly. "Thanks. Don't think I could have done it myself."

Someone had thrown pillows and blankets on the floor. There were nearly a dozen of them, all embroidered and made of brilliantly colored fabric. There was a fur, too, and it was draped in the middle of the big pile. Some of the pillows were beaded in intricate patterns that formed griffons, bears, eagles, and lions, while others were plain and soft. Johann kicked the beaded ones out of the way before he gently put David down in the middle.

"Do you know who attacked you?" Johann murmured. He lay beside David and rested one scarred hand on the younger man's belly.

"I just heard him," David whispered. He coughed and rolled over, wincing when pain stabbed through his body. "Someone threw something at me and Snowflake, but I didn't get a good look at it."

"I don't think it was a bandit." Johann leaned over David and traced his lips. "I get the feeling most of the bandits here are elven in nature."

David nodded weakly. He didn't mind what Johann was doing; it felt good, in fact. He curled up beside the man and sighed softly. Exhaustion wrapped around his body. He didn't know why someone would try to kill him. The elves were right; none of the horses they had were fine and they carried no money. Even the dogs were simple hunting hounds and herding dogs. A body could find ten more just like them for a few coppers.

"I don't even know who tried it." David coughed and winced when the movement jarred his head. "How long is it gonna be before I heal up? Because this shit sucks right now!"

Johann shrugged. "Could be a few hours, could be a day. Your body just has to heal itself."

"That sounds fun," David said. He propped himself up.

"Why did you join us?"

Johann looked away for a few minutes. Then, "Because that's what I wished someone had done for me. Before I came here, I was exiled to a place where I was all alone. A guardian, of sorts. I saw many people die trying to take something that belonged to the gods, and I wasn't allowed to stop them. The greatest torture is seeing someone walk to their death and be unable to stop them. Once I managed to free myself from the curse, I came here."

"And the kingdom you had?" David asked. "What of it?"

"It's been gone for a very long time," Johann said. He sighed. "Bringing it back would only cause more suffering. I don't have the taste for ruling anymore. I pity those who do."

"That makes sense," David mumbled. He cried out and all but collapsed into Johann's lap. "Tell–tell me it gets better. *Please.*"

"You were hit very hard," Johann whispered. He brushed through David's hair, kindness in his eyes. "You'll heal. Just be patient."

"David!" Wilhelm came racing into the tent, followed by Toman and Myla. "Is he all right?"

"He's going to be just fine," Johann replied. He patted the pillows beside him. "Just being close to him will get him better. He needs us right now."

Wilhelm nodded and lay down on the other side of him. For the first time in a long time, David felt safe, and he allowed himself to relax.

CHAPTER TWENTY-ONE: FALLING

◆ ◆ ◆

Wilhelm didn't know how long he was away from the others. He heard a commotion behind him, along with the dogs barking, but he paid it no mind. He just wrapped his arms around himself and stared into the forest. The wind dried his tears. He could hear the distant bird calls, but even that did little to lighten his mood. Wilhelm stuffed his fist in his mouth and tried not to scream. If the others heard…

Well, it probably wouldn't go so well for him.

"I was never meant to be king," Wilhelm whispered. He stood up and turned around, his eyes wild. "I was never meant to be king!" He sank back down and gripped at the sandy earth. "That was Emil's job…"

The wind wrapped around like a silken shawl. He reached out, like he could touch it, and imagined he was holding his brother's hand. He *missed* Emil. His brother, the true king, the one who had been educated for this job, would have known what to do. He would have gathered up that dun mare and galloped back to the others with a plan of action. Wilhelm just found himself sitting on the ground, wondering what the hell he was going to do next.

Something prickled at the back of his neck. The dun mare snorted. She tossed her head back, pinning her ears to her skull. Wilhelm slowly stood. He grabbed the mare's reins and looked around. Only the dark forest met his gaze. That didn't comfort him, not like it usually did. His heart raced in his chest. The trees seemed to crowd in around him, like they were going to capture him and do horrible things with his unwilling body.

"Let's get out of here," he said. "There's something out here, and I don't want to find it."

He mounted his mare again, wincing when she shifted under him. She pricked her ears forward and snorted again. Only the silent forest answered her. Wilhelm tugged on the reins. He tried to ease her away from that spot, but the mare stood firm. She pawed at the coarse ground. She half reared and whinnied her challenge a second later. And then—moving as silently as a ghost— a white mare slipped out of the forest.

She was lean and lithe, her legs fine and clean, and her neck arched like she was from the steppe. Her eyes were a cool amber color, and her pearl-white mane had been formed into a long running braid shot through with gold. Her coat was as white as the driven snow, and her hooves had been polished into a silvery glow. Her saddle and bridle were made of a soft, elegantly tooled leather set with bits of polished bone and worked gems.

"We have a horse," Wilhelm said. "But where is her rider?"

The white mare snorted when Wilhelm urged his mount toward her. She tossed her head back and pawed at the ground. Her tail lashed to one side, and she pinned her ears back. The dun mare snorted. She tossed her head, like she was going to yank the reins from Wilhelm's hand. Wilhelm pulled her back. The white mare started backing up. Her small, delicate hooves made no sound on the fallen leaves and muddied moss.

Wilhelm was just about to give chase when something crashed in the forest. The mare cried out in fear. She wheeled around, bolting through the thick underbrush before Wilhelm could even hope to catch her. The dun mare snorted. She chewed on the bit, pulling at it, before she finally calmed and allowed Wilhelm to guide her back down the forest road. He didn't know how he was going to face the others, just that he had to.

"Wilhelm!" Holly came galloping up the road on her fuzzy pony. "There's been an accident! David's hurt!"

Wilhelm's heart froze in his chest and the world seemed to stop. "He's...hurt? Is he–is he?"

If he dies, I don't think I could keep on living.

"I don't know," Holly said. She wheeled her pony around and waited until Wilhelm did the same. "Johann says it's bad."

Wilhelm could hardly breathe as he urged his mare after Holly. He gripped the reins with shaking hands and spurred her to a gallop. The mare snorted. She tossed her head and tried to yank the reins from his hand. Wilhelm swore under his breath. He urged her as fast as he could and charged that horse right into the camp. David's horse reared. The spotted mare jerked her reins free from where she was tied and bluff-charged the dun mare.

Wilhelm didn't care. He dismounted, tossing the reins to the ground, and ran for David. He could hear Holly yelling but couldn't bring himself to care. He had to find David. He had to know if his—well, Wilhelm didn't know *what* he was—was going to die. If David did, it would be his fault. Tears burned at Wilhelm's eyes as he ran. He ran right into someone and nearly raked his nails down their face.

"Easy!" Johann yelped. He grabbed Wilhelm's wrist. "I'm not going to hurt you, I swear it. Nice of you to join us, by the way."

"Is–is he dead?" Wilhelm whispered. He collapsed into

Johann's arms and didn't bother trying to hide the sobs. "If he's dead, it's my f-fault…"

"It's not your fault, and he's not dead," Johann said. He swung Wilhelm into his arms, carrying him to a tent. "He just hit his head pretty good, that's all."

"I saw a white horse," Wilhelm said. He swallowed and rested his head against the man's shoulders. "I didn't see her rider. I think something killed them."

Johann settled him down on a pile of soft blankets and brushed a kiss against his cheek. Wilhelm found himself leaning into the touch. His eyes fluttered closed. He all but crawled into the older man's lap. Johann's hands were rough and strong, the hands of a working man, and they felt so good against feverish skin. Wilhelm had never really been with anyone before. He wanted to feel good right now, wanted to feel like someone was caring for him.

"We can find that horse tomorrow," Johann murmured. He nuzzled Wilhelm's neck and nipped over the soft skin.

Wilhelm took a shuddering breath. He could see David's chest gently rising and falling. He reached out, jut brushing the other man's cheek. David seemed to lean into the touch. Wilhelm felt his heart sing, and a small smile played across his face. Johann nuzzled under his ear, making Wilhelm gasp. The older man's hands felt so skilled and strong that Wilhelm found his tension melting away. It was like he was drifting, floating almost, and shuddering with pleasure.

"Is he going to be all right?" Wilhelm asked. He curled up close to Johann and allowed the man to pull his shirt off. "Holly said he was hurt bad…"

"He'll be fine," Johann said. A half smile tugged at his lips. "I've hurt myself worse falling off a horse."

Wilhelm nodded. He didn't stir when the man stripped off his own clothing. He could feel the warmth Johann gave him and could smell his scent. He sprawled on top of the man, resting his head right above the man's heart. Wilhelm did his best to ignore his body. Johann wouldn't want to be burdened with his needs, and Wilhelm wasn't going to impose. If he couldn't control himself, that was on him.

"Do you want me?" Johann asked. He brushed a soft kiss against the back of Wilhelm's neck.

"I've never been with anyone," Wilhelm said. He swallowed and tried to control his flush. "It–it wasn't proper. I'm the prince, my body belongs to—"

"No." Johann gave him a long look. "Your body belongs to *you*. Tradition be damned."

Wilhelm wished he could believe that. Tradition was a powerful thing in Talla Gael, and he didn't think that he could go against it. A prince was to marry royalty, no matter what he felt. Then he smiled slowly when he had an idea. If what Johann had said was true, then he was royalty. He just didn't have his kingdom anymore. The tradition said that he was to marry another prince or princess, not that said prince had to have a kingdom.

"Do I want to know why you're smiling, or..." Johann trailed off, concern in his eyes.

"I think you could have me," Wilhelm said. He snuggled close to the other man and dared to kiss him. "And keep with tradition."

"That sounds good," Johann replied. A small smile played at his lips as he ran his hand through Wilhelm's hair. "I think I would like to have you. And what of David?"

"Yeah." David rolled over, the shadows playing across his expressive face. "What of David?"

"I want both of you," Wilhelm said. He bit his bottom lip. "Is–is that bad?"

"I don't think so." Johann kissed him, long and deep, leaving Wilhelm breathless. "I think you can have both of us. I wouldn't mind sharing."

"It's pretty common in Alsace," David said. He propped

himself up, wincing as he did so. "Please tell me when this head wound is gonna get better, because this sucks."

"It'll be a few days," Johann murmured. He leaned over and kissed David's hand. "You should be able to ride tomorrow though. The sooner we get back to Talla Gael, the sooner we can do away with Steven."

"Do you think we'll get there in time?" Wilhelm asked. His voice was little more than a whisper, and he couldn't keep the fear from bleeding into his words. "I don't want them to be killed for something we did."

"There's nothing you can do," Johann carefully said. "Please don't blame yourself. I made the same mistake when my kingdom fell."

Wilhelm swallowed. He curled up close to Johann and allowed David to do the same. If Johann didn't like having both of them on him, he gave no indication. Wilhelm took advantage of the warmth and made sure that David's head wasn't cocked to the side. Johann was so warm underneath him, so strong. Wilhelm felt like nothing bad could happen to him, not now. He had the man he loved and the one he would marry, right there with him.

"What did you do?" David whispered.

"I lost myself." Johann looked away and swallowed.

"Tried to kill Steven. I...only got my closest friend killed. No matter how much I hurt him, he simply bounced back. After that, I went away. It was the easiest thing to do."

"Wil's and my people are at war," David said. He winced and stretched out. "Does me being with him make me a traitor?"

"I don't think so," Johann replied. He simply held the both of them, waiting for the longest time to speak. "It's not like either of you are fighting and the war has to end sometime. Why not now?"

"Yes, why not now?" Wilhelm asked. "I don't know what the demands of either side were—"

"Nor do I," David quickly said. "But I'm not royalty. I'm just a soldier."

"Does it matter?" Johann asked. "If your government has a lick of sense, they'll give you some kind of rank. I'm not...I'm not really the marrying type. You two can be the royal couple, just as long as you come home to me at night."

Wilhelm nodded. That sounded fair. He moved over, letting David take his place on Johann's chest. Wilhelm tucked himself under Johann's free arm. He could still hear the man's strong, steady heartbeat, and it was more than enough to calm him down. Johann would be more than enough to take care of Maria once they got back. Wilhelm supposed that he needed to tell Johann about that situation sooner or later.

"What would you do if there were someone trying to kill me?" Wilhelm asked. "She already killed my brother. Maybe she invited Steven over to do his thing."

"She?" Johann gave him a long look. "What the hell am I getting myself in to? Wait. I don't want to know, because this sounds like I'm going to be dragged into court politics."

Wilhelm just smiled. He had a feeling Johann would do the right thing when it was time.

CHAPTER TWENTY-TWO: LOVE

❖ ❖ ❖

David woke up sprawled on Johann's chest. The early morning light spilled through a crack in the colorful material, resting on the older man's face. It highlighted his expressive, almost arrogant features and made David's heart beat faster. He wanted to cling to this man. Wilhelm shifted in his nest, and blue eyes slowly fluttered open. David couldn't resist; he leaned down and brushed a kiss against the man's face.

"Hey," David whispered.

"Hay is for horses." Wilhelm ran his hands through David's sleep tangled hair. "How are you feeling?"

"Better." David nuzzled Wilhelm and nipped his bottom lip. "My head's not killing me, which is nice. Let's see if we can get him up."

David wished he could lay in that bed forever. It wasn't really a bed—it was really more of a pallet than anything else—but it was nice and warm. David brushed a kiss against Johann's lips. The man squirmed some, and he flushed when David deepened the kiss. Wilhelm nuzzled the older man, nibbling the tender skin at the base of his neck. Johann groaned. His eyes fluttered open, and he stared at both of them in confusion before realization slowly dawned in his eyes.

"I take it you're feeling better?" Johann asked. He yawned and squirmed. "Your eyes look better."

"I'm a little sore, but otherwise fine," David said. He yawned and rolled his shoulders before curling up beside the man. "I don't have a pounding headache anymore. That's nice. And I feel good enough to get sexy with you, if that's what you want."

Johann grumbled some. He kissed David, though, and peeled off his shirt. David shivered when his soft, tender skin met the cold morning air. He didn't see a brazier, meaning this tent was heated by their own bodies. David grinned. If they were heating the tent, it would work better if there was bare skin instead of thick, heavy clothing. He stripped off the rest of his clothes and played his hands against Johann's shirt buttons.

"I want to see you," David whispered.

"Me too." Wilhelm kissed Johann's cheek and lowered his eyes. "If we're to marry—any of us—I want to know what you look like before we're supposed to consummate."

"We're supposed to what?" Johann asked. He grimaced and sighed some. "You have the weirdest way of putting things, you know. You take all the romance out of it. Make it sound like we're a bunch of animals instead of human beings."

Holly cleared her throat a moment before lifting the tent flap. "Everyone still alive in here?"

"We're fine," Johann called. He sighed softly and kissed David's cheek. "We need to get going. As much as I would like to have you, we still need to get back to Talla Gael." He stood and grabbed his coat. "Come on, you two. Wilhelm, you said you saw a white horse with no rider. We need to see if we can find her again."

David grabbed his clothes. He knew they needed to get going. As much as he might want to stay and love these two, they had a kingdom to save. He dressed as quickly as he could, pulled on his boots, and slipped outside. Toman barked sharply. The big dog looked up from where he was resting with Myla. The white dog completely ignored him. That was fine; David didn't mind being ignored. Sometimes that was the better option.

He caught Snowflake when the hair at the back of his neck stood up. Snowflake shifted and pawed at the ground. David touched the back of her cheek to calm her. He could hear someone behind him, and he forced his racing heart to calm. The back of his head throbbed. Even the wind shifted, warning him of some strange danger. He grabbed the mare's bridle and had just slipped it over her head when someone cleared his throat.

David whipped around. "Hey!"

"Easy!" Henri yelped.

"You scared me," David weakly said. He tried to ignore the fear in his veins or the way he wanted to bolt. "I– that's all. You just scared me."

"Whatever," Henri said. "Quit looking like a scared rabbit."

"Someone tried to kill me yesterday!" David said. "I think I have a right to be nervous."

"Whatever." Henri grabbed his roan stallion's reins and jerked the horse over.

David grabbed Henri's shoulder. "What crawled up your ass and died, Henri? Because this isn't the man I know!"

Henri shrugged him off. "You really wanna know? You really wanna know why I'm pissed off right now? Because you picked that stupid prince and that–that old, scarred-up son of a bitch instead of *me*. You could have had someone pretty, young, and did I mention beautiful and you picked *that*."

"Are you jealous?" David asked. He saddled Snowflake and mounted her to keep from laughing. "Is that why you're acting like this? Because you're jealous of Johann?"

Henri gave him a dark look. David noticed that he was rough with his stallion and even slapped the horse when it nuzzled him. He winced as he guided Snowflake toward the road. The dogs took their place by his side and yipped when the elves got the tents all packed together. Henri, for whatever his reason, kept his distance. That was fine; David didn't want to start a fight if he could help it.

Johann cleared his throat as he urged his dun gelding beside David. "The only way to Talla Gael takes us through Wattling Street."

"Then how did they get Wilhelm here without being caught?" David asked. He shook his head as he peered into the dense forest. "Wattling Street isn't exactly like this road. It's crowded with traffic!"

Most of Alsace's money came from tariffs and protection from bandits, if David were to be honest. It wasn't that a kingdom known to be mostly forest would have a great deal in the way of trade. There just wasn't enough land to farm on, nor were there the sort of precious metals that made a place rich.

Johann just shrugged.

David knew that Wilhelm wouldn't know—he had been out for the duration—but there had to be some kind of magic involved. Something made David look around. He swore he could see a flash of white fur deep in the forest, like the stag was watching them. David shook his head and swore under his breath. He needed to keep his focus.

Toman barked. David jerked his head toward the dog. He couldn't see what the dog was upset about, but David knew something was there. Toman's hackles stood straight up. He snapped and snarled at what looked like a patch of brambles. David almost slid off the horse to grab the dog before he thought better of it. He didn't need to get in the middle of a fight, especially if it was a fight between a wolf and the wolfhound.

"What are we waiting for!" Ruari yelled. "You're Alsatian; take us down this Wattling Street so we can get that land!"

"I love how direct he is." David laughed. He shook his head, a small grin playing at his lips. "All right, I'll take you down Wattling Street."

Wattling Street started near the headwaters of Kileo

River. David didn't think they were that far from the river—the Kileo was the largest river in the continent and almost all roads ran into it at some point. David urged Snowflake into a trot. He rested one hand on the pommel and used the other to guide his mare. The two seemed to move as one now. It was like David could see every movement she was going to make and guide her to the best one.

Henri galloped up behind him. The roan stallion snorted and pinned his ears to his skull. He acted like he was going to bite, only for Snowflake to buck. The mare's hoof almost caught the stallion in the cheek. The dogs snapped and snarled, like they were trying to drive the other horse away. David took Snowflake over the bridge. Snowflake started when she almost tripped over a loose board.

The roan stallion stopped short. He pawed at the ground, snorting, and refused to take another step. Henri struck him, but still the stallion stood. Snowflake crossed over the bridge easily enough. She turned around, her ears pricked forward. David was just about to slide off the mare when a pale gray horse picked its way through the forest. His breath caught. It was still tacked up, and its mane was braided.

Then he saw the blood splattering its side. The horse moved slowly, like it was favoring one leg. Its ears flicked forward as soon as it saw Snowflake. Snowflake snorted a warning. She pulled on the reins but allowed David to hold her back. David ignored the fear pulsing through his body. He slid from Snowflake and crossed the moss-covered ground. This close, he could see that the gray horse was a mare, and its coat was so pale that it was nearly white.

"Found your horse!" David yelled. He led the nervous animal back to the group. "Is this the animal you saw yesterday?"

This close, he could see the soiled gold in the horse's running braid. The animal trembled as it walked after him. It even ignored Snowflake when she tried to nip at it. David petted the gray's nose. The horse must have been running for hours; otherwise, it would have tried to fight back. It just hung its head low, completely ignoring the others and even the dogs as they raced at it. David wished there was something he could do.

"That's the horse I saw!" Wilhelm said. He pulled his own mount to a stop and stared. "But where's the rider?"

"Dead." Johann dismounted and took the reins. "Look at the blood on this one's tack and sides. Whoever killed the rider did so a good distance away. Most horses won't leave their riders, especially if the rider was hurt this bad."

David nodded. He stripped the trembling mare's tack and took a step back. She completely ignored them as she lowered herself to the ground. David feared that she would die, just like her rider had, but there was nothing he could do. The mare extended her leg like it was hurting her. It even sighed and dropped its head to the cold, unforgiving ground. David petted her head one last time before he mounted Snowflake and guided her away.

"Poor thing," he said.

"I know," Johann said. The man sighed as he nudged his own gelding down the winding forest road. "Where exactly are we heading?"

"The headwaters of the Kileo River," David replied. "It's the biggest river in Alsace and also where Wattling Street starts. There's a settlement there and we should —"

"Yeah, we know the settlement," Ruari said. He rolled his eyes. "They don't like elves."

"Why am I not surprised?" Henri said. He sneered and gave Johann a nasty look. "I don't like washed-up old mercenaries!"

Johann ignored him, even though David could tell that it hurt. He wished he could comfort the other man. He just spurred Snowflake into a gallop and raced her on ahead. David had to scout the road to make sure there weren't more bandits. Not everyone was going to be as friendly as the elves. The soft morning light filtered through the tangled trees, pooling on the ground and crawling over more exposed bits of stone.

Dust motes and pollen seemed to hang in the air. Dew drops glittered on the slowly uncoiling ferns. David slowed Snowflake to a walk and allowed the mare to nibble at a few sprawling vines. She seemed at peace in this forest, likely because she was born in it. David patted her side. He pulled her away from the vines after a second and walked her under an arch made of tangled branches and ancient vines.

"It's beautiful," David whispered. He turned around, a smile playing at his lips. "I never thought about the forest like this, not until it was taken away from me..." He trailed off.

Snowflake just flicked her ears toward his voice, like any horse would, and she ambled to a crystal-clear stream. David let her drink. The forest seemed to sing around him, and it felt like he was the only person in the world. Something tugged at his mind—the idea that he could just vanish into the forests of Alsace and never be seen again.

Then David banished it. He loved Wilhelm and Johann, even enough to give up Alsace...forever.

CHAPTER TWENTY-THREE: HEADWATERS

◆ ◆ ◆

Wilhelm kept close to Johann. He didn't know what to say to Henri, nor did he know if he wanted to even try and say something. Calling a man—a *good* man, at that—a washed-up old mercenary seemed beyond the pale. Wilhelm didn't know why Henri disliked Johann. The man was nothing but kind to all of them. Hell, he was the reason why Wilhelm hadn't died in the forest. Wilhelm shuddered to think what might have happened if Johann hadn't been there.

Wilhelm risked a glance over at the man. Johann seemed lost in thought, his teeth nibbling at his bottom lip, as he rode. There were lines across the man's handsome face. Scars, too, if you knew where to look. He wasn't as young as they were, and it was clear that he had lived a hard life. Yet, Wilhelm didn't find anything to fault the man on. He was a good leader and an even better fighter. If not for him, they wouldn't have made it this far.

Wilhelm nudged his mare in the side and guided her beside Henri. "He saved my life, Henri! We owe him something!"

"Yeah, we do," Henri said. He stared at the road, his jaw clenched. "And it's not you sleeping with him!"

"Is that what you're angry about?" Wilhelm asked. He gave Henri a long look. Then, "Henri. You're my brother. My *cousin*. As much as I love you, we couldn't be together. Besides...that's not the way I love you. I have a brother's love for you. I thought I wanted to marry you, but..." He trailed off and looked away. "I couldn't give you what you wanted. I don't love you in that way, Henri. But I can't give you what you need."

"And a stupid soldier and a washed-up ex-mercenary can." Henri's voice was tight with grief as he spoke. "I always knew he was no good!"

"We need an alliance." Wilhelm bit his bottom lip and tried to ignore it when David rejoined their group. "Steven's no fool. Even if we do kick them out of the palace, we're going to have a hard time keeping them out of Talla Gael. Alsace is small, but they are mighty."

"David's a soldier!" Henri yelled. He gestured wildly as he spoke. "A *soldier!* He has no rank, no money, no land, no connections! All he has is a sweet voice and pretty words! And what does your mercenary have? Claims of a title that no longer exists because the country he came from is *gone!* So forgive me, Wilhelm dear, if I think you're making a terrible mistake. This isn't Vitor; I can say you're a fool to your face without being killed!"

"Then what do you suggest?" Wilhelm hissed. "Both of us be miserable and Talla Gael be invaded anyway?"

"My family has connections to Azania," Henri said. He kept his voice even and calm, but every fool could see the rage just under the surface.

"So does half of Talla Gael," Wilhelm replied. "You're not that special, Henri."

Henri winced as if he had been struck. Wilhelm knew that he had gone too far with that last remark, but he couldn't bring himself to care. He just clenched his jaw and jerked his mare away from Henri. So maybe he was being a stubborn fool. But damn him if he wanted to be happy for once. It was bad enough that he had to be a prince. Wilhelm didn't think he could do it if he had to marry someone he didn't love.

He sighed as he took his place by David's side. The forest seemed to wrap around them in some strange kind of living blanket. Sunrise burned away most of the morning mist, allowing the light to pool on the forest floor. Wilhelm could hear trickling water that slowly, oh so slowly, became a roar. Bits of mice-flecked granite poked through the mossy forest floor, and mountain laurel clung to exposed sheets of stone as they rode.

"It shouldn't be that far now," David said. His soft voice shattered the stony silence. "We can rest in the village if we need to."

Toman barked sharply. The dog darted out from the middle of the pack and started running toward a cluster of wattle and daub homes. Smoke coiled from a brick chimney, filtering through the dense branches and filling the air with its heady scent. Myla ran under the dun mare's legs and made the horse rear some. Wilhelm held on. He patted the side of her neck as soon as she settled down, just to make sure she wasn't terrified.

"Who're you?" A young girl, her hair the color of spun gold, wandered toward the group with one hand on Myla's back.

"I'm Wilhelm." Wilhelm dismounted his mare, petting her nose to keep her calm. "We're looking for the village near the river."

The girl chewed on her hair as she thought. Then she pointed to a path that branched off toward a rocky patch of forest.

"Down there," she said. "Mama says that the Kileo's the strongest, swiftest river in the world. Where're you going?"

Wilhelm glanced to Johann as he made a snap decision. "Talla Gael."

The girl's eyes widened like he had suggested they go to the ends of the earth. Toman's tail wagged back and forth. He licked the girl across the face, making her squeal, as he bounded back to Wilhelm's side. Myla followed after a minute. Wilhelm thought he saw a flash of white in the forest, and he turned around to see what it was. He opened his mouth, words lingering on his lips, but they died when Henri cleared his throat.

Wilhelm mounted his mare again and guided her down the forest path. He could smell the water in the air now. Bird cries—strange and harsh, like nothing he had ever heard before—echoed through the air. A white-winged bird suddenly dipped between the trees. It darted between the little group, nipping at them and spooking the horses. Henri's roan reared. The man jerked on the reins harshly and slapped it in the jaw.

"Easy!" David yelped. "You're just scaring him!"

"What do you know about horses, Alsatian?" Henri growled. He forced the nervous stallion back under control. "If I want your opinion, I'll ask for it."

David rolled his eyes and gave a dramatic sigh. "You know," he brightly said, "no one's ever gonna sleep with you if you keep talking like that."

"Shut up!" Henri screamed.

"Make me." David flashed his most winning smile. "Come on, Henri. Get that stick out of your ass; this isn't you! What happened to the guy who saved my life, huh? What happened to him?"

Wilhelm tried to tune them out. This was his fault, wasn't it? It was his fault that he got captured and also his fault that Henri was in a foul mood. He patted his mare's shoulders when she stepped over a rough cattle guard. Her hooves slipped over the rusting iron bars and she popped her head back, but still she crossed. David jumped his mare, as did Johann and the elves, leaving only Henri and the dogs.

"Let's go, Henri," Johann said. "We don't have all day."

Wilhelm turned around, dread building in his belly. He didn't know how he knew, but he knew something was about to go down. He had just opened his mouth to speak when a shot rang out. Wilhelm didn't know what caused the sound, just that it came suddenly and the mare reared. She cried out in fear, tossing her head wildly, and galloped down the forest trail. Another shot rang out, causing a tree trunk to explode into a shower of pulpy shards.

"Not now!" Henri screamed. He tried to hang on as best he could as his stallion raced down the narrow road. "You idiot!"

Wilhelm had no idea what that was about, but he didn't intend to stay around to care. He spurred his mare in the side. She took off after Henri. Her neck stretched out low to the ground and her long stride seemed to swallow the distance. Toman raced past them, barking all the while. His teeth flashed in the dappled sunlight as he ran and his bays filled the air. David kicked his spotted mare in the side, urging her closer to the runaway stallion.

"Hang on!" David yelled. "Just hold on!"

Wilhelm pulled his horse to a stop. He knew his mare couldn't run that fast. The others didn't even try to keep up. They pulled their own horses in a stop, watching as David raced after Henri. Wilhelm's heart seemed to freeze in his chest. He wished there was something he could do, even if that meant he got in the way. He seemed to shake like a leaf in a rainstorm as the two men vanished.

Wilhelm suddenly kicked his mare into a gallop. She snorted as she took off, her ears pinned to her skull. Bits of craggy stone poked through the dense clay road. His mare almost tripped more than once, and it was all Wilhelm could do to hold on. He wanted to yell, wanted to chant that none of this was fair, but he forced himself to keep going. Tears burned his eyes as he rode. The mare half bucked under him, like she wanted him off her back, but he held on for dear life.

He rounded the corner, just in time to see Toman launch himself at Henri. Someone screamed—some distant part of him hearing his own cry. Before Wilhelm knew what happened, he slid off his mare's back and *ran*. Henri's stallion reared. The horse lashed out with his razor-sharp hooves, catching Toman in the shoulder. The dog screamed as he fell. He bled heavily from his shoulder, and his eyes were wild.

"Toman!" Wilhelm screamed. "Stop it!"

"Get that beast away from me!" Henri screamed. He forced his sweating, scared stallion under control and just barely kept his seat. "He tried to kill me!"

"Someone tried to kill us!" David slid off his spotted mare and grabbed the stallion's reins. "So forgive him for being scared!"

Wilhelm just grabbed his dog. He held Toman close to him, not caring that his hands were covered in blood. Toman couldn't die. He just *couldn't*. Wilhelm wrapped his arms around Toman, trying to bite back the tears. If his dog died, it was going to be his fault. Johann knelt beside him. Wilhelm didn't know where he came from, nor did he care. He curled back against the other man and allowed a broken sob to spill from his lips.

It seemed like daggers speared his chest. He could feel those spectral blades twist through his very soul, gashing their way through his body and allowing an abyss inside. Wilhelm choked back a sob. Toman licked his face, thumping his tail against the ground. Johann didn't say a word. He just crouched there, his hand a warm, comforting weight on Wilhelm's back. Wilhelm did his best to ignore the others. This was about Toman, not them.

"The dog's going to live," Johann said. "He might have a nice little scar on him, but he's going to live."

"But he got kicked!" Wilhelm cried. "Kicked by a dangerously wild stallion!"

Henri rolled his eyes. "Dangerously wild stallion? Try not to have your dog attack me!"

"Toman did launch himself," David said. "Damnedest thing I ever saw. You would think Toman was a guard dog with how he was acting! I don't blame Henri for being upset. On the plus side, we're near the headwaters. Should be just a few minutes around the next bend. We can make it before high noon."

Wilhelm stood up slowly. He ignored the others, only vaguely aware of the blood on his own clothes. He glanced back to the elves. Holly looked concerned, as did Bracken. Even Ruari looked like he was concerned. Wilhelm petted Toman's head as he walked back to his horse. He couldn't look at Johann. How could that man want him, as weak as he was? Wilhelm couldn't even hide it now.

Bracken hung back from the others and gave Henri a long look. "I don't trust that one."

"Why?" Wilhelm asked. "He's my cousin; he would never turn traitor!"

"Well," Bracken said as Wilhelm mounted his mare, "there's a first time for everything."

CHAPTER TWENTY-FOUR: RIVER

❖ ❖ ❖

The roaring river drowned any unease David might have had. He patted Snowflake's neck as he mounted the mare again. She seemed nervous, much like he was, and she kept flicking her ears toward the underbrush. David wished he could hear what she did. He nudged Snowflake forward as soon as the others were ready, taking care to stay at the rear of the group. Whatever had attacked them was still out there—it simply *had* to be.

"Why do you think Toman went wild?" David asked as soon as Johann was in earshot. "I've never seen him act like that before!"

Johann bit his bottom lip. "Fear, maybe. It's been a hard journey on all of us. He's probably just as scared, tired, and grouchy as we are. Henri happened to annoy him, I guess."

David didn't know if he believed that or not. He forced

a smile on his face, though, and guided Snowflake away from Johann's mare. A cool breeze—a far cry from the bitter chill Talla Gael had—wrapped around his body and slipped through his hair. The road they were on took them close to the river. Where the rushes broke, David could see hints of blue gray and dense tangles of water-logged boulders.

A thick, dense tangle of laurel bushes stretched up the other side of the river. David could just see hints of gray where the laurel hadn't grown yet. Water splashed down the cliff face, adding to the swollen waterway below. Voices floated on the wind—voices of the travelers and those who called the headwaters home. Something in David's heart sang as he followed the twisting, winding path. This place, though not the village where he was born, was *home*.

A young woman wearing a long, heavy skirt and a blue headscarf stopped them. "Who're you?"

"David." David dismounted and looked toward the river. "What's the first port in Talla Gael?"

The woman shrugged. "I don't know; I don't live on the ferry."

"Could you ask them, please?" David asked. He resisted the urge to get short with her. "It's urgent that we be in Talla Gael as quickly as possible."

The woman rolled her eyes as she turned to go. "Fine, I'll ask my husband. He runs a ferry from between here and the Sija, so he should know."

"Sija?" Johann dismounted and wandered over. "Damn, we have traveled far!"

David nodded. He squeezed Johann's hand and wished that would calm his racing heart. Snowflake reared her head back when two muddied men wandered out of a half-overgrown path and toward a few low stone huts. They looked older, with streaks of gray visible in their mire-soaked hair, and the one on the right walked with a pronounced limp. Snowflake stamped her foot in warning when they came closer.

"Is she safe?" the first one asked. He favored his right leg, and his dark eyes darted around the little clearing. "Last thing I want is to get bit."

"She's safe." David tugged on her reins to calm her. "You might want to watch out for the roan though. He does kick."

Toman flopped down in the dirt. He eyed the two men and bared his teeth when they came closer. Myla stiffened. She lowered her head, hackles slowly standing up. The white dog stood in front of Wilhelm and seemed to dare the men from coming closer. Wisely, they decided to stay where they were. David didn't have the energy to figure out what was going on.

He glanced around, trying to see where that woman was.

"Where are you going?" the second asked. His voice was rougher and his hand rested a dagger hilt.

"Talla Gael," David said. "I'm David. You are?"

"Call me Hawke." Hawke bit his bottom lip as he examined the little group before them. "My friend over there with the bum leg is called Keevan. You know you have elves traveling with you, mate? Those bastards'll stab you in the back if you give them half a chance."

David barely managed to keep a civil tongue in his head. "I know they're elves. They're my friends, so you need to watch your tongue."

Hawke snorted. "An elf's only friend is an elf."

"Hey!" The woman waved her arms as she came back over, followed by a burly man. "You're in luck; my husband's leaving for the Sija in just a few minutes!"

"Who are you, beautiful?" Hawke purred. He stalked toward her like a large cat after a mouse and reached out to touch her skin.

"Back off!" The woman slapped him across the face.

Behind her, a long-haired tricolor dog growled. The animal's hackles slowly stood, and it pinned its ears to its skull. The dog snapped at Hawke when he moved closer. It was clear some kind of guard dog—David thought it looked like one of those black-and-tan shepherds the Korisans kept—and it clearly wanted no part of Hawke. The man grumbled under his breath. He backed off and gestured to Keevan.

"Let's get on the stupid ferry," Hawke muttered.

David took Snowflake's bridle and stroked her nose before leading her after the others. Snowflake nipped at Keevan when he came too close to her. The mare snorted in anger when the man glared at her, like she was daring him to start something. Even Toman kept his distance. The big wolfhound stood in front of David and nipped at anyone who dared come close. Henri, too, looked unnerved.

He struggled to control his stallion and finally slid off the horse to walk it. Wilhelm followed his lead, as did the elves. Soon, there was a long line of travelers walking nervous horse toward a pier jutting into the river. David thought that the ferry moored to it didn't look like much. It was a simple raft made of logs lashed together, planks nailed atop that, and a split rail fence all around it. There were oarlocks for the captain to steer it and a small gate to limit access.

Henri made a sour face. "Is that what we're supposed to

ride on?"

"It is." David couldn't help but grin. "What, have you never seen one of these before?"

A massive gray draft horse raised its head as the burly man drew near. The first thing he did was take the long leather line it was attached it and shorten it until he had a lead. Then, he led the horse on to the ferry before tying it to the railing beside a pile of hay and a bucket of water. David figured the horse was how he got back to the pier. If he looked closely, he could see a path in the reeds near the riverbank.

"It'll be three coins a head," the man said. He eyed the two dogs. "They can ride free, as long as no one bites."

Johann searched through his pockets and came up with a small handful of coins. "There. Keep those two ruffians away from us, then, Master...?"

"Call me Lebe." Lebe turned to open the gate. "All right, you two hunters! Keep away from this other lot!"

Hawke rolled his eyes as he walked upon the deck. The man reeked, like he had been laying in a bag of rotting onions, and his clothes were soaked with more filth than David thought they could hold. The man clearly didn't care about keeping clean. David drew back, making sure to keep away from him. Even when he had been a prisoner, he had tried to keep clean. How Hawke dealt with that amount of filth on his body, David didn't know.

Wilhelm pressed his body against David's. "Do you think they'll want me back?"

"We're their only hope," David whispered. He ruffled Wilhelm's hair and brushed a kiss against his forehead. "Of course they're going to want us back."

Maybe Steven had pretty words, but he came with a sword instead of peace. From what David knew of the Tallans, they didn't like being told one thing and given another. When—not *if*—Steven tried his attack, he was going to meet a well-primed army. David hated cheering for the Tallans, but he thought they were better than some renegade knight and his band of merry murderers. David didn't even know if Rogarshall was a place.

"I'm scared," Wilhelm whispered. He clung to David, wincing as the rapid caught the ferry once it was unmoored. "We can't fight a knight!"

"I can," David said. He kissed Wilhelm fiercely to chase the fear away. "So can Johann and every knight in Talla Gael."

He hoped that was enough. Wilhelm clung to David, resting his head under the other man's chin. David stroked Wilhelm's back gently. He could feel eyes ripping into his back, though, and David feared that malice was aimed at Wilhelm, not himself. David braced himself. He could hear whispered conversations between the two hunters and they, too, couldn't keep their eyes from Wilhelm.

"What are you looking at?" David snarled. He braced himself for a fight.

Keevan cocked his head like a hungry dog. "Does it matter, pretty boy?"

"Yes," David growled, "it does."

"That's fine, that's fine," Keevan said. "Hawke and I were just wondering what sort of people let filth like you live."

Myla snapped to attention. The white dog flashed her teeth at both men. Her hackles went all the way up, and her snarl sounded like rumbling thunder. Toman did the same. The wolfhound was half a head taller than Myla. His scarred, lean body screamed threat. The wolfhound pinned his ears to his skull and stalked toward the two men. Tension draped over the entire group.

Hawke swallowed. He took a step back, wincing when his back met the railing. Toman stopped a few feet in front of the men. He lowered his head, still snarling all the while, and his dark eyes seemed to scream a threat.

David's breath caught. He didn't know if he could stop this. Toman sat down heavily. He eyed both men, and they wisely decided not to take a step closer. Wilhelm clung to David, his breathing rapid and fearful.

"Easy," David whispered. "They're not going to hurt you."

"A righteous society would kill you!" Keevan screamed. "Let the river take you and get you out of my sight! Just as long as you don't pollute this world anymore!"

"Gladly." Johann took a step forward and drew a sword David didn't know he had. "Only I figure I'm better at fighting than a pair of filthy has-beens like you two."

"You wouldn't dare." Hawke took a step forward. "I knew you were filth! You travel with elves and dogs, not men!"

"Then come fight me," Johann taunted. "We'll see who's the man here."

"Easy, easy!" the ferryman yelped. "Can we stop the fighting? Please?"

All three men ignored him. Hawke drew his own sword —a jagged little thing that had seen better days—and lunged. Johann swatted the sword away in two strokes. He caught it with his boot, held it up so he could get a look at it, and kicked it over the side. Hawke stared at Johann in horror. His eyes went even wider when Johann swung his sword and casually put the tip right over the hollow of his throat.

"Do you yield?" Johann asked.

Hawke stared at the sword for a few long seconds. "Fine. I yield. What kind of dirty trick did you play, you freak?"

"It's called being good." Johann stepped back and snapped his fingers to get the dogs' attention. "When I was a boy, my father decided to teach me fencing. I decided I rather liked the sport and progressed until I was training with a broadsword far heavier than this one. And"—he sneered now, his face the very picture of arrogance—"I know how to maintain my weapon."

Hawke took his place by Keevan's side. "The son of a lord, then."

"No," Johann replied, "the son of a prince."

"Your *Highness*," Keevan drawled. Scorn dripped from his words as he mock bowed. "Good to know that not just anyone can kick his ass."

David kept his own opinions about that to himself. He stroked Wilhelm's hand, trying to calm his racing heart. Those two knew they were beaten. They weren't going to try something. After all, that would be foolish and David was sure they were smarter than that. Still, try as he might, he couldn't banish the thorny fear settling deep in his chest.

It didn't help that he saw the stag standing in a sea of twisted laurel.

CHAPTER TWENTY-FIVE: HOMELAND

◆ ◆ ◆

Wilhelm didn't look at Hawke and Keevan. They didn't like him, and the feeling was mutual. Wilhelm glanced toward Lebe, trying to understand what was going through the man's mind. Lebe kept his gaze focused on the churning river. The brown water foamed as it splashed over jagged stones. Wilhelm could see dark shadows from fish and large turtles as they darted under the surface.

There was no snow on the riverbank, only slick patches of mud that hinted at its presence. The thick tangle of laurel that clung to slick granite cliffs had already started to bud. The air was warm now, heavy with promise and hope. A few birds—many of them white gulls—flew over the river. Snow melt had swollen the thing, and waves crashed over the side of the raft every so often.

No one spoke. Johann's brawl had killed any conversation, and it was clear that neither Hawke nor

Keevan wanted to start another one. Wilhelm didn't mind that. He just stayed close to David and tried not to look those two in the eye. They weren't worth it. They would never be. Wilhelm would have to remember that, no matter how much he might have wanted to plead with them for acceptance.

David wrapped rested his arm on Wilhelm's shoulder. "You okay, love?"

"They scare me," Wilhelm whispered. He pressed his body into David's like that could save him. "I wish–I wish we could find another ferry."

"This is the only one on the Kileo that won't rob you blind." Lebe lashed the rudder to the railing and stepped around the dogs. "And I let you take the dogs. Those two look like they could do some damage. The elves got to ride, too, and not everyone would do that."

As if on cue, Toman stood up. The big wolfhound ambled over and sat in front of Wilhelm. Toman kept his dark eyes trained on the two men. Keevan took a step forward, like he was going to start something again. Johann gripped his sword. The man leaned against the railing like a large cat, his body tensed and ready for action. A muscle twitched in Johann's jaw, and murder glittered in his blue eyes. Henri just stared at his nails, completely indifferent to the brewing brawl.

"If you start something, I'll kill you," Johann softly said.

He snapped his fingers, getting Myla's attention. "You might not like me, but you will fear me."

Keevan smirked. "So maybe you got the drop on us one time. You won't do it again."

"Hey!" Lebe yelled. He stepped between the bristling men and held up his hands. "Can we try to not kill each other? At least until you get off my boat?"

Ruari casually reached for his sword, as did Holly, Bracken, and the other elves. Wilhelm's breath caught. He didn't know what was going to happen. He didn't want another fight starting, especially if it were to be over him. Tension draped over the entire ferry. Toman growled softly. Myla did the same, her hackles rising up. She snapped at Hawke when he dared take a step toward her.

"Easy!" Lebe yelled. He put his hand on a short sword stuck in his belt. "Look, if you idiots are going to start a fight, do it on your own time. Not mine. That means you —and I do mean *all* of you—need to cut it out."

Wilhelm grabbed Toman's collar. The dog growled. He tossed his head and dug all four feet into the wood as Wilhelm tried to drag him back. David did the same with Myla. The white dog whipped her head around like she was going to bite him, only to calm once she realized who it was. Myla stood in front of them as soon as David let go of her collar. Tension draped across the little group. No one said anything for the longest time, and the air seemed heavy with the promise of violence.

Lebe's eyes narrowed. "I mean it. If you keep trying to start a fight, I'll kick you out in the middle of the river!"

His threat worked. Johann forced his body to relax and nodded for the others to do the same. Wilhelm sat down. The rough wood bit into his hands as he worried at. Chill river water swept over the sides; it soaked his feet if the ferry tipped enough. Wilhelm listened to the wind and tried to send himself far away from here. He watched the shore, smiling when the current caught them and yanked them downriver.

The Kileo cut through the heart of the forest. Miles of winding roads, fraught with bandits and wild beasts, could be avoided in just a few hours. Here and there, slick rocks broke through the water's surface and barren willow boughs dipped into the flow. Wild horses drank from the shallow places along the sandy banks. The stallions reared when they caught sight of the tame horses and challenges rang out over the waves.

Ruari sat beside him. "Are you feeling all right?"

"I don't want a fight," Wilhelm whispered. He fought the urge to bury his face in Ruari's shoulder. "I'm tired of fighting!"

Emil would have known what to do. Unbidden,

Wilhelm's mind flashed back to his brother. If he looked just right, he could see the barest hint of Emil's shade. The rough wood seemed to jut through the man's body and linger in the transparent flesh. Only Emil's eyes could be clearly seen. They were the color of molten gold, much like the stag, and haunted pain echoed through their depths.

Wilhelm lowered his head. Finding Emil's killer would put the spirit to rest, but Wilhelm was no closer to that than when he had begun. All he had to show for his efforts were a dun horse, his cousin's silence, the elves, and Johann. Wilhelm glanced toward Johann. Johann, for his part, watched Hawke and Keevan like they were mice and he a cat. Every move they made was noted by his sharp gaze.

After a few hours, Lebe cleared his throat. "We're nearly there."

"Thank the gods." Ruari stood, making sure that Wilhelm did the same. "I thought we would never get off this boat!"

"You're free to ride next time," Lebe said. His tone was light, but his gaze was sharper than new steel.

"Maybe I will." Ruari grabbed his horse as Lebe guided the ferry to a half-rotted pier. "You do let any old riffraff foul this place. If we wanted to be insulted, we would have gone to Cymri. There's no need for what they said."

Hawke grimaced as he stepped on to the pier. "And there's no need for being foul!"

"Why do you say that?" Johann asked. He mounted his horse and charged the animal off of the pier, nearly hitting Hawke as he did so. "It's not like we started the fight!"

Wilhelm turned his head. He petted his mare's nose before he mounted her. She shifted under him, likely out of fear, and tossed her head when he asked her to step on the pier. Parts of the wood had already fallen away. Water vines clung to the grayed wood and pulled apart the rusting metal supports. Wilhelm could see water through the holes. Luckily, it didn't look like it would be too deep, but his mare was still frightened.

She clearly didn't want to go on. Wilhelm was just about the dismount when Henri slapped the mare. She half reared and took off toward the shore. Keevan yelled as he dove out of the way. Wilhelm thought he heard a splash, but he wasn't sure. He forced the mare to a stop as soon as she could. She locked her legs together, sliding for a few feet, and half reared. The mare tossed her head in fear. She snorted and pawed at the ground as her sides heaved.

"What the hell was that for?" Johann yelled. He caught Henri's reins just as Wilhelm turned around. "He could have been killed!"

"That stupid horse wouldn't get out of the way!" Henri snapped. His eyes narrowed as he jerked the thin strips of leather back. "If we're going to have a hope of dealing with Steven, we can't waste time waiting for neurotic nags to get their act together!"

"I don't know what's gotten into you," Johann growled. He backed his gelding up and ran a hand through his hair. "Look. You grew up around horses, right? You can't spook a horse like that!"

"It's okay," Wilhelm said. He tried to calm his racing heart. "Really, it's fine. Can we go now?"

David frowned as he took the lead. "I still don't like it, Wil. You could have been killed!"

"But I wasn't." Wilhelm shook his head as emotions warred inside of him. "I'm...I want to get home, okay? Is that too hard to do?"

No one answered him. Wilhelm watched as Keevan and Hawke took another one of the forest trails. Henri's gaze lingered on them too. There was something odd about that relationship, but Wilhelm did his best to put it out of his mind. Instead, he took his place behind Ruari and started to ride. They had spent several hours on the river and that had taken them into Talla Gael. There were road signs now, and the winding path they were on lacked cracks and pits.

Wilhelm's mind wandered as he rode. He couldn't help but keep sneaking glances at Henri. Henri held himself bowstring taunt. His stallion, too, seemed similarly nervous. The roan kept popping his head up at every sound and pawing at the ground. Henri yanked the horse's reins every time. Wilhelm wanted to say that Henri needed to stay out of the stallion's mouth, but he knew when his opinions weren't welcome.

Bracken urged his pony to David. "We need to stop for the night. It's going to be late soon."

"All right." David turned his spotted mare toward a grassy clearing. "That looks as good a place as any. Someone has to keep watch; I don't trust those two. There's a good chance they'll try and start something."

Wilhelm dismounted. He pulled the tack from his mare and hobbled her. The others did the same, and a tense silence draped over most of them. Only Henri looked relaxed. He dumped his belongings in a pile and all but kicked Toman when the dog wandered over. Toman growled softly. The wolfhound tensed, like he was going to attack, but clearly thought better at the last minute. Wilhelm didn't know what to think. He just tried to force the incident from his mind.

"I'll take first watch." Johann stood at the ready and glanced towards the forest. "David, you do second. Ruari, you take third. We'll do a few hours each and cycle through."

"Why not me?" Henri asked. He put his hands on his hips, and his words were laced with rage.

"Because I don't trust you," Johann said. He narrowed his eyes. "Don't take it personal; I hardly trust anyone."

Henri muttered something that Wilhelm couldn't quite catch. Wilhelm was just about to comfort him when he spun around and vanished into the forest. After a second, Wilhelm followed. Toman trotted along after him, his tail wagging. The big wolfhound moved silently through the thick forest and showed Wilhelm the best path. Henri seemed to know where he was going. He stopped in front of a half-rotten tree and waited for a few minutes.

Keevan picked his way out of the underbrush. "You didn't tell us about the mercenary."

"I didn't know." Henri's words were clipped and hard.

Wilhelm's breath caught. *He knows them? But why didn't he stop the fight? He could have done **something**!*

"That's no excuse," Keevan said. The man's eyes narrowed. "Deal with the mercenary so I can deal with the boy king and his pet soldier."

"You want me to kill that thing?" Henri asked. "You know I can't fight!"

"Then you just have to be clever. Use that special talent of yours or some shit like that." Keevan sneered as he turned to leave. "I'm sure you can think of something."

Wilhelm's breath caught. He couldn't help but stare at Henri through the brush. He couldn't believe it. His cousin. His greatest friend. A traitor. His mind raced, and he was just about to bolt when Toman snarled.

The big dog burst into the clearing and ran straight for Keevan.

CHAPTER TWENTY-SIX: FOUND

◆ ◆ ◆

David paused after helping set up the camp. It seemed... quiet somehow. Like something was missing. He bit his bottom lip as he walked around the little clearing. All of the horses grazed peacefully on their lines. The elves sat in a little group and murmured amongst themselves. David didn't know what they were saying, and he didn't bother to ask. He didn't see Henri, and if he were to be honest, David didn't care about his whereabouts.

Darkness fell across the forest. Johann sat beside the fire and examined his nails. Myla rested beside his feet. The big dog raised her head as he walked past. Her tail thumped against the ground for a few seconds and then she stood. David didn't say anything as she took her place at his side. Then dread slowly filled his belly and he could hardly breathe. Wil and Toman were nowhere in sight.

"Johann?" David asked. He could hardly keep the terror from his voice. "Have you seen Wil?"

Come to think of it, where's Henri?

"He was with us when we stopped," Johann said. The man stood and bit his bottom lip. "Though I don't see him now."

Myla whined. The white dog put her nose to the ground, tail wagging slowly, and darted into the forest. David followed without a second thought. Thorn vines yanked at him as he ran and branches slapped him in the face. Moss-covered stones seemed to jut out of the forest floor, like they were put there just to trip him up. Myla barked. She forced her way through a mound of bracken and emerged beside an old forest road.

A stunned Toman lay beside an algae-stained mile marker. The dog's chest still rose and fell, but his fur was matted with blood. David crouched beside him. His hands shook with fear, and he forced himself to stay calm. Panicking wouldn't do anyone any good. He swallowed. The fear seemed to grip him, and he could hardly breathe. David gripped the dog's fur. Toman whined softly and licked at David's fingers.

David petted the wounded dog. "Where is he, Johann?"

"If I knew, I'd be going after him right now," Johann grimly said. He pulled his sword and prowled around the little clearing. "Myla!"

Myla jerked her head up. The big dog growled softly. She prowled around with him, then started barking when she saw a scrap of fabric fluttering on a broken branch. David grabbed Toman. He dragged the dog toward the bush and ignored it when he started to whine. He had to find Wilhelm. If that man was dead or dying... Well, David didn't know what he would do. He just knew that it wouldn't be good.

Johann grabbed the scrap and held it up to the light. "Well, he didn't go willing."

"You can tell it's him just by looking at it?" David asked. He couldn't keep the fear from his voice.

"Who else wears silk?" Johann asked.

"You have a point." David sighed and rubbed his face. "I know this isn't the time to ask, but where the hell's Henri?"

"Oh, gods..." Johann trailed off. "Look, leave the wolfhound. He can take care of himself. We gotta find Wilhelm before Henri kills him."

David's heart hammered in his chest. *Henri*. He was just about to open his mouth when a cry ripped through the still forest. Myla didn't even wait for them; she just took off into the underbrush. David followed him. Some dim part of him knew that he had no sword, but he couldn't bring himself to care. The branches ripped at him all over again, reopening wounds that had attempted to close just a few moments before.

He burst into yet another clearing and almost tripped over his own two feet. Foul black mud seemed to grab to him. His boots sunk into it up to his ankles, and he struggled to drag himself through it. The mire made a foul sucking sound as he staggered forward. David grabbed at the tangled vines for balance, swearing as the mud soaked his pants. His heart hammered in his chest. He couldn't give up, not now.

He had to be close...

Myla barked. She paced at the edge of the swamp, her tail wagging back and forth. David did his best to ignore her. He couldn't carry her and get across this mud at the same time. The dog whined softly. David staggered across to firm ground and grabbed the long rushes to get his balance. He had just climbed to the banks when Myla took a flying leap. The dog screamed when her snow-white fur touched the muddy water.

She crashed through the swamp, sending up a wall of filthy water, and clawed her way to the bank. David grabbed her by the collar and dragged her up on the bank. Myla shook herself out. Her tongue lolled out to one side, and she completely ignored the mud that now splattered David and the ground. David stepped around the panting dog. He wound his way through the now silent forest, hoping against hope that Wil wasn't hurt.

"Wil?" he called. "Wilhelm!"

Only silence answered him. The forest crouched around him like some silent animal. David could hear the rustle of last winter's leaves and the snakes as they slithered over the muddy ground. The wind rattled the tall reeds as it wound through them and bent the spring green boughs. David might have thought it beautiful, but now wasn't the time. Myla trotted beside him. She seemed to have lost the scent, and that filled his soul with dread.

Fucking hell! David thought. *This is the one time I need Johann and he's nowhere to be found!*

"I hope he's not dead," David whispered. He petted Myla's head and crouched when he saw what looked like drag marks. "They brought him here, it looks like. Think you can pick up the track, Myla?"

Myla cocked her head and gave him a look that could only be described as extremely put out. David rubbed her head. He pressed his finger in the marks, trying to decide when they were made. It couldn't have been too long—the marks looked fresh enough that the mire hadn't yet receded into the wet earth. David bit his bottom lip. He reached for his sword and cursed when he realized he was unarmed.

He gave Myla a long look. "I really need to keep my sword with me."

Myla jerked her head up. The big dog growled softly and pinned her ears to her skull. She lowered her belly to the muddy ground before crawling toward an overgrown trail. David followed her. The drag marks weren't as clear now—David thought that the ground wasn't as soft—but he could see disturbed leaves and bruised spring grasses. He swore under his breath as he followed the dog.

Already, the setting sun cast sharp shadows in the dense forest. The night dew had started to form, ruining any trail that Myla might have been able to pick up. Davit bit his bottom lip as he stepped around a thick stand of bracken. He couldn't hear anything, and he didn't know if that was good or bad. The idea of Wilhelm being hurt sickened him. His heart fluttered in his chest as he slipped through the shadowy forest.

He came up to a small earthen mound. David dropped his belly to the ground and crawled under a thick tangle of laurel. The mud soaked into his trousers as he slipped over the ground. He could feel the thorns as they raked over his back and every single one of the stones hiding under forest leaves. Wet moss soaked into his shirt as he lay on it. His eyes narrowed when he came to the embankment's crest.

What he saw stunned him. Henri crouched over Wilhelm's still body, his own body pressed against a stone wall. The white stag reared, tossing its bloodied antlers. David could see blood splatter on crumbling stone columns and a dagger tossed beside a moss-covered stone. He found himself moving before he knew what he was doing. Henri whipped around. He struck David in the cheek and sent the other man sprawling to the ground.

"Leave him alone!" David screamed. He sat up, rubbing his cheek. "Just leave him alone!"

"Why should I?" Henri sneered. His eyes glittered with madness. "If I can't have him, no one can!"

"Is that what this is about?" David asked. He backed up and wrapped his fingers around the dagger's hilt. "You're mad because Wilhelm won't sleep with you?!"

"He chose a *mercenary*," Henri growled. "You're one thing, but that washed-up old mercenary is something else."

David slipped the dagger behind his back. His heart hammered in his chest. His mind seemed to race in a thousand directions at once. He could see Henri and Wil's body at his feet. The stag stood on the other side of the clearing and pawed at the ground. Myla crouched the ground. She seemed confused, like she wasn't sure what to do. David forced himself to ignore them. He focused his entire being on Henri.

"So you're jealous." David stood and forced himself to be calm. "You're jealous of me and Johann."

Well, I guess I'm not surprised. He's been with Wil longer than any of us.

Henri's lips twisted into a sneer. "That stupid deer—"

He moved and David saw the blood on his shoulder. David took a step back. His heart hammered in his chest, and he couldn't help wondering if Henri had something to do with Emil's death. Henri stepped toward him. He pulled a second dagger, this one free from blood, and his eyes glittered with madness. Henri moved like a cat now and lunged. David jerked back. He dropped his shoulder, trying to knock Henri on the ground.

The stag reared. Before David could do anything, the animal charged. It caught Henri on its antlers and tossed him to the ground. It struck at him with sharp hooves, making him cry out in pain. David ducked under the stag. It reared in terror this time and kicked him so hard that he fell to the hard stone ground. Something in his wrist gave on impact. David couldn't help the scream that ripped from his throat. He rolled over, cradling the throbbing wound.

Beside him, Wilhelm moaned.

David fought through the pain. He staggered to his feet, only for a flying hoof to strike him in the head. Everything went black for a few long seconds, and he collapsed on top of Wilhelm. He seemed to float in the darkness, unaware of everything that went around him. Then he felt a warm, wet tongue lick over his face. Sharp teeth worried at his ear, followed by more licks and a soft, almost timid, bark.

David's eyes fluttered opened. "M-Myla?"

The big dog lay beside him. Everything seemed blurry, and blood dripped into his eyes. David wiped it off with one shaking hand. He managed to push himself to a sitting position and allowed someone to brush his hair out of his face. David licked his lips. Thirst grabbed at him, and he murmured his appreciation when Johann tipped his head back. Johann's hands were sure and gentle; the water he offered was cool and sweet.

"Took you long enough," David slurred. "Where the fuck were you?"

"Seeing if I could do something other than go charging off," Johann said. "You know, trying not to do things that might get me killed!"

David tried to roll his eyes, but winced when the pain stabbed through him. Johann petted his hair to try and soothe him.

"Wilhelm?" David asked. He pulled back and tried to tell himself that Wilhelm was all right. "Is he okay?"

"He's still out of it." Johann sat beside him, sighing

softly. "I don't think he's going to die."

"That's good," David mumbled. His head throbbed and he couldn't help but moan. "Damn deer kicked me."

"I know." Johann pulled his eyelids back. "Looks like it got you pretty good. What the hell were you thinking?"

"I had to get him," David whispered. "I had to get him. Henri was gonna kill him."

"Henri," Johann growled. He rubbed his face. "I *knew* it!"

"Did you kill him?" David asked. He didn't know if he hoped Henri was dead or not.

"He was gone when I got here," Johann said. "Probably for the better, because I was going to take his head for this stunt."

"Don't," David whispered. "He's not worth it."

"He still hurt you," Johann said. He let David curl up in his lap and seemed to stare off into the distance. "We need to get Wilhelm up, darling. It's a long walk back to camp."

David nodded. He staggered to his feet after Johann did and watched as the man woke Wilhelm. He felt numb inside, like he didn't care that Henri had betrayed them.

He should have felt something, he knew, but David just couldn't bring himself to care.

CHAPTER TWENTY-SEVEN: BETRAYAL

❖ ❖ ❖

Wilhelm floated between darkness and light for the longest time. He could hear muffled voices in the distance speaking of him and Henri, but he paid them no mind. Some part of him didn't want to believe that he had seen Henri with those men. More of him didn't want to believe that Henri had tried to kill him. Wilhelm still didn't know what Henri had done to him. He just remembered pain—agonizing pain that blossomed through his entire body—and his body falling to the ground.

Why? Why would anyone do that to him? Wilhelm didn't want to be the crown prince; he certainly didn't want to be king. If there were a person he could palm his responsibilities off on, he would do it. He would find that person and give them the crown as he rode off into the sunset with David and Johann. He wished he could have asked Henri why he had flown at him. Henri hadn't said a word; he had just lashed out.

The scene shifted from darkness to a cool and shadowy forest. Moonlight dripped between tangled tree branches and pooled on closed flower buds. Laurel tangled the trail margins, offering a dark and twisted tangle to the silver light. Wilhelm moved down the trail slowly. The air hung heavy with promise around his shoulders. He could taste ozone on his tongue, like lightning was soon to strike. Nothing else stirred, though, and Wilhelm found himself standing in a clearing.

The grasses danced as if they were caught in a breeze. They rippled in pond waves, and Wilhelm imagined the field mice swimming through them. The sky overhead was filled with stars that seemed so close he could touch them and constellations that he couldn't recognize. A pool lay in the middle of the clearing; it was filled with still, cool water and glistening white stones. Wilhelm sat at the edge of the pool and stared at his reflection.

When he raised his head, the white stag picked its way from the forest.

Still wet blood covered its chest, like a hunter had tried to cut its throat. Its back and legs bled freely from the bites of wild hounds, and it favored its right foreleg. Ivy tangled in cracked and broken branches, like it had been caught in a snare, and one of the animal's golden eyes was cloudy and faded. Wilhelm slowly stood up. He found himself holding out his hand, and the stag pushed its velvet muzzle into his touch.

"Who *are* you?" Wilhelm whispered.

The stag blinked slowly. Wilhelm felt like he should know the beast, like there was something he was missing, but he couldn't quite find it. He rested his head against the stag's cheek and trailed his fingers through soft fur. The world seemed to fall away from him for a few seconds. The only thing grounding him—the only thing he felt aware of—was the stag in front of him. He didn't know how long he stood there, just that he did.

Then Wilhelm drew back, his eyes filled with wonder. "Are you... You can't be!"

The stag lowered his head and huffed softly. Wisdom seemed to filled the animal's golden eyes. It allowed Wilhelm to climb on its back. Then, slowly, it turned around and started picking its way through the forest. Wilhelm clung for dear life. The world shifted around him like spilled water. He found himself standing in a small room, staring at himself and David. Echoes of pain ripped through his body, followed by a wave of dark, all-consuming rage.

Wilhelm's breath caught. He stared at himself through Henri's eyes and felt what the other man felt. Pain wrapped around his body, sinking into his soul with white-hot barbs that cauterized living flesh. Wilhelm opened his mouth to cry out, only for no sound to come and for his limbs to feel like lead. He stood there, rooted to the spot, as he stared at his face. Then, out of the corner of his eye, he saw David and Johann.

He was just about to get a better look at him when cold crashed over his body. The vision shattered in a thousand pieces, and the darkness wrapped around him. Something held him, pinning him to the ground. Wilhelm lashed out, kicking wildly and raking his nails down whatever he could reach. Something grunted and strong hands caught his wrists. Wilhelm kicked as hard as he could, anything to hurt whoever held him.

"Let go, you fucking son of a bitch!" Wilhelm screamed. "I'll fucking kill you!"

"Easy!" Johann yelped. He dropped Wilhelm as soon as blue eyes flied open. "What the hell, Wilhelm? Don't you know me?"

"I had a vision," Wilhelm whispered. He curled into Johann's side. "I was Henri and I saw the stag. He seemed…so familiar to me. Like I was supposed to know him and he was so sad that I didn't."

"Stag?" Johann asked. He held out a small cap of water for Wilhelm to drink. "What stag?"

"A big white one," Wilhelm said. "He has eyes the color of a gold coin, blood staining his throat, and ivy in his antlers. He's showed up before, but I don't think you ever saw him. Every time I look at him, though, I feel like he's a part of me. I just wish I knew who he was!"

"That stag is real, too. I've seen it," David said. He sat beside Johann, one hand on Toman's back.

Guilt jabbed Wilhelm when he looked at the dog. Toman had tried to defend him, but Henri had been too fast and too vicious. He had moved like a tiger, striking Wilhelm with a weapon he had no chance of seeing. Pain—pain that left no mark—raked across his body. Wilhelm shuddered to even think of it. Did Henri know magic? That the stag even existed implied that magic was a very real and very powerful force.

"Why didn't you say something before?" Johann asked.

Wilhelm looked at David and shrugged. "You never asked," Wilhelm finally said. "How was I supposed to know you wanted to know?"

Johann rubbed his face. He didn't say anything, though, and simply helped Wilhelm to his feet. Long shadows crawled over the trees now. Shadows pooled over the tangled forest floor, and hints of moonlight filtered through barren branches. There was warmth on the wind, though, along with the promise of rain. Wilhelm stuck close to the other two. Toman limped after him, at least half of his weight supported by Myla.

The elves had the camp ready when they came back. Wilhelm sat in front of the fire, murmuring his thanks to Bracken, and all but collapsed against the hard earth.

The coldness of it, not to mention the wet soil, bit through his trousers. Belatedly, Wilhelm realized he bled from a cut to the temple. He didn't know where it came from and feared that it would bleed until he died. He clung to Johann as soon as the man sat down.

"A white stag, huh?" Johann asked. He stroked Wilhelm's hair and pressed a kiss to his forehead. "Is he one of your gods or just a friendly spirit?"

"I don't know," Wilhelm admitted. "He started showing up after my brother died."

David bit his bottom lip. "Wil?"

"Yeah?" Wilhelm sprawled out so he was in David and Johann's lap at the same time. "What?"

"What if he's Emil?"

Wilhelm stared at David. Words seemed to die on his tongue, words that would have told David how wrong he was. The stag *couldn't* be Emil! Emil had been buried in the proper way with the proper songs sung over his body. Even Maria had sung her songs over him, whatever that meant. There was no need for Emil to come back like that. Tears beaded at the corners of Wilhelm's eyes. He didn't know what to say or if there were words to describe what he felt.

Unless... the alternative was too horrible to think of, so Wilhelm refused.

"But that can't be," Wilhelm finally said. "We buried him the right way. There's no need for him to come back!"

"Wil, he was murdered. If that ain't reason for a body to come back from the dead, I don't know what is!" David yelped.

Bracken looked up from a bowl of spiced stew. "I'm not dealing with any dead body or a ghost. That was not part of our deal."

"I don't think he's a ghost," Johann said. "If he's carrying himself like one of the old gods, he probably is one."

"Is that supposed to make me feel better?" Bracken asked. "Because it doesn't."

Wilhelm didn't say anything. He simply drifted off to sleep, curled up as he was in their laps. Johann petted his hair every few seconds, and David curled up beside him. It was as if they needed to be touching the older man. Johann, of course, had little choice in the manner. He let them do as they needed and kept guard all night long. The wolves might have howled and the dogs answered them, but no harm came to their little camp.

"Let's get going," Johann murmured. He woke Wilhelm

at the crack of dawn with a gentle shake. "We have a long ride to go."

Wilhelm didn't want to, but he had to. He got his dun mare and saddled her, mounting her before the others had broken camp. Johann didn't say anything; he just passed Toman's wounded body up to the mare's back and arranged him so he could ride. Wilhelm gritted his teeth. His body ached from his wounds last night, and he couldn't shake that fuzzy feeling in his head. Wilhelm hoped he wouldn't slow the others down, especially if he fainted.

He hung his head as he rode. David followed him on his spotted mare, Myla trotting at his side. The white dog kept her gaze trained on Toman. Something strange seemed to pass between the dogs, and Wilhelm swore they were in love. He petted Toman's side to soothe him before kicking his mare in the side. He didn't want to talk. Wilhelm didn't know how he could explain what Henri did to him, and he didn't want to find the words.

"Hey!" David urged his mare beside Wilhelm. "What's eating you?"

"I don't want to talk." Wilhelm kept his gaze straight ahead.

"Are you pissed about Henri?" David asked. "Because there was a guy like that in my unit. His name was Pru, and he was a right pain in the ass. He betrayed us to the

Tallans as soon as he could."

"I'm a Tallan."

"You're also not a cold-blooded murdering bastard," David said. He shrugged when Wilhelm growled at him. "What? I love you, Wil, but you're also not the only Tallan in this realm. Some of you are right bastards."

"I don't want to talk!" Wilhelm screamed. "Please! David! *Leave me alone.*"

He jerked the dun aware from the spotted mare, only for David to grab his reins and give him a long look. Wilhelm stared at him helplessly. How would he explain this? How would he be able to tell another about how Henri had betrayed him? A helpless laugh escaped Wilhelm's throat as he looked at David. Did David even know what he had done? Wilhelm snatched the leather strip back before he said something that shattered what they had.

"I can't do that," David said. He shook his head, his eyes gentle. "I know you don't want this, but I can't let you ride off like this."

"I trusted him," Wilhelm whispered. The words spilled from his lips unbidden, and his shoulders shook. "He was my cousin and I loved him and he tried to kill me."

David gingerly rubbed the back of his head. "I think he tried to get me, too. Someone threw a dagger at me and I got cracked upside the head with a tree branch."

"It may not have been a branch," Wilhelm admitted. "I think he knows magic."

David made a face like he had bitten into a sour melon. Wilhelm didn't blame him; magic was a wild thing and it could be easily twisted. On a whim, he reached out and squeezed David's hand. He couldn't apologize with his words, but maybe this would be a start.

CHAPTER TWENTY-EIGHT: RAIDER

◆ ◆ ◆

David didn't know how long they rode in silence, just that they did. His shoulders ached with the strain of sitting upright in the saddle, and he couldn't help but jump at every noise. Snowflake didn't seem to appreciate his nerves. The mare pinned her ears to her head every time he jumped. David patted her side. He spurred her into a quick trot as they came to a bridge and held on tight as she went over it.

"Hey!" A young man in a faded tunic waved his hand as David rode up. "What are you doing here?"

"Heading toward the palace," David said. He cursed when he realized he didn't even know what its name was and prayed the man wouldn't ask. "Is there trouble or something?"

"Depends on what you're looking for," the man said. He was a shepherd by the looks of it, and he leaned on his crook as he examined David. "We had a band of mercenaries go through the village last night. They burned two families out and stole every horse they could find. We won't let that happen again."

David caught the implied threat. "Don't worry about us," he said, "we're just passing through. What did the mercenaries look like though?"

The man scowled, his blue eyes dark with anger. "Their leader had a blue roan stallion."

"Are you sure?" David asked. He could hardly keep the fear from his voice. *Wil isn't going to like this.*

"I'm sure!" the man snapped. "Bastard let his horse trample my dog! He had a band of others with him too. Two of them looked like they had just crawled out of the gutter, and they could hardly control their mules; he had a blond that's good with a sword, and a couple of others. They took what they wanted and killed the rest. Only reason why I didn't get it is because I don't have much of anything."

"I'll tell the others," David said. "We've been tracking them for some time. We think their leader—the one on the roan stallion—killed the crown prince and kidnapped the next in line. His name's Henri."

"Do I look like I care?" the shepherd asked. "Go! Do something about it and leave me the hell alone!"

David nodded. He knew when to make an exit, and he turned Snowflake around. He didn't know what he would tell Wil though. A part of him still loved Henri, David knew, and Wil would have a hard time accepting what he had done. David's face hardened as he spurred Snowflake into a trot. He regretted his mercy now. If Johann had killed Henri, none of this would have happened. That village would probably still be standing, and Toman wouldn't be wounded and riding on a horse's back.

"They got the village." David pulled Snowflake beside Bracken and Johann. "Henri, his friends, and probably Steven."

"Damn!" Johann snapped. He rubbed his face. "Okay. We go after them. With any luck, we can catch them before they reach the palace. It looks like Steven was waiting around for Henri."

David bit his bottom lip. "You think they were working together?"

"I do." Johann spurred his horse into a gallop. "Let's go!"

David did the same. Snowflake tossed her head as she ran and she flicked her head toward the forest. David tensed. He reached for a sword he no longer had and, once again, cursed himself. He didn't know the last time he had had a weapon, but he knew he needed one. He shook his head as he held on. The forest soon thinned as they rode closer to the village. Or, well, what was left of it.

He smelled it before he saw it. The scent of charred wood and burnt meat hung heavy in the air. The dirt track through the middle of the village was scarred with hoof marks, burns, and drag scuffs where stone walls had been pulled down. Snowflake picked her way through the piles of stone and mortar. She pinned her ears to her head and snorted softly. David patted her side. He didn't know what else to do and feared that she would bolt.

Wil pulled his horse beside David. "What happened here?"

He pointed to a charred house. Streaks of soot covered the whitewashed outer walls and a burned-out wagon rested beside it. Its wheel rims, covered in iron as many were, were half melted and dripped into the stone. The thatch still smoldered when the wind caught it. A body lay in the doorway, its head a few feet from the rest of the corpse. Dogs—scarred and burned things—picked around the rubble. They scattered when David rode near them.

"Henri," Johann said. His voice was cold and grim as he urged his gelding on. "He was with Steven and the others."

"But why?" Wil asked. His voice cracked on the last

word, and his eyes were filled with pain. "Why would he do this?"

"Because he can," David said. "He was angry at you and he took it out on them."

He didn't know what else to say. Ruari gave him a long look, as if to say that he had pushed things, but David ignored the elf. He just kicked Snowflake into a gallop again. The horse seemed to know the way home. She pulled David in the directions she wanted to go and splashed through the mud puddles with ease. The destruction ended as soon as the village did, but David could still see the hoof marks. He didn't think they were too far behind.

They came to another patch of dense forest. The spring hedges had already sprouted new buds and white flowers that trailed in the wind. David ducked his head under some of the boughs. The wildflowers—strands of gold and white blossoms that clung to the ground and looked like pieces of the sun—filled the air with their sweet scent. Water dripped from pools in the rocks, and the verdant mosses hugged the cliff face as they rode under it.

No one spoke. Wilhelm turned his head when they found the body of a young man, no older than they were, twisting in the breeze. Going by the scratches in his throat and the terror in his cloudy eyes, he had fought until he could fight no more. David turned his head. He had seen this kind of cruelty before. It only ended in blood, and he had no desire to inflame things any more than they already were.

It took some time, but they came to a place where the road was wide and straight, the trees cut back, and the path more marked with travel. An ox cart took up much of the path ahead of them, and the large animals didn't even raise their heads when David rode past. The driver, a woman with a gentle expression, waved David over. David took a breath. It never did to irritate the locals, so he guided Snowflake over and hoped for the best.

"Are you after those bandits?" the woman asked.

"You might say that." David petted Snowflake as the mare danced under him. "They tried to kill some of my comrades, so I thought we would return the favor."

The woman nodded and clicked to a black-and-white ox. "Well, I hope you deal with them soon enough. They tried to steal these two and couldn't get them to run. Fucking bastards, I wish we had Emil back!"

"So do I," David said. He took a breath as he turned Snowflake toward the others. "Do you know where they went? It would help us greatly if we knew where they were going."

The woman pointed to a small side road leading into the shadowy forest. "They went somewhere down there. If you hurry, you might catch them."

David nodded. He kicked Snowflake in the side and galloped her down the path. She leapt over a fallen log, nearly unseating David as she did so, and splashed through a swift moving stream. The cold water soaked David's pants, and mud splattered the spotted horse. She tossed her head as soon as David slowed her. He could hear voices drifting through the trees and the barking of a camp dog.

He dismounted the horse and dropped her reins to the forest floor. Snowflake snorted as she started to graze. She wouldn't wander too far—she never did—and David felt like he could leave her. He pressed his body to the forest floor as he crept forward. He could smell the rich rotting leaves and the spicy sedges as he brushed passed them. St. John's wort sprinkled his back with tiny golden flowers, and tangled tree roots seemed to reach from the earth to trip him.

"Did we have to do that raid?" Henri asked. He sat in front of a fire and sipped something from a waterskin. "All that's going to do is make them mad."

"If you don't remind the peasants who's in charge, they'll forget," Steven said. He leaned his arm over the younger man and gave him a cruel grin. "Besides, you had fun! And I heard what you did with Emil. That, my soon-to-be prince, was a work of art."

David's eyes narrowed. *I knew it! That bastard!* He could

hardly keep from bursting from the forest edges and, instead, pressed himself in a small gully. A tan-and-white dog wandered around the camp. Its tail wagged a little as it begged food from the raiders. Henri looked a little worse for the wear, his hair filthy and his cheeks unshaven, but he held himself like a seasoned warrior.

"I know," Henri murmured. He rubbed his forehead. "The prince was supposed to be mine, dammit! And then I had to let that stupid Alsatian in!"

"When you're king, you can get rid of them," Steven soothed. He rested his hand on Henri's knees and rubbed his thumbs across the tender flesh. "Start with the prisoners. It shouldn't be that hard to get rid of them. And then, as soon as they're dead, you can take Wattling Street."

Not if I have anything to do about it. David almost saw red as he thought those words. He slipped through the tangled forest, doing his best to not make a sound. He held his breath as much as he could and nearly worked his way to Henri when the camp dog started barking. David froze. Keevan stood slowly and drew his sword. The man looked just as ratty as he always did, and rage lingered in his dark eyes.

"Permission to see what the mutt's barking about?" Keevan asked. He tossed his sword from hand to hand as he waited.

"Fine," Henri said. "Just make sure you come back."

David pressed his body against a tree and waited. Keevan stepped out of their little camp and prowled through the forest. He paused right before he came to David's hiding spot, like he could sense David was there. David tensed. He picked up a stone and prepared to bash this one in the head. As soon as Keevan wandered close enough, David sprang into action. He struck the man in the head and stepped over him as soon as he crumpled to the ground.

David kicked him in the side and took his sword. "I should cut your head off. Just to make sure you're dead."

He tossed the sword in his hand as he studied the man. Keevan moaned softly. He stirred a little on the blood-soaked forest floor and his eyes fluttered open. He opened his eyes slowly. Confusion swam in them, and his mouth opened like he was going to cry out. David swung the sword in a smooth arc, severing the man's head from his body. Then he slipped through the forest, holding the bloody sword close to him.

He didn't feel anything after killing Keevan. The man honestly deserved it, and David didn't think there was anything wrong with killing him. Keevan had threatened to kill him. Turn about, as the old saying went, was fair play.

He grabbed Snowflake's reins and urged the horse back

to the others. He needed to get them so they could end this once and for all.

CHAPTER TWENTY-NINE: MAGIC

❖ ❖ ❖

Wilhelm looked up as soon as David galloped toward them. "David! Where were you?"

"Finding this." David threw a bloodied sword to the ground and dismounted his sweating horse. "It belonged to Keevan. He's not going to be a problem for us anymore."

"What do you mean by that?" Wilhelm asked. A sick feeling started to build in the pit of his stomach.

"Well, it's hard to be a problem when you're dead," David replied. He kissed Wilhelm lightly on the cheek and gave him a crooked smile. "Unless his dead body starts attracting rabid vultures that don't want to wait for us to die, that is."

"You killed him?" Wilhelm yelped. He jerked back from the other man. "Why?"

"Because he probably would have killed us," David said. "Look, Wil. You might not like killing things, but sometimes you have to do what you have to do."

David's words were calm and slow, almost patronizing, like he was talking to a slow child that never bothered with their lessons.

Wilhelm bristled and almost kicked the sword away. He didn't know what to say; he would have never thought to kill Keevan. Yes, the man had done vile things, but that didn't mean he needed to die. Wilhelm didn't know if he could look at David the same way again. If he was so blasé about taking a human life... Maybe it was because he had been trained as a soldier. Or maybe it was an Alsatian thing. Wilhelm didn't know and he didn't want to find out.

Johann picked up the sword and tossed it up in the air. "You know, this is absolutely shit quality. I don't know why you took this."

"Because we need weapons," David said. "Look, they've camped a few miles from us. If we go for them now, we could probably take them out right now. They probably haven't figured out he's gone yet."

Bracken looked at Ruari. "We can do it."

"I'm in," Johann said. He grabbed his own sword and handed the bloodied one back to David. "Let's get this done."

"What about me?" Wilhelm heard himself asking. "Please, I don't want to fight."

He didn't. He didn't even know if he *could* fight. Wilhelm had never picked up a sword before, not even in training. His breath caught as he looked at the others. Holly bit her lip. She looked like she was going to say something, probably to snap at him and tell him to be a man, but at least she didn't say what she clearly thought. Wilhelm took a breath. Would they send him away because he didn't want to fight?

"You need to come with us," Johann said. "The dogs too. I don't trust them; there's a good chance they'll break up and send a few toward our camp."

Wilhelm nodded. He petted Toman's back as he crouched down. The dog whimpered softly as he raised his head; pain still clouded his amber eyes. Wilhelm took a breath as he pulled the dog close to himself. He hoped the wolfhound recovered. He still didn't know how Henri had hurt them—all he remembered was falling to the ground with pain raking its way down his vulnerable body. If that wasn't magic, he didn't know what was.

"Let's go," David said. He stuck the sword in his belt and

grabbed his horse. "Shouldn't be that hard. They were bedding down for the night."

Wilhelm gestured to Johann. Together, they managed to heave the whimpering dog on the dun mare's back. She shifted nervously, likely thinking that the wounded dog was a wolf, but she calmed as soon as Wilhelm mounted her. He followed the others and ducked under low-hanging branches. Being back in Talla Gael didn't make him feel like he thought it would. Instead of being relieved, all he could feel was a strange sort of terror.

The mare paused as something stirred in the underbrush. She jerked her head up, chewing at the bit. Her ears swiveled forward, and she tossed her head a little. Wilhelm petted her side. Holly's pony did the same. That one even pawed at the ground, tearing great gouges in the soft soil. Wilhelm tensed. He backed the mare a few steps, careful to keep her on the path, and was just about to raise an alarm when someone burst out of the underbrush.

The mare reared. She pawed at the air, tossing her head in terror, and cried out. Toman started to slip from her back. Wilhelm grabbed him with one hand, desperate to keep his dog safe, and yanked at the terrified animal's reins. The mare bucked. This time, Toman did fall. The dog hit the ground hard, making him cry out in pain. Wilhelm tried to keep the panicking, thrashing animal under control.

Ahead of them, a man on a jet-black horse raised his

sword. He wore armor made of burnished steel overlaid with gold, and his helmet was in the shape of a roaring dragon. The horse trembled under him. Its legs were fine and long, like it was built to run on the steppe, and it pawed at the sandy ground. Wilhelm's mare backed up. The animal snorted, her nostrils trembling, and she half reared again.

David jerked his spotted horse down toward the intruder, bloody sword held high. "Who are you?"

In response, the knight kicked his horse and lunged. Wilhelm jerked his mare around. He didn't have a weapon, but that horse had hooves. He charged his mare right at the knight, only for her to rear at the last moment and send him flying. Wilhelm struck the ground so hard that he was stunned for a second. Out of the corner of his eye, he thought he saw the stag. Then he heard a crashing sound through the strand of dense trees, and the beast charged into the road.

"You!" the knight screamed. "I thought I killed you!"

Wilhelm stared. The animal's snow-white fur seemed to glow in the weak sunlight. Its eyes flashed like they were made of flame, and the ivy wrapped in its antlers trembled. Johann cursed loudly. His gelding reared in fear as it saw the stag and Johann fought to stay on his mount. Even the elves looked at it in awe. Wilhelm didn't even register the knight's voice as he stared at the stag. It seemed so familiar, yet so strange, like it was from a place no human could understand.

David recovered first. "Get out of here before I kill you!"

He swung the sword wildly as he kicked the spotted mare. She tossed her head in fear, refusing to get near the stag, and bit at David when he kicked her again. Myla and Toman cowered against the forest floor. Wilhelm found himself standing. Time seemed to slow to a crawl as he approached the stag. The animal lowered its head, ears pricked forward, and sniffed at his hand. Wilhelm let its warm breath wash over his body as he rested his palm against its flat nose.

"Is it really you?" he whispered. "Emil?"

The stag didn't answer. Wilhelm forced his way past the burning feeling in his throat and rested his head against the stag's shoulder. It trembled under his touch. The animal seemed so alive, so vital, that Wilhelm simply couldn't believe it was one of the spirits. Something strange came over him then, something that found Wilhelm climbing on the stag's back. It all seemed so familiar somehow, like he knew this animal from before.

Then the knight whipped off his helmet and broke the spell. Henri's wild eyes met all of theirs; he trembled with rage and seemed to be filled with some strange power. The forest seemed to close in around them. A low hissing sound filled the air as snakes—hundreds of them—crawled through the tangled underbrush to their master's feet. The stag snorted. It tossed its head, backing up some, and stamped cloven hooves against the well-worn road.

"Why are you doing this?" Wilhelm yelled. He clung to the stag's back and tried not to vomit when the snakes started climbing up Henri's arms. "You don't have to, I promise! Whatever it is, we can fix it!"

"I want what is mine," Henri growled. He drew his sword and a sickly light emanated from a small red gem set in the hilt.

"I hate to break it to you," David said as he dismounted his nervous horse, "but people don't belong to anyone. Get your head out of the gutter."

"You took him from me!" Henri screamed. He took a step toward David. "You and that filthy mercenary!"

"Hey!" Johann yelped. "I took a bath last week; I'm perfectly clean, thank you!"

Henri whipped around and swatted at him. Johann grunted as something that looked like a mass of shadows slammed into his body. Then he crumpled to the ground, slowly falling from his horse, and landed in a still heap. His skin seemed unnaturally pale, and the shadows hovered over his body. Wilhelm heard himself screaming. He slid off the stag before he could even think of something better and rushed to Johann's side.

Only the slight rise and fall of the man's chest showed that he was still alive. Wilhelm pulled Johann into his arms. Behind him, Ruari let out a battle cry and raced toward Henri. A shower of sparks filled the air as the two clashed. Henri dodged and wove like he was a master swordsman, landing blows on Ruari's pony that had it bucking the rider. Ruari landed on his feet, his green eyes wild with rage.

He swung the sword like a wild thing, driving Henri back a few feet. David seemed to regain his composure. He raced at Henri, sword drawn. Henri paused. He held out his hand and twisted his fingers just so. David screamed when the metal turned white. He dropped it quickly, cursing as it fell into a pile of leaves. A thin tendril of smoke rose through the air as the sword turned into a pile of molten slag.

Ruari crumpled seconds later. The elf also lay unnaturally still, and his eyes seemed clouded somehow. The stag lowered its head. Just when its horns had touched the elf's pale skin, a deep cut appeared in its shoulder. The animal bellowed in pain. It reared up on its hind legs and sent great drops of blood all over the road. The others drew back. Even Myla pressed her belly to the ground and licked her lips in fear.

Wilhelm trembled as he stared at the man who was once his friend. "Why are you doing this?" he whispered. "Who taught you this? Please, whatever it is..."

Then a horrid thought struck Wilhelm, and he stared at a rapidly approaching Henri in horror.

"You killed Emil, didn't you?" Those words tumbled from Wilhelm's mouth before he could stop them, and they tasted of bitter ash.

"He was in the way," Henri growled. His eyes glowed like they were filled with red hot coals, and his touch burned when he cupped Wilhelm's chin. "You know, there's a strange thing about magic. They say you lose a bit of yourself every time you use it, but I never see that happening. I think they lied."

"They're not." Wilhelm jerked back and tried to protect Johann's body with his own. "Henri, this isn't you! I swear it! I don't know who's forcing you—"

"No one's forcing me to do anything!" Henri slapped Wilhelm hard enough to stun. "You and that stupid soldier! I thought you would tire of him quickly enough, but you're too stupid to see exactly what he is!"

"Hey, buddy, I didn't let me into his rooms," David said. He picked himself up slowly and gingerly flexed his bleeding, burned hand. "That was all your doing. Didn't your mama ever tell you *not* to fuck around with nature?"

One of the snakes wrapped around his feet. David snarled something and tried to kick it off, but the animal sunk its fangs into his leg. His cry of agony seemed to split the still forest air. Then he fell to the ground, his skin parchment pale, as blood dripped from the corner of his mouth. Wilhelm watched it all in horror. His legs seemed rooted to the ground, like they were made of lead, and he couldn't fight it as those hot hands wrapped around his bicep.

"Now," Henri said, "you're going to come with me. I have a throne to take and a kingdom to run and you're just the man for the job."

Then he forced a kiss on Wilhelm, and it tasted like fouled, rotten honey.

CHAPTER THIRTY: SNAKE BITE

❖ ❖ ❖

David lay in a heap on the forest floor. His blood seemed to burn where the venom coiled through it, and the world was laced with shadow. His breath tasted of blood, his heart hammered in his chest, and it seemed like lead had draped over his body. More of the vipers —thick, black and gold things with red eyes like their master—crawled over his body. Their slick scales left a foul, reddish oozing rash over his skin that felt like it was made with hot coals.

One of the snakes peered into his eyes. Its forked tongue darted out to taste the air, and the ends of it brushed against David's nose. Water from the leaf litter soaked into his clothes. The chill eased the heat under his skin, though David knew that the relief wouldn't last. He could feel the throb of every heartbeat in his fingertips and taste cold iron in his mouth. The snake in front of him coiled its cold, slick body around his arms in a sick parody of a lover's touch.

The stay lay beside him. Blood stained the beast's snowy white fur, and its heavy antlers were tangled in the underbrush. The snakes seemed to avoid it, almost like something in the stag's very nature repelled them.

David tried to force his leaden limbs to move. The effort made the world spin around, and his body collapsed to the forest floor. The snakes hissed at him. One even reared up like it was going to strike again. All David could do was look at it. It calmed down after a second, though those red eyes still stared at him. David reached out with a trembling hand. He buried it in the stag's soft fur, almost expecting to feel the warmth he was used to.

Instead, he felt nothing.

Johann stirred from where he lay. The mercenary looked a little worse for the wear, and blood streaked his handsome face. The snakes reared back as soon as he moved. Johann stood up quickly. He kicked the snakes away, even as they tried to strike through his leather boots. The man cursed at them as he drove the beasts away. David wished he could help. He opened his mouth to speak, but no sound came out.

Johann knelt beside him. "That looks bad, darling."

You're telling me! David wanted to snarl at him, wanted to force him to understand the pain. More of it lanced through his leg. He heard himself cry out, and his back arched. Johann cursed. The man grabbed him, forcing him to sit up, and ripped the blood-soaked fabric back from David's leg. Angry red flesh met a sharp blue-eyed gaze. The snake bite had swollen up into a fist-sized mass, and two spots of darkened flesh—the same places where the snake had bit him—leaked blood and a thin yellow fluid.

Johann took a breath. "You're going to hate me for this, but I don't have any other choice."

Then he took his dagger, sliced across the wound, and pressed down with the flat of his blade. David arched his back and *screamed*. Foul yellow pus shot out of the wound. Agony lanced through David's body. He thrashed as best he could, trying to break free from the pain. Johann wrenched David's arms behind his back. The leg wound stunk as it drained, and the filth slowly crept down David's leg as it subsided.

"Magic snakes," Johann muttered. "Now I've seen it all."

David panted. "What the fuck was that for?"

"Probably saving your life," Johann snapped. He helped David rest against a tree and grabbed his sword from where he had dropped it. "If I had known there was going to be black magic and snakes, I would have fucked off before I even came on this trip! Not to mention the stag!"

He aimed a kick at the beast, only for the stag to

scramble to its feet and toss its head. Johann picked up a rock and threw it at the animal. The stag snorted. It pawed at the ground, like it wanted nothing more than a fight.

"Some old god you are!" Johann screamed. "You can't even protect a kid from...from whatever that was!"

Myla whined. The white dog dragged herself to David's side and rested her head in his lap. David scratched her ears. He didn't have the strength to do much more than that, let alone help Johann with whatever he was looking for. He didn't see any more of the snakes. That, of course, didn't mean that they were gone. It just meant that they had hidden themselves so he couldn't get a good look at them.

The stag snorted as it circled Johann. It limped down, and brilliant red blood stained its once pristine hide. Johann held up his hands. He didn't seem too impressed, though, and wisely backed up once the stag pawed at the earth again. David couldn't help but laugh softly. Then he sobered when he realized that he didn't see Wilhelm at all. He could see the elves, the horses, and even Toman, but Wil had vanished.

Dread pooled in David's heart. He dragged himself up, using the tree for support.

"They took Wilhelm!"

"I noticed." Johann grabbed his horse and swung up in the saddle.

"What the hell are you doing?" David asked. "Tell me that you're not going to screw with black magic on your lonesome."

"Then I would be lying," Johann said. He wiped the blood from his forehead and turned the horse around. "Besides, it's not the first time I've done this."

"Is that supposed to make me feel better?" David shot back. "Because really, it doesn't. All it means is you're a hothead who goes charging off at the drop of a hat!"

Johann ignored him. He spurred his horse in the side and galloped into the underbrush. David gritted his teeth. He didn't know if Johann was going to get himself killed and, for the moment, couldn't bring himself to care. His head throbbed like someone used it to play the drums and waves of pain washed over his body. David moaned. He sat down slowly, his still bleeding leg extended in front of him.

Toman picked himself up from where he lay. The big dog staggered as he walked, blood coating his shoulders, and almost collapsed when he reached David's side. David pulled him into his lap. He couldn't bring himself to look into those big brown eyes. They had failed. That crushing sense draped over David's body and his mind played images of every horrible thing Henri could be doing to Wilhelm at this very second.

"Some bodyguard I turned out to be," David mumbled. He stroked Toman's ears. "I can't even protect him from his own cousin!"

The stag snorted. It lowered its head, resting its chin on David's shoulder. The animal's golden eyes were clouded in pain, and it kept its weight off its right foreleg. It stayed there for the longest time, almost as if it were waiting for something. David didn't bother trying to find out what it was. Very soon, it wouldn't matter anymore. Every beat of his heart spread the poison through his body.

The venom discolored his skin as it slipped through his body. It left trails of inky darkness as it climbed up his wounded, swollen leg. The bite itself had stopped draining now in a mockery of healing. David rested his head against the rough bark. He hated waiting like this. He had thought that he would go with a sword in his hand, not half dead in the forest. And to think that a snake bite, of all things, had done him in.

"I guess this is it," David murmured. He petted Toman and watched the dog with tired brown eyes. "You and me tried our best, but we got outclassed. I just wish I saw it coming."

The stag sighed. It rested its antlers against his swollen

wound, but only a weak golden glow spilled from the wound.

"It's all right," David whispered. He petted the animal's ears and smiled sadly. "I promise it's okay. Save your strength, sweetheart."

The stag sat down beside him. It, too, seemed like it was waiting. David wished he could ask what was on its mind. This close, he could see the faint scars under its neck. Something bubbled up through his pained mind. He touched the scars, careful not to hurt the stag, and ran his fingers over the twisted, raised flesh. If it bothered the stag, it gave no sign. David bit his bottom lip as he thought.

"I'm sorry." David hung his head. "I'm so, so sorry."

He didn't know what else to say. The stag was all he had now, and if Henri was able to defeat it... Well, that didn't say much about the great and the good. David wanted to cry out, wanted to rage, at the injustice of it all. Something stabbed his leg, and he threw his head back. A pained cry ripped from his throat. It seemed to echo through the dense forest and startled the resting birds.

"David?" Ruari knelt beside him and rested his hand on David's arm.

"Hey." David closed his eyes. "Kinda sucks, you know. I thought I was going to die in battle."

"Don't talk like that!" Ruari hissed. "You're not going to die! If–if I had talked to myself like that when I was a captive I wouldn't be here today!"

"You were a captive, too?" David asked.

"Yeah." Ruari looked away. "I'm not proud of what I did."

"That's all right." David petted the elf's soft red hair and tried to read his expression. "You survived. That's all that counts. Besides..." He trailed off and looked away. "You need to go with Johann. I promise he needs the help more than me."

Ruari hung his head. "I can't do that."

"They have Wilhelm." David coughed and tasted blood. "You have to help him. If Henri gets his way..." He trailed off and let the silence do the speaking for him.

Henri wanted nothing good for Wilhelm. If the stag couldn't stop him—and David had thought that it would be invincible or close to it—there was no force in this entire realm that could stop him. David didn't know if he wanted to cry out or rage, maybe both; at least he would feel like he did something. He took a ragged breath, lolling his head to one side as he waited.

Waiting. He hated waiting. It seemed like he had waited

for all of his life. First to become a man, then to defend Alsace, then to become free, then to share his love with Wil and Johann, and now to die.

"I can't leave you." Ruari kissed his knuckles. "If Wilhelm and Johann die, you will be king."

David barked a sharp laugh. "Me, a king! Are you *mad*?"

"You and Wil—"

"Wil and I never did anything but kiss," David said. "Maybe I love him, but that doesn't mean they would give me a crown! Not unless all seven hells froze over!"

He didn't mean to snap like that. Maybe it was the pain talking or maybe he didn't care at all.

"Those people need a leader!" Ruari hissed. "I didn't come to my people's aid when they needed me and look what happened to us! A proud nation, destroyed! All because I had to run off to the forest because I couldn't face the shame in my head!"

"These aren't my people!" David screamed. He spat a foul-tasting wad of blood and darkness to the ground. "My people are Alsatians! To hell with Talla Gael!"

His chest heaved as he stared at the elf. Ruari jerked his head back like he had been slapped. David couldn't bring himself to care. He ignored the stag and the way it jerked away from him. Even the dogs moved back from him.

"That's where they will go if you don't help them!" Ruari hissed. He grabbed David by the arm and hoisted him up. "Come on; if you start walking, you'll drain the poison. Both the leg wound and your charming personality."

David let the insult slide as he hobbled after the elf. He was going to regret this, he knew, but he didn't see any other choice.

CHAPTER THIRTY-ONE: CROWN

❖ ❖ ❖

Wilhelm pressed his body into the corner and tried not to stare at Henri. He didn't know his cousin, didn't know the reddish light that now colored his once beautiful eyes. Henri cocked his head like a hungry jackal as he prowled around the room. His skin was pale now, almost as pale as that of a corpse, and he muttered to himself. A lacy black shadow clung to his skin. If Wilhelm looked at it for too long, he swore he saw a pair of golden eyes.

"Why aren't you looking at me?" Henri asked.

His voice was little more than a growl now. It was animal like now—whatever human had lived in him was long gone.

"Because you aren't my cousin," Wilhelm whispered. The words tasted like bitter ashes in his mouth. "You aren't the man I knew and loved."

Henri whirled around and grabbed him by the collar. "Don't speak of love to me, you filthy blood traitor!"

"Let me go!" Wilhelm struggled, his nails scratching at Henri's wrists. "And I'm not a blood traitor! An alliance with Alsace—"

"An alliance built on the back of a common soldier has no worth!" Henri spat. He shoved Wilhelm away from him in disgust. "I don't know what you see in them. Really, I don't. A common soldier and a washed-up mercenary from gods know where. Is that really what you want in your life? Or has Emil's death driven you mad?"

Wilhelm took a breath. He wanted to fling himself out the window of this rotting palace, but the arrow loops were too thin for him to do so. Hell, he could hardly fit his hand through them. Henri knew what he was doing when he chose this place —the curtain walls were covered in thorny vines that ripped a man's flesh just to look at them and the moat crawled with all manner of foul and sick beasts.

Wilhelm sat down on a mildewed rug and played his hand over the faded pattern. Sheets of rotting silk hung from the walls, and more of the silk ivy crawled in through a window crowded with broken glass. A few of the rotting tapestries had silver thread poking through; that alone escaped the rot. Dead leaves had blown in from broken bay windows and the wild foxes made their homes amongst the lower quarters.

A fine layer of death and decay seemed to hang over the little room they were in. The long-dead hearth hunched in the corner, its gaping maw filled only with half-cemented ashes and the feathers of hundreds of birds. Beady black eyes stared at Wilhelm if he glanced into the chimney. The wind, heavy with the scent of rain, came whistling through cracked and broken glass. The bronze and gold that would have decorated such a room had long since been stolen; the bare spaces on the wall hinted at the distant splendor.

Wilhelm waited for some time before speaking. He didn't trust himself. A wild thing lived in Henri now, a wild thing that he could neither trust nor tame. A black swallow perched on the other man's shoulder. It had the same bloody red eyes of the dagger on Henri's belt, and it hissed if it looked at him for too long. Shadows seemed to prowl across the walls. They moved independent of the candle or the setting sun, and Wilhelm never could escape the feeling of being watched.

"Why do you want this?" Wilhelm whispered. He hugged himself and feared the answer.

"Why not?" Henri asked. He pulled a cracked and warped mirror from under a crumbling desk. "Your family has held power for the last five hundred years. Isn't it time that someone else get a chance? Besides, you deserve better than a *mercenary* and a *soldier*!"

He spat those last two words, and Wilhelm didn't have to imagine the scorn and derision behind them.

"But what if I want a mercenary and a soldier?" Wilhelm asked. "Johann saved my life!"

Something wild passed in Henri's reddish eyes. He murmured something that Wilhelm couldn't quite hear before slinging a silver circlet at Wilhelm's feet. Wilhelm picked it up. It was light and delicate, made of finely wrought metal shaped like tangled ivy and the tiny leaves were set with pieces of pale green peridot. It looked like something an elven prince might have worn and was so delicate that Wilhelm feared he would break it if he put it on.

"Wear the damn crown," Henri growled. He bared his teeth like a cornered dog. "I said wear it!"

"And if I don't?" Wilhelm tried to keep a brave face as he stared at the man.

Henri marched over. He ripped the circlet out of Wilhelm's hands and shoved it on the other man's head. The jeweled leaves ripped at delicate skin. Blood beaded where skin had been torn and dripped down Wilhelm's face. Wilhelm jerked back. He grabbed at the circlet to fling it off, only for Henri to grab his wrists. Wild red eyes stared into his. There seemed to be something wild there, something dangerous that chilled Wilhelm to his very bones.

"You'll do what I say if you know what's good for you," Henri said. He gave a sickly-sweet smile as he released Wilhelm's wrists. "You know, I could make you do anything I want. This,"—he pulled out the dagger with its bloody red jewel—"gives the power to do it."

Wilhelm's blood ran cold when he saw the weapon. "But that's Maria's dagger!"

"Not really." Henri smirked and, for a second, some of his old charm seemed to show in his features. "I just told her to say that. Magic is funny like that. It lets you do all sorts of things you couldn't otherwise."

Wilhelm backed up and pressed his back against a crumbling stone wall. "Why are you doing this?"

"Because I want what was taken from my family!" Henri's chest heaved as he flung those words into the little room. "And because I can."

Wilhelm nodded like he understood. His mouth went dry as his heart pounded. He swore he could hear the shadows whispering vile things to him. Those strange curses said in a soft tone seemed to bore their way into his very soul, and the icy words offered him a way out. All he had to do was give in. That was it. No more fighting. No more pain. No more fear. No more worry about what it would be like to be king.

All he had to do...

It was so simple, really.

He didn't know why he hadn't thought about it before.

Simple. So simple. All he had to do was take the shadowy hand in front of him.

An inhuman face stared back at Wilhelm; only red eyes poked through the veil of mist and haze. He stared into the void of that thing for the longest time. Its ragged black cloak seemed to shift in a nonexistent breeze, and its hands were as pale and wrinkled as a water-logged corpse. Broken black beads littered its gown. Strands of blonde hair—rotting and splintered—poked out from under its cowl.

"Go on," Henri whispered. His voice was soft now and layered like a thousand people were speaking at once. "Take it."

Something warred within him. Some part of Wilhelm wanted to run away screaming. It felt like ice flooded his chest as he looked at the thing, yet his boots felt rooted to the spot. He could just see the gleam of white teeth hidden in that shadow-wreathed mouth. A strange warmth touched his face as the shadow hovered over him. It cocked its head, like it didn't understand what he was, and that pale hand traced down his face.

Pain blossomed across every centimeter of skin it touched.

Wilhelm jerked out of his stupor. "Get away from me!"

The shadow jerked back like it had been scalded. Wilhelm bared his teeth. He didn't know what came over him, only that he screamed at the shadow and ran right at it. He tackled the thing, likely before it could vanish, and slammed the beast into the ground. He fastened his hands around its cold, crooked neck, placing his entire weight on it, and forced the thrashing being to the ground.

His heart hammered in his chest. He could taste iron in his mouth and dimly hear horrific screeching. Arms fastened around his middle. Wilhelm threw his elbow back, making the other man grunt, and slammed his head back. Henri cried out in pain. The dagger clattered to the ground. Wilhelm sprang up, leaving the stunned shadow where it lay, and flung the weapon out of the broken window.

"What have you done!" Henri screamed.

"Saved you!" Wilhelm took a deep breath and tried to look braver than he felt.

Something twisted on Henri's face as blood ran down it. His eyes were still the blood red color and the shadows seemed to swarm together. The thing on the floor slowly started to stir. Wilhelm's fingers twitched before he reached for a weapon that wasn't there. His mouth seemed to go dry as he stood there. Time seemed to slow to a crawl. Wilhelm could taste that iron in his mouth again.

The rotting door behind them swung open. A dirty blond man poked his head in, probably to check on them, and that was when Wilhelm bolted.

He shoved the blond aside and raced toward the slick stairs. They were sharply pitched and narrow, the stairs used in fortresses, and they clung to the tower core like a snake did a branch. Wilhelm raced as fast as he could. He ripped the circlet from his head, throwing it down a tower shaft, and picked one of the levels at random. He forced the wrought-iron door open and raced inside.

A tangle of rooms and corridors met his eyes. Dust billowed with every step he took, and cobwebs clung to the door frames and furniture. Long-dead potted vines spilled into the hallway. Candles made of dried wax still clung in their holders, and pools of shadows draped across the floor. Wilhelm swallowed bitter fear. He ducked into an old stateroom at random and slipped inside a splintered armoire.

His heart hammered in his chest as he waited. The

shadows there flickered, but only because light passed over the windows. Wilhelm couldn't see any sort of demonic creature. Just the natural light that came from the end of the day. He almost wished he was home. The Henri he knew would have never acted like this. Perhaps, if he went there, he could pretend that everything was right in the world.

Something sighed, and the same golden creature crawled into the armoire.

Wilhelm froze. His eyes went wide, and he couldn't help but stare at the creature. It cocked its head like a hungry, confused dog. He could just see the fear alongside curiosity in its eyes, followed by a strange sort of pain. A hysterical part of Wilhelm's mind wondered if it were trapped there too. It didn't seem like it was going to hurt him, even though it did seem wary. Wilhelm supposed it had a right to that, seeing as he had tried to kill it.

"What *are* you?" he whispered. Wilhelm cupped its soft, cool head. "I'm used to a stag—he's the great lord of the forest—but I've never seen something like you before."

The shade drew back quickly. Wilhelm knew that it remembered his attempt to kill it, and he couldn't help the shame that spiked through his body. He hung his head. Then he heard boot steps outside the hall and went very still. Ice seemed to flood his body. He could hardly think for the fear of it. The shade froze. It turned its ragged head, keen eyes focused on the door. Wilhelm offered a silent prayer for mercy.

"You see anything?" a gruff voice asked.

Wilhelm thought it was Steven and cursed his bad luck.

"Nope," his companion answered. "If the little brat's here, there's a good chance we'll find him at the bottom of a vent shaft."

"What about the shade?" Steven asked. "Last time I checked, it fucked off."

"Who cares about that stupid thing?" the other laughed. "I don't know what our glorious leader sees in them! They're dogs, nothing more! Let's go check the other levels. I don't trust that Tallan bastard not to lay a false trail."

Wilhelm thought he would faint by the time they were gone. He even tried to ignore the way the shade crawled into his lap.

CHAPTER THIRTY-TWO: RESCUE ME

◆ ◆ ◆

David rested beside Ruari and petted Toman. "You think he's going to be okay?"

"Nope." The red-haired elf drew something on the ground with a stick and didn't meet David's gaze. "But do I think you could have stopped him? Also nope. That means that we need to go along after him to keep him from getting his fool self killed."

David winced. He stared at his bad leg and how it awkwardly rested to the side. He couldn't fight like this. If he fell off Snowflake, there was no way he would be getting back up. Hell, he didn't even have a *sword*. How was he going fight off Henri and his men without a weapon? David glanced over to the stag, trying to judge how strong it was. Even Toman looked down for the count.

David couldn't speak for the rest of the elves, but he had to imagine they wouldn't be spoiling for a fight. Perhaps

Ruari was the only one who wanted to fight in that entire cohort.

"I don't think I can fight," David said. He gestured to his still swollen leg. "I can hardly walk, let alone ride. We don't even have weapons, Ruari! Besides, the stupid stag healed Toman and none of us!"

Toman looked up from where he rested against the stag's side, his tail wagging slightly.

The stag sighed, almost like it was apologizing. David buried his hand in its side to comfort the beast and tried to ignore how cold it was to the touch. He felt as if he were touching frozen starlight, not something living. After a second, the stag struggled to its feet. It favored its right side, almost like it was still wounded there, and pawed at the ground. David stared at it intently. He wasn't quite sure what the beast wanted.

Ruari cleared his throat. "We don't need weapons."

"Ruari." Bracken gave him a long look as he poked the fire. "Don't."

"Do we have a choice?" Ruari asked. "Hiding lost us our old home. I, for one, am sick and tired of it! What kind of forest prince am I if I can't protect my own kingdom?"

"Do you want me to answer that?" Bracken asked.

"Because I can and you won't like what you hear."

Ruari flinched like Bracken had just slapped him. Something strange passed between the two men, something that David couldn't hope to understand. The air seemed to thicken around them. Ruari and Bracken stared at each other, eyes narrow. Ruari's hand dipped to his belt as he stood. The elf moved like a cat, and *danger* seemed to roll off of his entire being. Bracken glowered.

David struggled up and took a step back. He had no idea what was about to happen, nor did he want to find out.

"Can we stop now?" Holly asked. She stepped between the two men and pushed them back. "I know you two don't like each other, but this isn't the time to make trouble. We need to work together."

"She's right," David said. He caught Snowflake's bridle and swung up on her back. "Come on; Johann couldn't have gone too far!"

He tried not to think about what he was doing as he rode off. They didn't have a chance. Henri had magic. David didn't even have a sword. His leg still throbbed from the snakebite, and faintness clung to his sweaty skin. He gripped the reins as hard as he could. Toman walked behind him, as did the stag. David ignored them. He braced himself against the mare's neck and tried to tell himself that his racing heart was fear rather than exhaustion.

The forest seemed to close around him. Walls of bracken, vines, ferns, and twisted young trees seemed to blot out the sky. Tangled tree branches seemed to form into one moss covered mass. The path ahead of them grew narrow, so narrow that David thought he was following a dusty thread through the forest. He could hear the birds singing in the dense underbrush, along with the soft wind and trickling water.

After a little bit, he came to a clearing. Mist clung to broken down ramparts in front of him and a rusted iron gate hung off its hinges. The grass was dark, burnt almost, and the path ahead of them was twisted and rocky. A stagnant pond rested near the decaying gate. Its waters were foul and filled with all sorts of slime; the stench of wet, rotting vegetation clung to the air. Nothing stirred in front of them.

It felt as if the entire world waited on them. David's leg throbbed as he urged Snowflake forward. The mare's ears were pricked, her eyes wide, as she took delicate steps. A strange silence settled over him and unease wrapped around David's body. He patted the mare's side to calm himself. Toman still trotted at his side, but the dog's hackles were up and his teeth bared. Snowflake tensed under him like she was going to rear at any second.

The mist started snaking toward them in long, thin tendrils.

Snowflake snorted. She half reared, her eyes wild, and lashed out. David kicked her. She bolted seconds later and leapt over a wall studded with half-curled ferns. The mist fled as soon as she crashed through it, almost like it retreated to the ramparts.

Toman tucked his tail between his legs. The big dog whined, his eyes wild. He jumped every time he heard something, and his entire body trembled. David wished he could comfort him. Still, though, he urged Snowflake deeper into the ruins and tried to keep an eye on his dog.

Water dripped down crumbling stones in black streams. Bits of rusting metal, often surrounded by rainbow-colored pools, lay in many of the corners. Thorn vines wrapped them around the remains of sheds and other structures, while golden eyes stared at him from every darkened place. Rotting banners draped over more walls and collapsed arches cut off much of the courtyard. The air seemed frozen here, like it hadn't moved for a thousand years.

A golden hunting dog yipped as it ran toward them.

It was a lithe beast and wore a thick leather collar. Its entire body jerked from side to side as it wagged its tail. David dismounted Snowflake, cursing as he did so, and caught the dog by the collar. Toman growled a warning. The golden dog ignored it, instead covered David's hands with wet licks and his trousers with muddy paws.

David petted it absently. He examined the collar to find out who it belonged to.

"Henri..." he whispered.

At the mention of its master's name, the dog's floppy ears pricked up. David petted it absently. He could just hear someone behind the inner curtain walls, so he paused and tried to keep as quiet as he could. Heavy foot falls seemed to echo through the crumbling stones. Sour air hung heavy, almost making David gag. Toman still stared at the golden dog, tense like he wanted to fight, but even he calmed when he heard voices.

"What do we do with the mercenary?"

David's breath caught. *Johann! They must have found him!*

"Wait 'til Henri gives an order," the second said. He sounded older and tired, like he wanted nothing more to do with this. "They still haven't found the little prince yet."

"I still can't see why he didn't just kill them both," the first whined. "Really, Jonathon, it's not that hard! As long as he's still alive—"

"It was Steven's orders." Jonathon's voice was as cold as the winter winds.

David pressed his body to the wall. He crept toward the men, praying that none of the dogs would bark. He knew that they had to have watch dogs. Some of them would be wild things, like the panther dogs his people preferred, and others would be hunting dogs like the golden one. That animal went running toward the two guards. David froze. His heart leapt into his mouth as he waited.

The first one must have caught the yipping beast. "Ahh, damn. Henri lost his dog again."

"If that thing goes running through the forest too much, a wolf's going to eat it," Jonathon laughed.

"Good riddance. I hate the thing! It always gets in my way when I'm trying to do something!"

The dog yelped like someone had kicked it and both men laughed. Toman growled softly. Before David could say anything, the wolf hound jumped over a fallen section of wall and attacked the two men. Jonathon yelled. His eyes went wide as the dog sunk its jaws into his hand. The first man, a blond, drew his sword. David scrambled over the wall. He grabbed a fallen branch, swinging it at the man and catching him off guard.

"Hey! Intruders!"

"Damn!" David hissed. He ducked a wild blow from the sword and tried to fend the man off. "Leave my dog alone!"

The first man snarled at him. His gray eyes were wild, and he swung the sword like a man possessed. The weapon seemed to gleam in the humid air. David jerked away from him as he swung it again. He could hear people yelling and boots thundering toward them. He found himself standing back-to-back with the dog. His limbs trembled with pain and exhaustion. They didn't have a chance. He knew it and so did everyone else.

David dropped his weapon and held up his hands. "All right, I surrender."

"I say we kill them," the blond said. "We don't even have to tell Steven. Let the wolves have them."

"Tobias." Jonathon gave his friend a long look. "We do that and *we'll* find ourselves in some deep, dark pit. No, it's best that we take them in."

Tobias grimaced, but he still grabbed David around the arm and dragged him up an algae-covered staircase. The musty scent grew stronger when they stepped into the courtyard proper. David thought it came from a pile of rotting canvas tossed in the mud, but he couldn't be sure. Rotting, mushy vegetation and churned-up mud littered the entire area, after all. He tried not to make too much of a face.

Steven sat at the end of a splintering wooden table in the Great Hall. A single candle fastened to the table by its own grease rested beside him, and thick rushes covered the floor. Another golden dog rested at his feet, as did one with short, gray fur. Their ears were cropped and their tails cut off. The gray one had a face covered in scars. It growled softly when it saw the lean, rangy wolfhound, but otherwise made no move.

Steven closed his book and looked up at them. "So we meet again."

"We do." David held his head high.

"Sit down. Please." Steven gestured to the space beside him. "I assume you're here to find the mercenary, correct? The one who calls himself Johann?"

"I am." David tried not to look for the stag, even if he couldn't find it. "Prince Wilhelm von Hart., too."

"Johann is not the man you think he is," Steven said. He ignored what David said about Wilhelm and stroked the spine of his book. "He called himself the Deathbringer in my country and did much harm. He killed my best friend."

"I'm sorry to hear that," David said.

"He also unleashed a horror that ravaged our land. Even today, it follows me." A twisted smile spread across Steven's lips as shadows formed into wolves and wild cats. "These shadows were once his servants. The very same magic he used has found its way to Henri. In fact, this book I'm reading?" Steven held up the battered tome. "Your Johann wrote it."

"I never said he was a good man," David said, "just that I love him."

"A man like that isn't worthy of love," Steven growled. He leaned back in his chair and looked at David with hungry eyes. "But someone like me, someone who's done something in life? You could do worse."

David bristled. "And what of Wilhelm?"

"What of him?" Steven asked. He gestured for the two guards to leave. "Let him have his prize. The little prince isn't too much trouble."

"I heard you lost him," David quickly said. "That sounds like trouble to me."

The shadows seemed to cluster around Steven. Toman growled softly. The dog bared his teeth, but there was nothing he could do. David tensed as *something* brushed against his skin. He was just about to ask what it was when he knew only darkness.

CHAPTER THIRTY-THREE: SHADE

❖ ❖ ❖

Wilhelm stayed as silent as he could. The shade curled around him, likely seeking warmth, and its form shifted every few seconds. Its body flowed between a vaguely human, ragged-looking thing, a starved wild cat, and a large, wolf-like dog. Black smoke trailed off its sides if it held one form too long. Wilhelm found himself petting it and studying the thing. Unlike the stag, which was made of solid flesh, he found his hand sinking through the shade's body if he wasn't careful.

"What are you?" he whispered. Wilhelm tipped the beast's head up and stroked its ears. "I've never seen anything like you before."

He heard something move outside of the wardrobe. The beast tensed. It bared fangs that were long and sharp and focused on the movement. Wilhelm pressed his back against the dry and splintering wood. The dim light flickered as heavy boots tramped around the little room. Wilhelm could hear the heavy cloak. A sick feeling settled in the pit of his stomach. If that was who he thought it was...

"You can come out now," a soft voice said. "I'm not going to hurt you, I promise."

Henri's words were as soft and deadly as poisoned honey. They settled over Wilhelm's shoulders, seeming to bore into him with a sick precision. Henri seemed to relish in Wilhelm's fear. He stood there, right outside of the wardrobe, and waited. Tension draped through the air in a choking, deadly cloud. Henri paced a little. His dagger—the same blade that Wilhelm had thrown out the window—still cast that sickly reddish light from the center gem.

Wilhelm tried to hold as still as he could. His heart raced in his chest as sick bile spread to his mouth. He couldn't fight Henri. Hell, even the stag hadn't been able to do it. If something that was so clearly an old god couldn't fight back, Wilhelm knew that he wouldn't be able to. *Unless...* He glanced at the shade. The thing resembled an attack dog now. Its hackles stood strong, and its red eyes were narrowed as it glared at Henri.

Wilhelm took a breath and tried to calm his racing heart. Then he lunged, kicking open the dry rotted wood, and let the shade loose.

It went straight for Henri. Henri snarled as he jerked back. The shade sunk its jaws into his arm, tearing through skin and muscle, and started dragging him down. Wilhelm didn't wait to watch the fight. He turned and ran, racing for the stairs. Behind him, an inhuman scream tore through the air. Wilhelm forced himself to keep running. He could smell an acrid stench, much like the air before lightning struck, and *something* shook the castle to its core.

Wilhelm fell to the ground. Great chunks of stone and masonry fell from the ceiling. Ancient timbers groaned and holes opened in the floor. Painted plaster fell from the walls, sending up clouds of choking dust. Wilhelm picked himself up as quickly as he could. The hair on the back of his neck stood up. He could feel something watching him, almost like more red eyes were tearing into him, and he forced himself to run.

"Come back here!" Henri screamed. He staggered out of the little room, black fluid clinging to his body. "I order you as your king!"

Wilhelm turned around, his chest heaving. "You'll never be king!"

"Oh, really?" Henri asked. He cocked his head like a hungry dog as he prowled near. "That's what Emil said. Right before I killed him."

Wilhelm saw red. Then he let loose a wild animal cry and raced for Henri. He tackled the older man, pinning him to the ground, and slammed his head against the quivering floor tiles. Henri snarled as he threw Wilhelm off. Tendrils of inky magic climbed up Henri's arms. His eyes were wild, the eyes of a maniac rather than a man, and his nails lengthened into ragged claws. When he bared his teeth, he had a mouth filled with ragged fangs.

"Maybe you killed Emil," Wilhelm hissed, "but you won't kill me."

Henri took a step forward and ran his fingers over the dagger like it was his lover. "You rely on a stupid soldier to keep you safe and a dog that I beat half to death. Somehow, I'm not very scared."

Wilhelm bared his teeth as he reached for a dagger that wasn't there. "But I have something to fight for and you, you traitorous bastard, you don't have that!"

He lunged. He struck Henri upside the head with his fist, getting a slash to the cheek for his troubles, and dropped back as soon as he could. The castle groaned around them. Wilhelm could hardly breathe for the choking dust and falling plaster. It coated them, making them look like phantoms as they circled each other. Henri shook his head. His eyes narrowed, as if he was focusing, and that was when Wilhelm hurled a piece of plaster at his head.

Henri snarled when it struck him. He shook his head, sending droplets of blood all over, and came at Wilhelm with a wall of magic. It picked him up effortlessly and slammed him into the crumbling stone. Wilhelm cried out as soon as he hit. He rolled away as quickly as he could, shaking his head wildly, and scrambled for the door. Those massive expanses of wood and iron snapped shut just as he reached them.

Wilhelm whirled around. He raked his nails across Henri's face, drawing blood, and kicked him to the ground. Something welled up inside of him. Wilhelm had no idea what it was, only that it felt white hot, and he let it free. It struck Henri in the chest. Henri groaned as it pinned him to the ground. He tried to fight through it, his eyes wild. Wilhelm turned around. He wrenched the doors open with strength he didn't know he had and raced down the stairs.

His heart fluttered in his chest. He could taste old blood, and his lungs screamed at him. Wilhelm tripped on the slick, debris-covered stone, falling head over heels into the dark void below. He landed hard on a pile of rotting canvas and lay there for a few precious moments. He could still hear the movement and see the flickering shadows. They moved in animalistic patterns all around him, and a few materialized out of the darkness.

Wilhelm picked himself up slowly. "Does he hurt you?"

The scratches on his head, fouled now with blood, dust, and sweat, seemed to sting.

The largest shade—the one in the form of a crouching

wolf—growled softly. It lowered its anvil-shaped head as it sniffed him. Glowing, sickly green eyes seemed to rake over him, and Wilhelm feared that it could see right into his soul.

"I won't hurt you," Wilhelm promised. "You want to go home, just like I do. But you don't know how."

The wolf recoiled. It gave a low growl, the sound reminding Wilhelm of approaching thunder, and circled him on silent feet. The other two lowered their heads. They had the shapes of fine hounds, and their bodies rippled as they walked. Wilhelm couldn't help but touch the leader. It hissed at him as he caressed its head, yet didn't try to move away.

"Easy," Wilhelm whispered. He picked himself up slowly, cursing at the pain in his side. "I'll get you out of here, I promise."

He limped his way toward a once-ornate door. All three shades surrounded him, almost like they didn't want him to enter. Wilhelm pushed his way through them anyway.

"Wil!" David got up from where he was sitting and raced toward him. "We have to get out of here!"

Wilhelm wrapped his arms around David and held him close. For the longest time, the only thing that seemed to exist in the world were the two of them. Wilhelm buried his nose in David's neck to try and ground himself. Then a sinking feeling filled his stomach, and he forced himself to move back.

"They have Johann, don't they?" Wilhelm asked.

Steven slowly stood up from the table. "You mean the bastard who destroyed my kingdom? Yeah, we have him. And I'm going to give him the punishment our father was too weak to give!"

"I think Henri picked up a few nasty habits from you," David said. He wiped half-dried blood from a split lip. "Because he didn't act like this before you showed up!"

"You don't get it, do you?" Steven asked. He shook his head like they were slow children. "You just don't understand his mission! I might not like the kid, but you have to admit that he has some good ideas. Ending the war with Alsace, for one, and letting all the prisoners free."

David froze. Wilhelm turned to his lover and shook his head. Steven was lying. He *had* to be. There was no way Henri would do any of those things; if anything, he would continue the war and make it so much worse for the Alsatian people. Wilhelm could hardly breathe as he looked at David. He hoped against all hope that David wouldn't turn away from him. Wilhelm didn't know what he would do if Henri got his way.

"You think I trust you?" David laughed. It was a bitter laugh, the type that came from a man wounded in body and soul. "You honestly think I trust you enough to let Henri have his way."

Henri stalked through the still-open doors and bared his teeth. "Why wouldn't you trust me?"

"Uh, because you tried to kill us?" David asked. He nudged Wilhelm with his foot and gave the slightest gesture toward the far door. "Several times now. And you hang out in a place that looks like a rotting trash heap. Forgive me, but I don't exactly trust you after all that."

Wilhelm bolted as soon as Henri turned his attention to David. Henri snarled. He lunged with the grace of a wild cat, nearly catching Wilhelm, but fell to the ground when David struck him with an iron platter. Wilhelm didn't turn around. He scrambled out the door and raced to the courtyard. A battalion of soldiers turned as soon as Wilhelm rounded the corner. One of them opened his mouth to give a battle cry.

As soon as he did, the stag charged him.

Wilhelm didn't know where it came from, just that it lashed out with razor-sharp hooves and tossed men in its antlers. The animal bellowed as it reared. Hooves sliced into tender skin and ripped through canvas armor. Wilhelm ducked around the wild beast and scrambled over to an iron cage. Johann's bloody, unconscious form rested in the bottom of it.

His blond hair had soaked through with blood, and more of it clung to his shirt and trousers. Only his chest still moving betrayed signs of life.

Wilhelm grabbed an iron axe and bashed it against the lock. Johann bolted up. More blood clung to his lips and teeth, like he had been struck there, and he made a horrible, strangled sound. Wilhelm wrenched open the door as soon as he could. He grabbed Johann and dragged him out before turning to run.

"Oh, no you don't!" One of the soldiers struck Wilhelm in the head with the flat of his blade and sent him sprawling. "You know something, sweetheart? I'm going to take care of you once and for all!"

Johann snarled. He grabbed the axe, ignoring the way he swayed on his feet, and lashed out. He caught the soldier twice and rammed the weapon through a boiled leather helmet. Johann kicked the body away as it dropped before falling to his knees. Wilhelm picked himself up. His head throbbed, and the world seemed dim somehow. He could just barely feel the gravel biting into his hands and hear the raging battle.

He had to find the horses. They couldn't escape without the horses. He didn't know why those wild thoughts raced through his head, but they did and he knew he was going to obey them.

Wilhelm clung to that thought as he climbed to his feet. He ignored the blood in his mouth and the ringing in his head as he focused on the rearing stag before him.

CHAPTER THIRTY-FOUR: WARRIOR

❖ ❖ ❖

David shook as he looked at Henri. The young man lay sprawled across the ground and bled sluggishly from a wound to the head. The wound itself had seared around the edges, almost like the iron had burned him. David bared his teeth. His eyes narrowed as he glanced around the room. Dimly, he could hear fighting from outside. David took a step to join it, only to stop short when he heard Henri moan.

He grabbed a sword from a decoration set into the wall and held it at the ready. His heart pounded in his chest as he waited. Henri seemed oblivious to it all, his entire world focused on his bleeding head, and he drew himself into a small ball. Not for the first time, pity flooded David's heart. He found himself kneeling on the filthy, rotting rushes and gently rolling Henri over.

The red slowly faded from his eyes. Henri lay there, his gaze focused on the vine-covered ceiling as if it contained all the answers in the world. No shadows clung to his sickly pale, sweat-soaked skin. His gaze seemed unfocused and unsteady. David brushed his blood and sweat-soaked hair out of his face, only for Henri to grab his wrist. Those fingers—tipped with short, sharp claws now—dug into David's flesh and held the other man's hand fast.

"Let me go!" David snapped. He tried to yank his hand back, only for the claws to slice through his soft skin. "Henri! I said *let me go!*"

"Don't you see it?" Henri whispered. He still clung to David's wrist with one hand and stared at the ceiling. "The shadows are dancing. I hear them calling my name and telling me to join them."

Cold dread flooded David's chest. "Don't!"

A soft, almost broken smile spread across Henri's features as he lay on his back. He raised his free hand to the ceiling, and David swore he was reaching for something. A fine black mist—so fine and soft that David almost couldn't see it—wrapped around Henri's outstretched hand. The thing pulled back, taking something that looked like a thin silver aether from Henri's hand. David barely heard a sigh before Henri's hand went slack and fell to the ground.

David scrambled to his feet. He could hardly look at the body beside him and swung the sword in a wide arc. The fight outside seemed dim to him now, like it was coming from far away. The air temperature started to drop around him, and David's breath froze in the air. His blood rushed in his ears as he stalked around the Great Hall. He could see shadows from the corner of his eyes and that thin tendril of silver smoke.

"Where are you?" David snarled. "Show yourself!"

Nothing answered him. The silver mist hung around the floor, as if it couldn't decide what it wanted to do. David slashed at the dark mist and grabbed the silver tendril before it could be sucked away. He backed up, cursing softly, and tried to slip out the heavy door. The tendril sagged in his hands. He felt like he was holding frozen starlight in shaking fingers and that it would slip from his grip.

Steven burst into the Great Hall, his sword drawn. "Where's Henri?"

"Dead," David choked out. He pressed his back against the splintering wood, his eyes wild. "They–they killed him!"

"Do I look like I care?" Steven hissed. "I only needed him to get at Johann. You're just the icing on the cake."

David bored his teeth. "Over my dead body."

"You know something?" Steven asked. "That works."

Then he drew his sword and lunged. David dropped the tendril. He drew his own blade and slashed at the older man. The two men danced around each other, parrying and striking at each other's blows. Steven's eyes were wild, like some beast was taking over him. He danced around David with the grace of a man professionally trained, and his blade nearly severed David's head from his shoulders.

The fight spilled into the little courtyard outside the Great Hall. David tripped over a pile of cracked stones. He landed, hard, and cried out when he struck his wrist against that stone. Steven slashed at him and sliced his cheek. David scrambled up. He grabbed his sword from where it had fallen and lashed out wildly. Steven struck David's sword with the flat of his blade. The weapon clattered to the ground seconds later.

David jerked back. He scrambled up a small incline, cursing when his boots slipped on the lose rocks. He grabbed up another of the stones, one that glittered like starlight, and threw it at Steven. The man snarled as it struck his gambeson. Steven started picking his way up the incline. David slipped down the other side and cursed when the stag nearly speared him with its antlers.

David scrambled on the animal's back. He clung with every bit of strength he had and kicked the beast in the side. It tossed its head as it reared and caught Steven as he slipped down. The man screamed, his eyes wild. He struggled as the stag shoved him against the wall. David slid off the animal's back and lunged at one of the men at arms. He could just see Wilhelm out of the corner of his eye, and Johann slashed at two men by one of the many arches.

"Hey!" David yelled. "Why don't you pick on someone your own size!"

The man stalking Wilhelm turned. David grabbed an iron bar that had fallen by an old fire pit and smashed that one in the head. He stepped around the twitching, collapsing man and lunged at one of the men pressing Johann. He could hardly hear for the blood rushing in his ears. His heart raced, iron filled his mouth, and everything seemed to slow down around him. It was like the soldier was telegraphing his movements so David knew each one.

"Wilhelm!" David called. "Get out of here!"

Wilhelm picked himself slowly. He looked dazed, almost like he had been struck in the head, and he leaned against the wall. Blood trickled from a cut on his head. David tried to get close to him, really he did, but the soldier he was fighting struck him in the side. David cried out. He fell to his knees, hand flying to his arm to stop the flow of blood. He heard himself cry out and barely ducked the death blow.

Wilhelm grabbed a sword from who knew where and

swung it with all his strength.

The soldier stared at the blade sticking out of his chest. Then he looked up, confused, and collapsed to the ground. Johann finished off his own soldier and kicked the man away. He knelt beside David, strong hands pressing at the wound. David found himself sagging against the man's side. Words were beyond him now, and he wondered if this was what Henri had felt. He thought about the starlight again and if that was a human soul.

He rested his head on Johann's shoulder. "What's the deal, Doc? Am I gonna live?"

"I think so," Johann said. He tied off the wound with a strip of dirty shirt and kissed his forehead. "We just have to keep this wound clean."

The world narrowed around him. David focused on the soft bird calls and the rain heavy wind. Sunlight dappled through the thick leaves and pooled on the churned-up, sandy earth. The dead lay in their own heaps, their blood staining the earth and fallen leaves. David couldn't see Steven, but he knew the stag took care of that problem.

Then he felt soft breath against his neck. David turned around slowly and rested his good hand against the beast's nose.

Blood stained the stag's neck, shoulders, and antlers.

Bits of cotton batting clung to the animal's antlers and fluttered in the breeze. Steven had fought back, slashing at the stag's neck and revealing blood and pale silver tissue. The stag pressed its head against David's forehead. It sighed softly, and David swore it was trying to tell him something. He wished he understood it, wished he knew what it was trying to tell him.

Johann curled his lip. "You know, I don't like you very much."

The stag pinned its ears to its skull and snorted, almost as if to say that the feeling was mutual.

"Easy," David said. He smiled softly and stroked the stag's soft fur. "I don't think Emil means any harm."

"Emil?" Wilhelm's voice was soft and shaky.

"I think it's Emil." David stood up slowly and winced. "I don't see why it wouldn't be. From what I understand, old gods don't usually bother with humans."

The stag snorted. It allowed David to hug it, though, and rested its antlers against the wounded arm. David closed his eyes. He braced himself as the familiar warmth spread through his body. The stag drew back after a second, its body surrounded by a halo of golden light. David rested his hands on Toman's back as the dog wandered over. Toman seemed like he didn't mind the stag, and the stag returned the favor.

"Thank you," David whispered. "Thank you for all you've done. He's dead now; you don't have to stick around."

"No!" Wilhelm yelled. He raced toward the stag and wrapped his arms around the nervous animal's neck. "No! You can't leave me! Not now!"

The stag lowered its head. It drew back, and its form started to blur. A cloud of starlight surrounded the animal. David lunged and grabbed Wilhelm before that cloud could wash over him. Even now, magic scared him. He couldn't force himself to trust the stag even if it had helped them in the past.

The cloud faded away as quickly as it came. A young man, his hair the color of starlight and his body so frail that David could see right through him, crouched on the ground. The young man stood slowly. His eyes were the color of molten gold, and his tunic was pure white. Antlers poked through hair mixed with white blond and soft brown. A sad smile played across the young man's full lips and he bowed his head.

"Emil!" Wilhelm ripped himself free from David and flung himself into Emil's arms. "Please...*please* don't go."

"I have to," Emil whispered. He brushed his ethereal hand through Wilhelm's tangled hair. "I can't stay."

"I need you," Wilhelm sobbed. He pressed his face into the crook of Emil's neck. "I–I can't. I can't do this without you. I just *can't!*"

Emil gently pushed Wilhelm back. "You're not alone, *bruder*. You have Johann and David. You don't need me."

"But I love you," Wilhelm gasped. "Isn't that enough?"

The heartbreaking look on Emil's face said it all, and David swore he saw tears lingering in Emil's eyes.

David put his hand on Wilhelm's shoulder and pulled the sobbing young man into his arms. "Thanks. For everything."

Emil gently smiled. "Believe me, the pleasure's all mine."

"Thank you." David bowed his head as he stroked Wilhelm's back. "Do you need…?"

"No, I think I have it." Emil turned, almost like he was going to leave, and his form started to fade. "I'll be back if you need me. I swear it."

Then he was gone, and only Steven's cooling body testified that he had ever been there.

"I need you!" Wilhelm screamed. He jerked back from David and raced to where Emil last stood. "*I need you, you asshole!*"

"Let's go," Johann said. He turned to leave, something sad in his blue eyes, and gestured to Myla and Toman. "We need to find the elves. It's not too far now."

David ignored him. He pulled Wilhelm into his arms again and slowly sat down. Wilhelm all but collapsed into his arms. David could feel hot tears strike his cheek. He didn't know what to say and settled on holding Wilhelm until he felt better. Maybe that would be in five minutes or maybe in five hours. Whatever it took, David was willing to do it.

He pressed a gentle kiss against Wilhelm's blotchy cheek. "What Johann said. Let's go home."

"Home," Wilhelm whispered. His voice as thin and fragile, reminding David of spun starlight, and he wobbled on colt legs as he stood. "I think I would like that."

"All right." David couldn't resist another kiss, this time on Wilhelm's dry, chapped lips and smiled softly. "So would I."

CHAPTER THIRTY-FIVE: RAW

◆ ◆ ◆

Wilhelm heard raw sobs rip their way out of his chest, but he couldn't bring himself to care. He had seen his brother for a few brief moments and then...just faded away. Almost like he was made of mist set before the burning summer sun. The stabbing pain settled into Wilhelm's chest and made its home there. It seemed to wrap around his heart, squeezing and sinking its barbs deep into tender flesh.

David soothed his back. "You doing all right?"

"No," Wilhelm whispered. Tears beaded in the corner of his eyes. "I want him back. *Now.*"

"I can't do that," David said. His lips brushed against Wilhelm's overheated cheek. "I can't bring him back for you. Would that I could..."

Wilhelm turned away. He looked up, trying to find the stag out of habit. Only crumbling walls and sprawling vines greeted his eyes. Wilhelm seemed to look past all the others, barely noticing Johann as he saddled up his horse and rode off to find the others. He couldn't bring himself to care when Toman shoved his nose into his lap. Wilhelm wanted to push the dog away, yet couldn't find the strength to do so.

"I don't want him to go," Wilhelm whispered. His eyes fluttered closed and he let the tears burn his cheeks. "I– I want him…" He trailed off and rested his head against David's shoulder.

David stroked his back gently. If he wanted to say anything, he gave no sign of it. Wilhelm didn't know if he was supposed to be grateful for that or not. He had thought—some strange part of him thought—that his brother would be back if everything was put right. Maybe Emil would come back as a spirit or stay as the stag. Knowing that there was nothing—that his brother had left—almost seemed to be worse than not knowing at all.

"I'm sorry," David said. He nudged Wilhelm. "Come on. We need to get going."

Wilhelm couldn't bring himself to look at the dead as he stood. He saw a tiny scrap of white fur clinging to the stonework. He grabbed it before anyone could tell him not to and slipped it in his pocket. The fur was as cool as frozen starlight, proving that it came from the stag. *No, not the stag.* **Emil.** Wilhelm wandered after the others and tried not to let his sorrow show too much. If he was to be king, he couldn't be thought of as weak.

Distantly, he heard the dogs barking. Wilhelm couldn't bring himself to care. He mounted his mare with shaking hands and guided her out of the ruins. He could hear David calling out to the elves. He wanted to rant at them, wanted to demand why they hadn't been there. Elves had magic. They could have done *something* to keep Emil where he belonged. Wilhelm would have rewarded them richly for it too.

Ruari must have seen the expression on Wilhelm's face. "What happened?"

"Emil was the stag," David said. His tone was careful, neutral. "What happened to you?"

"Ruins wouldn't let us in." Ruari gestured to the moss-covered walls and sighed. "Used to be, they enchanted everything to keep us out. I guess the magic still works."

Wilhelm almost snarled at them, but turned his head and urged his mare down the forest road. It wasn't their fault. After Emil and all he'd seen, magic truly did exist. Henri found that magic. It killed him in the end. Maybe that was the way it was supposed to work. Magic seemed so wild, so strange. Almost like it was something from a distant world. Wilhelm glanced to Johann and tried to read the man's guarded expression.

"Why?" he softly asked.

"Hmm?" Johann jerked, almost like he was lost in thought. "Why what?"

"Why did you find magic?" Wilhelm asked.

Johann shrugged. "I was young, foolish even. I thought I could control it rather than it controlling me. As you see, that wasn't what happened."

He laughed dryly. Wilhelm didn't bother to return it.

Johann sobered quickly. "I can't stay with you. I've seen what you have with David. I would only get in the way of that. I can't...I can't take him away from you."

He leaned over and squeezed Wilhelm's hand, his gaze gentle.

Wilhelm jerked back. "You're going to abandon me, too?!"

"I'm not!" Johann yelped. "I have to go. I can't take you away from David, dammit! Don't you understand?"

"No," Wilhelm spat. His voice was bitter, and it seemed to choke him coming out. "I don't understand. First Emil and now you. You know what? You can go fuck yourself! I never want to see you again, you hear me? *Never again!*"

Johann set his jaw as he turned his gelding around. "As you wish, Your Majesty."

Scorn dripped off the title, but Wilhelm couldn't bring himself to care. He watched as the other man vanished into the dense forest. His chest heaved with unshed tears, and he wanted more than anything to tell Johann he didn't mean it. Wilhelm shook his head slowly. After a few minutes, sobs broke free from his throat and he collapsed against the mare's neck. He didn't care who saw. He couldn't; otherwise, he felt he would burst from the pent-up emotion.

Ruari rested his hand on Wilhelm's back. "Look."

Wilhelm raised his head. His breath caught when he saw Myla. The white dog looked a little worse for the wear, but she held her head high as she walked beside Toman. Wilhelm knew that he should track Johann down to give the dog back, but he couldn't bring himself to do it. Maybe it was a sign. Maybe his brother was looking out for him; Johann would *have* to come back to get his dog, right?

Right?

"Hey, Myla," he whispered.

The dog raised her head. Her brown eyes studied him

and something told him that he was being judged. Maybe it was the tilt of her head or the way her lips were drawn back and exposing just a hint of teeth. Wilhelm shuddered. He reached down to pet her head, only for the dog to snap and him. Her hackles went up as she softly growled. Wilhelm jerked back. He didn't want to bother her, especially if she looked like she wanted to bite him.

"Go with him," Wilhelm said. "I know you want to."

Myla stared at him. Her ears pricked up and her tail dropped a little. Toman whined. He nosed Myla and pulled at her fur with his teeth. She ignored him. There was something strange in her eyes, almost as if she was deciding. The world seemed to narrow down to just her and the way she stood in the rutted dirt road. Her white body caught the sun, and it seemed to halo around her. She looked ethereal, almost, like she wasn't from this world.

"Let's get going." David's voice shattered the spell. "We need to get back before everything goes to hell even more."

Myla lowered her head. She turned, almost like she was looking for Johann before she followed Wilhelm and the others.

On a whim, Wilhelm patted in front of him. Myla ran quickly for a few feet, gathered her legs under her, and leapt upon the mare's back. The horse popped her head up. She snorted and pinned her ears, but didn't otherwise react. Wilhelm rested his free hand on Myla's back. The white dog looked a little larger, if that were possible, and she seemed to enjoy riding rather than walking.

Wilhelm didn't know how long he rode. He lost himself in grief and squeezed the little scrap of fur. No matter how hard he held it, it never grew any warmer. There seemed to be something magical about it, something that linked it to the spirit world. Wilhelm could hear the elves talking quietly in their soft, poetic language and listened as Ruari started a song.

The words carried him, it seemed, across a swiftly flowing stream and through the dense forest. Birds exploded out of the trees as they rode, and the laurel hells teemed with life. The tangled masses of pink flowers and emerald-colored, slick leaves hid a world of splashing streams and glittering fish. A brown bear watched them from a craggy outcropping and wolves —massive, shaggy beasts that made Toman snarl— scattered as the group came closer.

All the while, Wilhelm's heart felt like it would wrench in two.

David held his horse back until Wilhelm caught up with him. "You don't look so good."

"Are you going to leave me, too?" Wilhelm asked. His voice was a ragged, raw whisper.

"Not by choice," David said. He grinned crookedly. "We're going home, Wil! We can sleep in a real bed, eat real food, and I can get a bath!"

"I don't have Johann," Wilhelm mumbled. He took a breath. "I told him I never wanted to see him again…"

David snorted. "If you think that man's gonna do what you told him, you've got another thing coming. He'll be back when he's good and ready, I promise. He probably wants to give you time."

Wilhelm nodded like he understood. He feared Johann wouldn't, mostly because the man never struck him as particularly reliable. He bit his bottom lip as he rode. Wilhelm couldn't help but glance to David. The fading sunlight struck his face and made him look even more beautiful than he already was. A kind smile lingered on his lips and he reached out to take Wilhelm's hand. Something in Wilhelm's heart seized.

"I think I love you." Wilhelm looked down and tried to banish the warring emotions. "I know I've said it before, but I mean it this time. You're not a way to get me out of a marriage I don't want. I want *you*."

"That's good to know." David swallowed, his voice suddenly rough. "And here I was thinking I was just chopped liver."

"Well, I rather like eating liver, so—"

"Hey, lover boys!" Ruari yelled. "We're almost home, so get your asses up here! I don't wanna get shot!"

Wilhelm choked back a watery laugh. "Gods above, I love him."

"Let's get him out of trouble," David said. He spurred his mare into a trot. "Come on, it shouldn't be too far. Knowing Ruari, he's probably started a fight."

Wilhelm cracked a smile. He didn't feel that he could argue. He nudged the mare forward and tried to look as regal as he could. All the while, the scrap of fur weighed heavily in his pocket. Perhaps he was imagining things. It was just a piece of moon-colored fluff. There was no way it could feel as heavy as wrought iron. Wilhelm took a breath. He wasn't letting go, not this time. Johann he could understand, but Emil was another story.

I can't let you go, his broken heart whispered. *If I lose you, I'll lose another piece of myself and I...I don't think I'd survive that.*

He tried to school his features into something approaching pleasant as he rode toward the front of the group. Bracken and Holly glanced at him, but he ignored them. He could just see Ruari, holding tight to his nervous, prancing pony and two knights with their large, brindle dogs.

The dogs perked up as soon as they saw Toman, and happy yips filled the air. Toman bowed, his tail wagging wildly. The mastiffs pawed at him, their ears perked, and pulled at his long fur coat. Myla scrambled off the horse. The white dog approached slowly, her belly nearly brushing the ground. Myla licked her lips like a wolf did as she approached the largest mastiff. The mastiff cocked his head, his tail wagging, before he bounded over to play.

Wilhelm turned to the knight. "Problems, sir?"

"You're alive?" the knight—Wilhelm thought he was Sir Leonid—started. "We thought you were dead!"

"I'm alive, thanks to these people," Wilhelm said.

He wanted to add Johann to that but decided to keep his hurt to himself for a bit. Maybe, one day, he would start to heal.

"I'll tell the court," Leonid said. He shook his head slowly, his eyes oddly light. "Vixen! Tyr! We need to tell the others!"

"I think we're going to get a hero's welcome," David said. "Shall we?"

Wilhelm nodded. He couldn't trust himself to say anything and prayed no one would ask where Henri was. He knew the ruins were a cold and lonely grave, even if that was what Henri deserved. It was better, he supposed, to let Henri lie in the forest, far from those who might want to continue his legacy.

CHAPTER THIRTY-SIX: CASTLE

◆ ◆ ◆

David ducked his head as courtiers swarmed the horses. Snowflake pranced under him. She reared her head back, twitching her ears nervously, and snorted. Her nostrils quivered, and she bared her teeth when a young woman drew too close to her. The woman jerked back, scorn covering her delicate, pretty features. Snowflake pinned her ears to her skull and pawed more, the threat clear.

"Easy," David whispered. His own turmoil matched that of his mare, and he knew she was feeding from it. "It's all right, sweetheart. They're not going to hurt you."

Banners snapped in the breeze, and the dogs barked. Yet more people, all of them richly robed in the tradition of courtiers everywhere, pressed Snowflake. The mare tossed her head in warning. David could feel her tense under him, like she was going to rear, and pulled her toward a more sheltered spot. Snowflake trembled from nerves. She tossed her head, nearly yanking the reins from David's hands, and whinnied loudly.

"Snowflake." David dismounted and pressed his forehead to her nose. "I promise it's gonna be all right."

Going by her pinned ears, Snowflake didn't believe him.

David petted her nose as he drew back. He stood on his tiptoes to see if he could get a good look at Wilhelm. Almost out of habit, his eyes searched for Johann too. He shook himself. Johann had decided to go his own way, as was his right, and David had almost expected as much. He smiled sadly. Maybe Johann would find what he was looking for. David just wished that Wil would be there to see it.

"Don't like the crowds or was your horse about to rear?" Ruari asked. The elf laughed wryly as he led his pony over. "I swear those idiots don't know how to give a body some space!"

"Yeah," David softly said. He handed the reins to Ruari. "Wil needs me."

He ducked under Snowflake's neck and waded his way through the crowd. Everyone drew back from him. David didn't know why, nor did he care, but soon he reached Wil's side. Wil's own horse snorted and pranced in fear. Those heavy hooves slammed against the flagstones, releasing clouds of dust, and that broad, flat head jerked back and forth. David grabbed the horse's head to calm it as Wilhelm dismounted.

"Everyone, *back!*" Wilhelm yelled.

Silence descended across the noisy crowd.

"Thank you." Wilhelm dismounted and clenched his jaw. "Where are the king and queen?"

David took his place beside Wil and grabbed a man by the collar when he got too close. "He said back *off*, buddy."

"And who are you to tell me what to do?" the man sneered. An unpleasant look lingered on his features.

"My intended." Wil growled that last word and started walking toward the castle gates. "Tell the king and queen that I'm alive and Henri was behind the plot to kill my brother."

A startled gasp rose from the crowd.

"What?"

"That's not possible! He was such a nice boy!"

"I don't believe it!"

David looped his arm around Wil's shoulder. "I think that story's going to be a hard sell."

"It's the truth." Wilhelm kissed David's cheek. "Besides, I have you with me. I don't think too much can go wrong."

David almost said something about tempting fate, but he decided to keep his mouth shut. He clicked his tongue to get the dogs' attention. Myla and Toman wove their way through the crowd. The big wolfhound was easy to see, and people naturally seemed to draw back from him. David felt his heart swell with pride. Maybe this wasn't what he had expected his life to be, but he liked it better than what he had before.

"You!" a familiar voice rang out through the crowd. "Get away from the prince!"

Uh oh. David leaned to the side and grabbed a sword as a tall woman strode through the crowd. Two tall tan hounds walked at her side. Toman bristled. The wolfhound barred his teeth, his scarred ears pinned to his skull, as Myla lowered her head. Her hackles rose and a low growl gathered in her throat. The hounds did the same. The four dogs circled each other, snapping some, as the tensions rose.

"And who might you be?" Wilhelm asked.

His voice dripped with the sort of sneered superiority

only royalty could muster.

"Warden Lotte von Rigel," the woman spat. "And you have a dangerous man with you."

"I know he's dangerous," Wilhelm said. "That's why I've made him both my guard and my intended."

David shivered to hear those cold tones. He never knew that Wilhelm could speak this way. Part of him liked it; the other half felt scared stiff.

Lotte, apparently, felt the same. "My prince, you have an Alsatian outlaw beside you. Why, he could take you out into the forest and kill you without a second thought! They devour like wolves—"

"I know what I would like to devour." David kissed Wilhelm deeply, provoking a gasp from the crowd. He pulled back and grinned a little. "I don't think you would like to see it though."

Myla snapped at the hounds. The biggest one jerked back, tail tucked between its legs. Toman took his place at his mate's side and growled at the second one. It glanced at Lotte. Lotte ignored it and kept her focus on David and Wilhelm.

David tried to keep calm. He could feel close to two hundred eyes boring into his body. His hands itched to use the sword. It would be so easy—lunge and swipe, take out the menace right in front of him. His blood seemed to rush in his ears. David's heart fluttered, and cold iron filled his mouth. Every fiber of his being screamed at him to fight, but still he resisted. He met Lotte's gaze with his own and dared her to take a step forward.

"Leave." Wilhelm's voice was a low growl. "And never bother us again."

"But, my lord—"

"I said *leave!*" Wilhelm snarled. "And that's an order!"

Lotte took a step back, gestured to her dogs, and left.

David lowered the sword and handed it back to the owner with a sheepish grin. He didn't hear what was said and only mumbled his thanks. His heart still raced in his chest as a strange exhaustion settled over his body. David shook his head to dispel it. He had to stay strong, both for himself and Wil.

"Damn," David whispered. He squeezed Wilhelm's hand. "I didn't know you had it in you."

"Let's just go," Wilhelm sighed. He pulled back some. "I have to keep a promise, and I don't know if it'll go very well."

David nodded. He ducked under another portcullis and kept at Wilhelm's heels. The dogs trotted beside them. Myla still seemed nervous—her ears were pinned and her body stiff—but didn't seem like she was going to attack. David scratched her ears in thanks. He didn't know what he would do if she *did* decide to lash out. He turned around to see who was following.

Bracken kept close to them, but he didn't see the other elves. Perhaps they were waiting outside. David didn't even know if they would be allowed inside the palace proper.

Gold leaf and crystal surrounded him. David had never seen such wealth and splendor. The flagstones he stepped on with dirty boots were made of richly patterned, inlaid marble. Words worked in gold ran alongside the edges of the pattern. Tapestries done in copper, gold, and silver thread insulated the halls and delicate chains that looked like vines held them in place. He couldn't help but notice the deer that seemed to poke out of every design.

The deeper inside the castle they walked, the plainer things became. The delicate marble was quickly replaced by creaking oak and rushes. Light poured through windows covered in oiled calfskin rather than glass. The tapestries became plainer, most only showing a single rearing stag, and the braziers were made of copper and iron rather than gold and crystal. Even the rush lights and candles were of a plainer sort.

They stopped in front of a large, carved oak door. The carvings had been blunted by the years and grime, but David could still make out the rearing stag and the forest that surrounded it. His breath caught. Perhaps Emil's spirit form wasn't an accident. Perhaps the white stag—the symbol that surrounded him now—was some sort of family guardian. David touched the stag's antlers before drawing back.

Bracken tensed. "He better keep his promise," the elf hissed, "or it will mean war."

"He will," David promised. "He always does."

His heart warmed when he saw Wilhelm. Sunlight and candlelight surrounded him in a golden halo, and he never looked more regal. His face might have been smudged, his clothing torn, and his hair tangled, but he looked like every ounce the king he was. David couldn't help but watch him. His mind buzzed with every kind of wicked thought. He found himself turning around, making sure that the others weren't paying attention to him, as he cleared his throat.

Wilhelm threw the door open and marched into the hall like he owned it.

David found himself looking up at the ceiling and gasping. Impossibly tall windows of intricately worked glass flooded the room with light. Banners hung from the ceiling trusses, each one of them worked with golden thread and glittering glass beads. Even the rushes on the floor looked clean. A large table dominated half of the hall, while a raised dais occupied by two gilt thrones, and a white doe took up the rest of it.

David found himself drawn to the doe.

She stood as he entered, almost like she recognized him, and ambled over. David reached out with one trembling hand. His rough, work dirtied fingers buried themselves into soft, white fur, and he found himself holding the animal close. Her lashes brushed his cheek. Her collar—a heavy thing made of gold and tooled leather—rested heavy on his arm. Yet David couldn't draw away from her, no matter how hard he tried.

A regal man wearing long, silken robes stood from where he was sitting.

Wilhelm's head snapped up. "Father?"

"My son." The man bowed his head and smiled. "We thought you were dead. What happened?"

David reached over and squeezed Wilhelm's hand. He could feel Wil's fear. This wasn't the place to discuss what Henri had done. The crowd following them—the same crowd that bothered the horses—would tear Wilhelm to shreds.

"Sir," David said as he stepped in front of Wilhelm, "may we find a place to discuss this privately?"

"And who are you?" the king asked.

David smiled crookedly and snapped his fingers for Toman. "Your son's fiancé. We are each other's intended."

"What?" Going by the look of shock, this wasn't what the king was expecting. "Who *are* you?"

"I am David Troy," David said. "Son of Lucius Troy, born of Alsace. I saved Wilhelm's life from an enemy under your very nose. You might say that I'm nobody from a nothing kingdom."

Toman tensed as the guards drew closer. Myla growled, her ears pinned to her head. The white dog looked like she was going to fly at the men, maybe she was, and her snarl sounded like approaching thunder. One of the guards grabbed his sword. He half drew it, just as Toman snapped at him. A hush fell on the entire court.

David locked eyes with the king. He took a step forward, not realizing what he was doing, and his sharp gaze dared the man to say anything. Hot blue eyes stared into brown ones. David didn't say a word. His heart fluttered in his chest. He wanted to blurt out what Henri had done, how he had killed Emil and nearly invited ruin, but he held his tongue. He hardly noticed when Bracken and Wilhelm stood beside him.

Wilhelm's voice shattered the silence.

"Henri tried to kill me," Wilhelm hissed. His eyes were full of rage. "He killed Emil, and he learned a dark art so vile that it consumed him. I am marrying David, *Father*, and there isn't much that you can do about it."

The king's lips flattened into a thin line and disapproval flowed from him.

"So be it," the man finally said. He sat back down. "Now go get cleaned up. You both look like hell."

Wilhelm grinned. David couldn't help it; he wrapped his arms around Wilhelm and drew him into a passionate kiss.

CHAPTER THIRTY-SEVEN: KING

◆ ◆ ◆

Wilhelm bowed his head as the cold wind whipped around his body. The grumbling gray sky threatened rain as the grasses danced in a frenetic mass. The white doe stood beside them. Her eyes seemed to reflect the growing storm. Toman stood beside him. The big dog growled at anyone who dared come near them.

David took his place by Wilhelm's side. His fur-lined cape rippled out behind him in the twisting, dancing wind. His eyes narrowed as he scanned the crowd of courtiers, and the ivy draped standing stones. A sacred fire burned in the middle of the stones, and haunting music drifted through the trees. No one dared speak. David's fierce gaze seemed to pin anyone who dared glance at them, and Wilhelm found himself drawing closer to the other man.

David took Wilhelm's hand and squeezed it gently. "Are you ready?"

"Are you?" Wilhelm kissed him gently.

"Nope," David replied. He smiled crookedly. "You're never ready for something like this though. You just have to go for it."

Wilhelm nodded as he turned to face the crowd. He could see well over a hundred faces, some that he had known since he was a child, staring back at him. He swallowed, his mouth suddenly dry. Wilhelm wanted to bolt back to safety, away from all of this, but he forced himself to stay. Thunder grumbled overhead as the wind picking up.

For a second, he imagined a white stag standing in the forest. The beast's white fur seemed to glow as it stepped between the dense, dark-green tangled sedge. Wilhelm's breath caught. He reached out, almost like he could touch it, before the stag bolted. It vanished into the thick forest, almost like it had never been there in the first place. A lump rose in the back of his throat. Wilhelm forced himself to turn away, but not before his fingers found that scrap of silver fur.

A young girl robed in white motioned for him to kneel. Behind him, someone started playing a haunting song on flutes, tambourines, and a long, thin drum.

Wilhelm did as she asked and lowered his head. He shivered as a crown woven of ivy and holly berries graced his head. The ice-cold berries seemed to burn his tender skin, and the ivy bowed under the weight of the coming storm. A cloak made of hawk feathers covered his shoulders, and three fine lines of white paint were smeared across his cheeks.

Wilhelm closed his eyes. The weight of a thousand years seemed to weigh heavy on his shoulders. He swallowed, suddenly aware of the blood rushing to his ears. He gripped the white fur. Things warred inside of him, things telling him to keep the fur or to let it burn. Wilhelm could hear the voices chanting around him, each one of them cajoling him to be a good and fair king. David added his own voice to the song, letting words in Alsatian dip and flow between the sacred verses.

When he rose and opened his eyes, a hush fell over the crowd.

Wilhelm reached into his pocket and pulled out the scrap of white fur. It weighed heavy in his hands, like it was made of lead rather than soft spun air. His hands trembled as he held it high. Then, and only by sheer force of will, he forced his fingers to open and let the breeze catch it.

The fur seemed to dance in the air. It tumbled end over end, rising and falling as the wind pleased, as it floated to the fire. Then it dropped and vanished forever into the roiling, bright orange depths.

Wilhelm's breath caught, and he forced himself to look

away. The wind picked up, almost like it was brushing slender fingers across overheated cheeks. Wilhelm felt tears burn in his eyes. He turned away so no one would see his weakness as he took a shuddering breath. Almost on instinct, he reached for David.

Wilhelm turned around, almost on instinct. His father smiled gently. Wilhelm knew he was more than ready to pass on the crown. His son was of age, after all, and the old man had his decades of rest coming to him.

Someone cleared their throat and jerked Wilhelm back to the present.

David took his hand. "My king."

The priest stepped forward. He was an old man, his cheeks covered in spiraling chiseled tattoos, and he touched Wilhelm's chin with one gnarled finger. Whatever he said, Wilhelm didn't hear. Blood roared in his ears, and he swore he heard a choir of the ancients.

"Long live the king!" David bellowed.

"Long live the king!"

"Thank you." Wilhelm took a breath and glanced to David as he stepped toward the crowd. "I will strive to do as my father did and lead my people well. To that end, I'm announcing an end to any hostilities with Alsace, and no preference will be given to any faith. Talla Gael is a place for all citizens, regardless of what they believe or where they came from, and I would like to keep it that way."

Wilhelm removed the ivy wreath as he walked between the standing stones. He tried to imagine that the wreath was his past and his old life as a second prince. Wilhelm held it high above his head as he stared at the fire. Then, with so much less effort than before, he let the wreath fall into the blaze.

He took a gray dun mare when she was offered to him and swung up on the saddle. Her fur glistened with swirling, spiraling painted symbols, and her mane was braided with feathers and beads. The mare arched her head as she turned to the castle. Toman trotted beside her, like he always did, and Myla stuck close beside David.

He had a horse of his own, a plain bay. He looked so regal in his navy-and-gold robes that Wilhelm felt his breath catch. Someone had braided gold in David's long, soft hair. He wore an ornate rose gold circlet, the crown set with rubies and small emeralds, and it seemed to glow in the gloomy light. David rode tall and proud on that horse, with one hand on his sword and his gaze ever watchful.

Wilhelm smiled softly. Then his expression turned bitter as he thought of Henri. He tried to imagine his cousin in the crowd of onlookers, yet found that he couldn't. Instead, his entire gaze seemed to be devoted to David.

He dismounted as soon as he reached the courtyard and handed the reins to a stable boy. "How'd I do?"

"Like a dream." David swept up Wilhelm in a hug and kissed him. "A beautiful, regal dream."

Wilhelm flushed and pushed at him weakly. "You're wicked, you know that? Absolutely wicked!"

"I try," David smirked. "Come on, your father's waiting."

Wilhelm nodded, but paused as he saw Maria. "Aunt Maria!"

"Yes?" She turned toward him, something distant in her eyes. "What is it?"

"You didn't complain," Wilhelm half-teasingly said. "Are you feeling all right?"

"Oh, I had some time to think," Maria said. "I think I'm going to visit a place called Albion and stay there for a little while. Talla Gael will always be home, but..." She trailed off before turning to her horse.

Wilhelm left her to it. Only Maria knew what went on in her mind, and perhaps, it was for the best that she go to this strange, far-off place. Maybe if Wilhelm was lucky, she would stay there and never come back.

Wilhelm squeezed David's hand as he crossed the courtyard. Heavy banners snapped in the breeze, almost like the very spirits of the air were saluting him. Even the hawks and ravens paused to take note. The scruffy brindle hounds, the ones who slunk around the kitchen, paused and watched with their soulful brown eyes.

David pushed open the heavy oak doors. "After you, my king."

Wilhelm flushed as he strode through them. He could hear the crowds outside chanting his name as he took the throne. David stood beside him, holding the sword like any knight, as the crowd spilled into the Great Hall. The doe danced between them, her golden eyes filled with joy and her motions light and free.

Wilhelm could see his father on the balcony above them. The older man bowed his head, smiling some, as the crowd gathered around.

Even the dogs fell silent after a moment. The tense, hushed silence seemed to fill the room as two courtiers came forward with a gold-and-crystal crown. White fur lined the base of it, and the gold had been worked to resemble trailing leaves. The two men carried it reverently, like the sacred object it was, and allowed anyone looking to revel in its splendor.

Without a word, David took the crown when it reached him. He held it up so all could see it before turning to Wilhelm.

"No turning back now," he murmured. "Are you ready?"

"I'm as ready as I'll ever be," Wilhelm said. He cupped David's cheek and smiled a little. "I know I can do it. With you at my side, I can do anything."

David placed the crown on Wilhelm's head before turning to the crowd.

"All hail Wilhelm Kessler von Hart, king of Talla Gael!"

Finis.

ABOUT THE AUTHOR

C. A. Wood

C. A. Wood is an aspiring author with a great love for the outdoors, medieval fantasy, and the comforts of a good book. They can be found writing, working their day job, or playing with one of the multiple rescue animals they happen to live with.

Made in the USA
Columbia, SC
16 May 2023